BOOK ONE OF THE BLUE WATER MYSTERIES

IN THE DEAD OF WINTER

LYN FARRELL

KENMORE, WA

A Camel Press book published by Epicenter Press

Epicenter Press
6524 NE 181st St.
Suite 2
Kenmore, WA 98028

For more information go to:
www.Camelpress.com
www.lynfarrell.com

All rights reserved. No part of this book may be reproduced or transmitted in any form or by any means, electronic or mechanical, including photocopying, recording, or any information storage and retrieval system, without permission in writing from the publisher.

No generative AI was used in the conceptualization, planning, drafting, or creative writing of this work. No permission is given for the use of this material for AI training purposes.

This is a work of fiction. Names, characters, places, brands, media, and incidents are either the product of the author's imagination or are used fictitiously.

Cover design by Scott Book
Design by Melissa Vail Coffman

In the Dead of Winter
Copyright © 2026 by Lyn Farrell

Library of Congress Control Number: 2024952547

ISBN: 978-1-68492-318-2 (Trade Paper)
ISBN: 978-1-68492-319-9 (eBook)

*For the Hoffman children,
Paul, Lisa and Carla who introduced me to Charlevoix
and for Tim, who left us too soon.
I was inspired to write this story after adopting
Stella, a Cavalier Spaniel.*

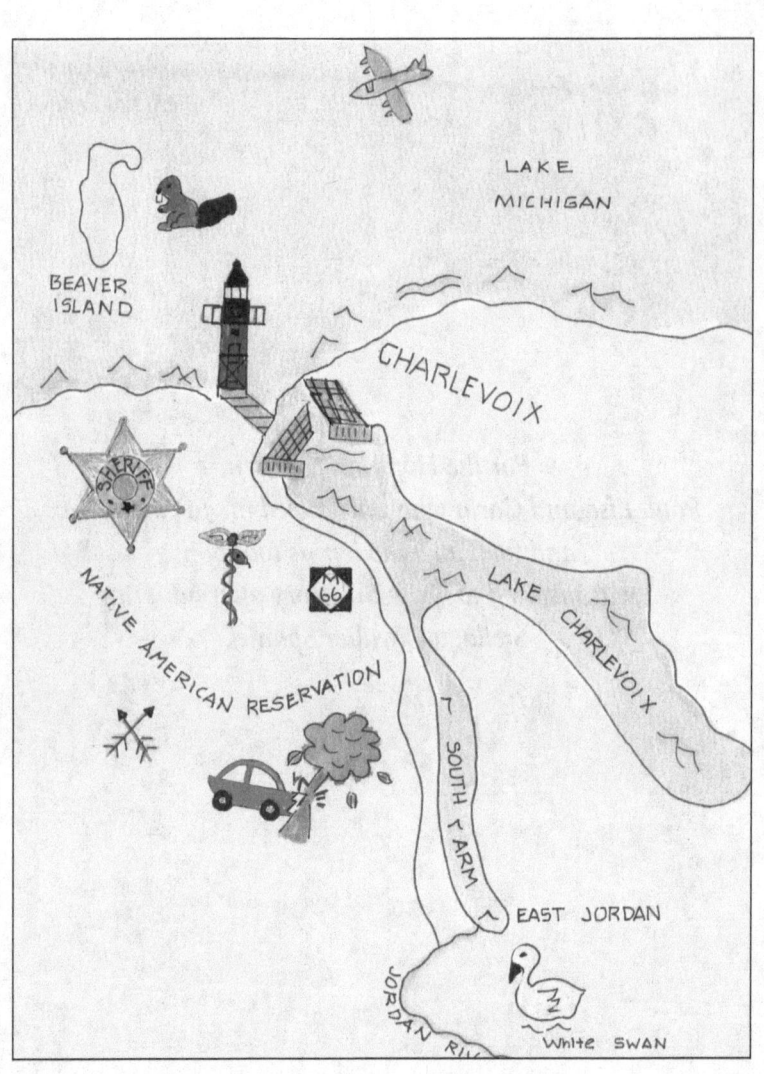

ACKNOWLEDGMENTS

"In the Dead of Winter" is the first of the Blue Water Mysteries and required more assistance from professionals than any of my previous books. My medical advisor, Dr. Robert Stuart, an ER physician for 40+ years and Medical Director for the Aurora Health system, provided his usual insightful help and expertise. Dr. Jane Turner, a top pediatrician at Michigan State University and a friend educated me about the medical and psychological complexities of a young child who had been traumatized. My niece, Emily Durkin, M.D. helped with the question of child guardianship. Will Schikorra, a paramedic, helped with information about CPR. My daughter, Lisa, who was my co-author for the Mae December mysteries, came up with the idea of Pete having been an EMT and having PTSD. "Rez Life" a book by David Truer was eye-opening in providing the history of the boarding schools and the immense love and commitment the Chippewa and Ottawa have for their children. Kathy Jacobs, with her long financial and personal support of tribes in Michigan, read and critiqued the pages dealing with the reservation. Joyce Benvenuto gave me the benefit of her long experience with the tribes in the southwest and appropriate nomenclature. Jacquie Paul, the receptionist for

Chippewa/Ottawa Social Services in Charlevoix County provided background on the services provided to the residents on the reservation. Jean Christensen, who has worked with the tribal children in Minnesota, read and critiqued the sections on Native Americans. Dr. Kevin Leonard, Director of the Native American Institute at Michigan State University, confirmed that a custody hearing would take place. Most importantly, Jennifer McCord, Executive Editor for the publisher, Epicenter Press, reminded me that the story had to begin with the "inciting incident" and with characters who would be continuing in the series. She was right. My personal editor, Linda Nuttall, did a superb job and paid me the compliment of calling the book "a real page turner." The map of the Charlevoix area was drawn by artist Jane Falion. While the story is set in Charlevoix and East Jordan, Michigan, which are real towns, and on the Chippewa/Ottawa reservation which is located there, all the rest of the story is fictional. If I have made mistakes in medical information, errors in police procedure or have in any way been disrespectful of the Charlevoix Sheriff's Office, or the Ottawa and Chippewa tribes, the faults are unintentional. All the characters in the story are fictional and are not based on the actual people who hold important positions in law enforcement or who feature in the tale.

MAJOR CHARACTERS

- Mike Dodgson, Charlevoix County Sheriff, who guided the murder investigation from a distance and returned to do the final interrogation of the perpetrator

- Riley Donovan, an employee of Inman's Snow Plowing service

- Ashley Hamilton, the Undersheriff's girlfriend and first grade teacher

- Peter Manstead, Undersheriff of Charlevoix County, a deliberate man, persistent as a bloodhound in his pursuit of a killer

- Charlie Pierce, Sheriff's Deputy, the real but unacknowledged hero of the tale

- Victoria Treadwell, Dispatcher for the Charlevoix Sheriff's Office, who found the last vital pieces of evidence to convict the perpetrator

- Carly Yellowwood, victim of premeditated murder

- Chenoa Yellowwood, two-year-old daughter of Carly

- Joe Yellowwood, ex-husband of Carly, Chenoa's father
- Doris Yellowwood, Joe's mother
- Ben Wilcox, Sheriff's Deputy

ONE

Friday, January 5th

THE FLUORESCENT FIXTURES IN THE CEILING of the evidence room at the Charlevoix Sheriff's office were buzzing, giving the room a tricky light that bounced off the boxes containing the records of cases investigated over the decades. Victoria Treadwell, the dispatcher for the station, was standing by the metal shelves in the basement that morning searching for a document the sheriff had requested. She was new to the job and the sole female in a place heavy with testosterone.

Before he left for his three-day conference in Minneapolis, Sheriff Mike Dodgson had given Victoria and his Undersheriff, Pete Manstead, the assignment to clean the evidence room.

"In addition to establishing *some* kind of order down there, I want you to pull out the cold cases and set aside those few labeled as Native American crimes," he said.

The sheriff was a tall guy with salt-and-pepper hair and chiseled features. He looked the very picture of a lawman from the old West and brooked no nonsense from his team. Their Undersheriff, Pete, was in his late thirties with the broad countenance and faded blue eyes of his Norwegian ancestors. He was a good second-in-command, being for the most part comfortably laid back. Victoria liked him.

It was a small office, just the two sheriffs, the jail sergeant, and two deputies who were based in Boyne City and on Beaver Island. The little towns of Charlevoix and East Jordan, Michigan, had their own police departments, but the sheriff's office was responsible for covering the remainder of the entire county. The size of the staff was proportionate to the amount of crime in their area—which was minimal.

Victoria had been dreading the cleaning job she'd suspected was coming her way ever since the sheriff had emerged from the basement a few days ago. He'd walked upstairs muttering irritably that it was impossible to find anything down there.

"It's the first week in January and *nothing* will be happening while I'm gone. It's too cold for the relatively few criminals we have around here to get into much trouble. You two may as well get something done instead of just standing around here gossiping," Sheriff Dodgson frowned. "The last time I was downstairs, I found two boxes with their tops off and one with its contents spilled all over the floor." He looked disapprovingly at the pair of them.

Victoria and Pete exchanged an uncomfortable glance.

"Once you finish helping Victoria with the evidence room, Pete, I'd like you to review all the cases involving Native Americans. When I get back, I have a meeting with the tribal police in Traverse City. You can brief me when I return."

"Yes, sir," Pete said.

THE MEN HAD LEFT THE STATION early. Pete was driving Sheriff Dodgson to the Traverse City airport to catch his flight to Minneapolis. Since Victoria fully expected him to duck the evidence room project, she'd located the three cold case boxes and lugged them up to the breakroom. Due to the sensitivity of the material, she closed the door behind her. Catching sight of her red hair in the small mirror on the back of the door, she frowned. Her unruly mane was normally worn in one long braid that fell below her shoulder blades. Because of its coarse texture, wiry curls escaped frequently. *No point in tackling my hair now,* she thought. *It's going to get messed up cleaning the evidence room anyway.*

Sitting down with a steaming cup of coffee in front of her, she'd taken the top off the first box when she heard two male voices. It was Pete, their Undersheriff, and their jailer, Sergeant Craig. Just as she had predicted, they were coming her way in search of hot coffee.

"Man, it's cold out there," Pete said, rubbing his hands together cheerfully as he muscled his way inside. Sergeant Craig was right behind him. The two big men took up all the space in the breakroom.

"What's the weather prediction?" Victoria asked.

"We're supposed to get two feet of snow starting Sunday afternoon," Sgt. Craig said gloomily. He grabbed a cup of coffee and then, spotting the evidence boxes on the small table, muttered something about having to check the cells and departed. They didn't have anyone in custody. He just didn't want to be roped into the cleaning job.

"Can you listen for the phone, please, Sergeant," Victoria called after him and they heard him mutter something incomprehensible in an irritated tone.

"I've already started with the cold cases," she said. Pete sighed.

IT WAS FOUR O'CLOCK THAT AFTERNOON when they mutually decided to call it quits. All the boxes were back on the gray metal shelves in order by month and year. Victoria had even found the broom and swept the floor.

"No idea how the boss expects me to find all the Native American cases," Pete groused.

"Without reading through all of them, it's impossible."

"We better check what the weather's up to," he said and darted up the stairs followed by Victoria.

Looking out the windows, it was apparent that the projected storm was on its way. The sky was blue-black and the wind was howling; its whine was audible even inside the building.

"How about we close up early?" Victoria asked. She had the weekend off and was looking forward to the break. She and her husband Matt had two sons, Max and Gavin. They were planning on driving over to see Matt's folks in Traverse City. Discussing the weather prediction, they thought if they got on the road first thing Saturday morning and left early Sunday to return home, they could beat the storm.

"You go ahead and take off," Pete said. "Absolutely nothing happening."

Pulling out of the lot, Victoria decided she'd pick up pizza for dinner for her family. BC Pizza was on her way home. *With the storm on its way, I might even get a three-day weekend,* she thought cheerfully.

ONCE VICTORIA LEFT, PETE PROWLED AROUND the station, checking locks and turning off lights. He and his girlfriend, Ashley Hamilton, were going to celebrate the winter weekend with a bus tour visiting a number of wineries in the area.

When he'd spotted Ashley across a crowded bar four years earlier, it was her hair that initially attracted his attention. Thick and luxurious, it was blonde, sun-streaked and curly. Plus, Ashley was tall and he was six foot five. Pete liked tall women. When he managed an introduction and finally summoned up the courage to ask her out (which took weeks), and she agreed to have dinner with him, he could hardly believe his luck. Sometimes, when Ashley smiled at him, he still found himself as tongue-tied as a schoolboy.

He walked out to the parking lot whistling to himself and started his car, feeling his spirits rise. With the storm expected to arrive Sunday afternoon, he assumed the criminal element would be confined to quarters and unable to get into much mischief. Although he was nominally in charge of the office (with Sheriff Dodgson away), he doubted he'd even get a phone call from the on-call service. The weekend was his and he intended to enjoy every minute of it.

Neither Pete nor Victoria had any inkling then, but unanticipated events were to unfold over the next few days that would be all-consuming. In hindsight, it was clear that they had been, at best, naive.

TWO

Monday, January 8th

WHEN VICTORIA TREADWELL GOT OUT OF the warm bed she shared with her husband, set her feet down on the cold floor and pushed aside their heavy bedroom curtains, she was unsurprised to see a thick veil of snow still tumbling from a steel-gray sky. The winter storm had started the previous afternoon and two feet of snow lay on the ground. They had barely made it back to the house from visiting Matt's folks before the storm hit in earnest. Their lights had flickered and the power went off just as they were putting the kids to bed. She touched her sleeping husband on the shoulder to wake him.

"I'm about to take off, Matt," she said. "Kids are already up. No school today. Hope you can get the generator going."

Victoria's two sons were wildly cheerful about having a snow day. They were pelting each other with couch pillows when she walked into the living room. She clicked the switch on their gas fireplace and was astonished when the flames came on with a whoosh. Electricity, she thought, was a continuing mystery.

"Come over here you two little ruffians," she said and gave them both sloppy kisses which they wiped away with their hands. At six and eight, they were already at the age when maternal displays of love were dreadfully embarrassing. "Dad is getting up now. He'll get you breakfast. There's enough snow that you can go out and make a snowman after you eat. Don't forget to wear your hats and mittens."

By the time she had found her coat, purse and cell phone and walked past the boys on her way to the garage, the pillow fight was again in high gear. Inman's plowing had come through and removed most of the snow from their driveway, but a layer of frozen ice remained undisturbed, glinting in shining patches beneath leaden skies. Turning the key in the ignition, she slipped her car in gear, crawled down the hill and turned right, keeping her speed down to thirty mph. The County snowplows had been working all night, but the continuing snowfall had since deposited another six inches on the road.

She knew she could have asked for the day off, but suspected there would be a lot of calls from people who required assistance. The sheriff's office had issued a "Stay off the Roads" message on the local TV and radio stations Sunday morning, but there were always people who took dumb risks. Getting the job working for the sheriff's office last year had been a blessing. Victoria's husband, Matt, found seasonal work in the area guiding fishermen and hunters. Plus, he watched the kids while she was at work, but she was the major bread-winner. Now that the kids were in school all day, Victoria found herself feeling a smidge resentful about their arrangement. Unless they decided to try for a third baby, she thought, it was time for Matt to look for a full-time job.

Although it was not her usual route to work, she decided to take Miles, wanting to see which of the side roads had been cleared. Approaching Detour Road, she reached for her car mirror. Tilting it down, she saw her lipstick was on straight, but her long red hair looked even more out-of-control than usual. *The power will be on in at the office. I can deal with it there,* she thought, before spotting a dark vehicle coming up rapidly behind her. The driver seemed to be having difficulty keeping the car under control. Then to her horror, she saw the car swerve wildly down into the snow-filled ditch at the corner, coming to a stop against a tree. The driver's head jerked back and then fell forward against the steering wheel.

Taking a moment to get control of her breathing, Victoria pulled her car over to the side of the road, got out and trudged back to the site of the collision as the wind whipped around her. She cleared a small patch of snow from the car's windshield and peered inside. A woman driver with curly blonde hair was leaning against the steering wheel. She wasn't moving. A surge of fear rose in Victoria's chest.

Working her way around the tree, she rapped against the window. The woman didn't move. Struggling to pull the door open against the powerful wind, she leaned into the car and said, "Can you hear me? Are you all right?" There was no response. At first, she couldn't tell if the driver was breathing, but by watching carefully, she could detect faint respirations. Then she looked into the back seat.

A tiny child in a pink snowsuit gazed silently at her. A fringe of dark curls had escaped her snowsuit hood and lay sweetly on her forehead. Her eyes were open, but as soon as she saw Victoria, the child shut them tightly. Pulling off her gloves and shuddering when the wind hit her fingers, she pulled her cellphone from her pocket and dialed 911.

"911 Operator, what is your emergency?"

"I'm standing by a car accident on Miles Road. The car veered down into the ditch at the corner before it was stopped by a tree. There's a woman at the wheel who's barely breathing and a little girl in the back seat. Please send an ambulance."

"Right away. Can you call Inman's Plowing and get them to tow the car out of the ditch so emergency personnel can get to the patient?"

"Will do, but please hurry. I can't get any response from the woman driver."

"Can you tell if she's breathing?"

"I think so, but it's pretty faint," Victoria said.

"What about the child? Is she okay?"

"She doesn't seem to be injured, but her eyes are shut and she's not making a sound."

"Okay, don't move either one of them. Stay where you are. We're on our way."

"What's happening?" Victoria's boss, Undersheriff Pete Manstead snapped when he caught her call a few minutes later.

"I was on my way to work this morning when I saw a car veer off Miles Road and hit a tree. There's a woman who's not moving at the wheel and a little child in a car seat in the back. I can't get any response from the driver and she's barely breathing. I've already called 911 and they are on their way. Inman's is coming to tow the car out of the ditch so the EMT's can transfer the driver into the ambulance, but something's not right about this situation, Pete. I want you to come out here."

"Okay. Can you see the license number on the vehicle? I want to see who it belongs to."

"Hang on. It'll take a bit of time to get around to the back of the car." Moments later, Victoria read him the number.

"Okay. Stay where you are. Charlie left a message that he was going to be here today. We'll both be there ASAP."

Charlie Pierce was their Deputy who was stationed on Beaver Island. He'd joined the staff after finishing a stint with the Navy as a Seal in the Special Forces. Although jokingly competitive with the other men, Charlie's military background meant he was good at following orders. He was a dark-complexioned guy with a short beard and a ready smile.

Leaving the station, Pete and Charlie drove past Castle Farms, Holy Island Road on the left and Otis Pottery on the right before taking Raney Road that veered sharply up the hill. It proved to be a bad idea. He was about half-way up the steep incline when his patrol car started sliding back down.

"Frickin' ice," he yelled, but managed to get the car under control and eased the vehicle back down the hill. It took another few minutes, making their way through the network of interconnecting roads before they reached the accident and Pete spotted the car in the ditch. His dispatcher in her red parka was standing beside it.

"Are you okay?" he asked when he reached Victoria. She'd been out in the elements for some time already and was white-faced and shivering. "I'm sorry it took so long to get here. There were a lot of unplowed roads."

"I'm pretty shaken up, but Inman's Snowplowing and the ambulance are both on their way," she said. "Do you know who the car belongs to?"

"Carly Yellowwood is her name. She lives out on Phelps Road."

"I'm afraid she might be dying, Pete," Victoria said with a shudder. "I couldn't get her to respond and she's hardly breathing. Can you check? You used to be an EMT, right?"

"I'll see if I can get a pulse," he said with a forbidding set to his mouth.

In the few minutes it took for Pete to get into position, the worst night of his life returned to hit him with a gut punch. He couldn't stop the awful memory of the snowmobile sliding off the ice and into a patch of open water—watching as it fell silently from sight, seeing the driver and his small passenger tumble down into the jagged black opening. No, he couldn't think about that now, how he had hesitated those few critical minutes before tearing off his coat, removing his boots and diving into the deep icy water. *Shut it off*, he told himself and bit the inside of his mouth hard enough to taste blood. It was a distraction technique he'd learned from the therapist he saw for a year after that terrible night.

Touching the still-warm throat of the young woman at the wheel of the car, Pete realized reluctantly that Victoria was right. The driver was in critical condition. He pulled her hood back, checked her forehead and the back of her head. There were no obvious injuries. The situation was puzzling because it looked like the car had just come to a stop by the tree—not that she had hit it at high speed. There was no bark torn off the trunk and it didn't seem like bumping into the tree would have resulted in this situation.

"She's unresponsive and apneic," Pete yelled to Victoria and Charlie. "I'm starting CPR."

"I'll radio the hospital that CPR is in progress," Charlie hollered back.

THREE

Ed Inman's back was killing him. He'd been plowing driveways and hauling cars out of ditches ever since the storm started, and was exhausted. They already had two feet of snow on the ground and the prediction was for more to arrive over the next few days.

"Morning, Mr. Inman," the seventeen-year-old high schooler named Trisha greeted him when he arrived at the office that morning. The girl occasionally subbed for his normal full-time office person who was out sick. Because schools were cancelled, she was available.

"Morning, Trisha. Thanks for coming in to help."

"No problem. We've had a little excitement here this morning. Victoria, the dispatcher from the sheriff's office called. There's been an accident. The car hit a tree and it's stuck in deep snow. She called 911 and there's an ambulance coming, but the car has to be towed out of the ditch so the EMT's can get to the driver."

"Has Riley come in yet?" Riley Donovan was Ed's assistant whose red hair stood bright testament to his Irish ancestry.

"He's just called. Almost here."

"Call him back and see if he will take the run, will you?"

"Hang on," she said. After placing the call, she told Mr. Inman that Riley would handle the emergency request.

"Okay, call Victoria back and tell her Riley's on his way."

"Thanks for taking this call, Buddy, I owe you," Ed said when, his assistant came into the office stamping the snow off his boots, removing his gloves and blowing on his hands to warm them.

"No problem. Trisha told me about the collision. How do I get there?"

"Take a right on County Road 48 at the light at East Jordan and then hang another right on Miles. It's only about a mile to Detour which goes off to your left. The County sometimes puts a barricade of straw bales on the corners of those seasonal roads so watch out for that."

"Will do," Riley said, tugging on his gloves and tightening the string on the hood of his parka before walking out of the office and climbing into the large red snowplow.

As the big rig pulled out onto M-66, Ed heaved a sigh of relief. *I'm getting too old for this job. Edna's probably right, it is time to retire*, he thought.

Except for blowing snow that skittered across the road's icy surface, Riley's drive down M-66 toward East Jordan wasn't as bad as he'd expected. The county had been plowing the road on and off since the storm started, barely managing to stay ahead of the snowfall. Reaching the stoplight at the city limits, he turned right on County Road 48 and drove slowly past the vet clinic before attempting the hill. He hit the gas hard and although the rig swerved on patches of ice, he managed to get to the top before pulling off the side of the road and peering ahead. There were no lights on in any of the houses. The storm had taken the power out throughout the county.

Putting the snowplow into gear, Riley pulled back onto the road. As he drove, the snow made huge exploding stars against his windshield. Ed had said it was about a mile to the turn-off and he watched his gauge intently. When he spotted what looked like a barely visible line of black trees going off to the left, he stopped the snowplow and climbed down. Ahead of him were three cars, an older blue Subaru, a sheriff's patrol car, and off to the side of the road a small black vehicle with its nose up against a tree. He could hear the distinctive siren of the ambulance coming from the north and saw an officer from the sheriff's office hiking toward him.

"I'm here from Inman's to tow the car out of the ditch," he yelled when the deputy arrived.

"Thanks for coming out," Charlie shouted.

Riley nodded. The wind was brutal and it was hard to hear. "What's the situation?"

"There's an unconscious woman at the wheel and a small child in the back seat. The sheriff is doing CPR on the driver. Let me check in with the ambulance driver to see if they want you to tow the car out now or wait after until they assess the driver."

"Yes, sir. No problem."

"I'm going to talk to the ambulance crew. I'll let you know what they say," Charlie said.

"Good morning, Officer," the paramedic said when they pulled up in the ambulance. "My name's Ward. This is Chrissy." The female EMT sitting in the rider's seat waved.

"Thanks for coming. There's an unconscious woman and a small child in that car in the ditch. Undersheriff Manstead; is doing chest compressions on the driver, but it's not looking good. Hopefully you can get her heart to start up again with the paddles," Charlie said.

"We'll give it a try," Ward said.

The wind shrieked around the two young medics as they trudged through the blizzard toward the car belonging to Carly Yellowwood.

"I got this, Sheriff," Ward said, gesturing for Pete to step aside and placing his stethoscope on the woman's chest. After a few moments, he said, "I'd rather treat her in the ambulance, but there's no time. I brought the portable defibrillator. I'm going to charge the monitor to 200 joules." He placed the paddles on the woman's body and connected the leads. Pete could hear the monitor charging, producing a low to high tone. Then the machine beeped.

"Clear," Ward yelled and Pete jumped back as the paramedic pressed the shock button. The female driver jerked horribly up and down as the current coursed through her body. After shocking the woman several times and listening to her heart, Ward looked at Pete and shook his head.

"No luck, sheriff. She's gone. Where should I take the body?"

Pete hesitated. He was a deliberate man, slow to come to conclusions but tenacious as a badger in pursuit of anyone who broke the law. "Take her to the Morgue at the hospital. Thanks, Ward. Appreciate your help today," he said and clapped the man on the back.

Charlie helped Ward lift Carly Yellowwood's body onto a stretcher. The two men carried her to the ambulance and loaded her inside. As the men were attending to the driver, Chrissy leaned into the back seat of Carly's car to check the child. After a few moments, she unbuckled the little one and lifted her out. Pete's dispatcher was standing nearby and they had a short conversation, after which Victoria disconnected the child's car seat and installed it in her own vehicle. Then she started her car while Chrissy buckled the little one in.

Backing her car down the road until she was alongside the ambulance, Victoria drew level with Pete and rolled her window down. "Chrissy and I are going to take the child to the hospital," she said.

"Why didn't they put her in the ambulance?"

"She's not injured and I'm not having this child ride in that vehicle with her mother's dead body." Victoria's teeth were clamped tight in determination.

Looking at Chrissy, who shrugged her shoulders, Pete decided not to argue.

As the ambulance pulled out, Pete gestured to Charlie and they hiked back to his patrol car. The situation was sufficiently troubling that he wanted to check in with his boss. They climbed into the car and he turned on the heat.

"What did you tell Riley to do with the victim's car?"

"Told him to tow it to our lot," Charlie said. "Figured you would want to get all the information we could from the vehicle."

"Good thinking. I'm calling the sheriff," Pete said and dialed the number.

"Dodgson speaking."

"Sorry to bother you, sir, but we have a fatal incident on our hands. A car belonging to Carly Yellowwood went off the road into a ditch this morning. The ambulance is taking her body to the morgue, so I hope to get a cause of death from the pathologist. She had a small child in the car with her. Victoria and the EMT took her to the hospital to be checked out."

"Okay. Call me after you talk to the coroner. And let me know if you want me to come back. As you know, I planned to take a week's vacation with my wife after the conference. She's flying in today."

"Will do," Pete said and clicked off the call.

FOUR

It had been a very careful drive through snow-covered rural roads in high winds before Victoria and Chrissy reached Charlevoix hospital. Chrissy had called the ER about the situation and Victoria was able to drive directly into the loading dock. Two nurses in heavy parkas were waiting for them and carried the child inside immediately.

After a thorough check by the ER attending, the doctor turned to Victoria.

"This child's lethargy bothers me. Did you notice how she doesn't react or smile? And her eyes are partly closed. She looks old enough to speak, but she's not talking. I'm wondering if she could be on the spectrum."

"Is she going to be okay?" Victoria asked. Her voice sounded pitiful.

"You have asked me that three times already, Mrs. Treadwell, and as I said before, she is breathing well, her heart rate is only a little lower than optimum, and her blood pressure is close to normal. She's been given IV fluids as a precaution and we put her in the warming device we call the bear-hugger. She wasn't in the cold for very long, but I thought it might help bring her around."

"Is she in a coma, doctor?"

"No, just lethargic. Without more tests, however, we won't know anything definitive about her mental state." He looked down at the chart before saying, "There's no name listed on this patient."

"The driver's name was Carly Yellowwood. I think she was the child's mother."

"How did you come to get involved?"

"I'm the dispatcher for the sheriff's office and was on my way to work this morning when I noticed a car that was pitching back and forth across the road behind me. The car slid off the road and came to a stop against a tree. I went back to see if they could use some help. The driver was unresponsive and I called an ambulance. They came and after multiple efforts to re-start the driver's heart, said she was deceased. Her body's been taken to the Morgue. I'm afraid this little person saw her mother perish."

"It's possible she's in shock," the physician said. "I'm going to put her name down as Yellowwood with an unknown first name."

Struggling to control her emotions, Victoria said, "Can't you give me anything else about her prognosis, doctor?" Her eyes caught the young man's gaze.

"I'm sorry, Mrs. Treadwell, you're just going to have to trust us. From what you tell me, this little girl's gone through a major trauma. It's going to be some time before we know the full extent of her condition. I'm going to have her taken for a psychological assessment."

"Can I go with her?"

"I'm sorry, but you are not her parent, so no," the doctor said.

Looking up at his solemn gaze, Victoria Treadwell's eyes filled with tears.

AFTER THE CHILD WAS CARRIED AWAY by a nurse, Victoria made a brief stop at the rest room to regain her composure. It was critical to learn more about the little person whose life she had likely saved, especially her name. Making her way through the maze of corridors to the hospital library, she found a room with multiple computers for staff use. Hearing about the situation, a competent IT tech helped her got on line. An hour later, having obtained the help of the Charlevoix High school librarian and calling the Vital Records office, Victoria had finished a pretty comprehensive background on Carly Yellowwood. Knowing Pete would want the news, she called the office.

"I have some information for you about Carly and her daughter," Victoria said when he came on the line.

"Good. Tell me what you found."

"Carly and Joe Yellowwood dated all through their teens. Both attended Charlevoix High School and they got married right after graduation. Their daughter, whose name is Chenoa Kai, was born three years later. Her first name means white dove in Chippewa. Her middle name means Willow."

"How did you get all this?"

"High School yearbooks and Vital Records. Carly is twenty-three so I figured she had graduated from high school five years ago. Joe was in the same class. There were lots of pictures of the two of them in the yearbooks, at prom and football games. The librarian sent the photos to my phone."

"With that last name, I'm assuming Joe's Native American. I'm going to have to inform him of his wife's demise. I've never had to do this before, and I have to tell him in person. At least his daughter's alive . . ." Pete's voice trailed off.

"There's a bit more complexity to this situation. Joe's mother lives on the local Chippewa/Ottawa reservation and he's living with her. After he and Carly got married, he worked multiple jobs, but showed up one night at the ER with bruises and a black eye. The guy who came off worse in the fight had to have stitches. All this was from a bar brawl. Joe was subsequently convicted of assault and served two years. Once he was released, he and Carly got a divorce, so he moved back home with his mother."

"Good information," Pete said. "I have an appointment with the pathologist for the results of Carly's autopsy at five thirty today. I think I'll wait to tell Joe about the crash until I talk to him. Meanwhile, you have to locate the appropriate hospital personnel and tell them that Joe Yellowwood is Chenoa's next of kin. The hospital will inform the family that she's there."

It was nearly six o'clock before Pete took the elevator down to the basement of the hospital where Dr. Maxwell Winter was standing in the hall outside the door to the Morgue. The doctor was a heavy-set man with a belly that curved roundly over his belt. He wore a pair of green scrubs, paper booties over his shoes, and was holding a pair of plastic gloves in his hand. They had met only once, years earlier. Violent death was extremely rare in the county and such events were the only reasons he would have been required to consult the coroner.

"Hello, Dr. Winter. I'm Undersheriff Peter Manstead. I apologize for being late. Have you had time to see the body?"

"I have already completed my preliminary work on the autopsy," Dr. Winter said crisply, pursing his lips. It was obvious he was irritated at the delay.

"Do you have a cause of death for me?"

"The cause of the woman's death has been difficult to pin down. There were no injuries to her body or any head trauma. However, her pupils were fixed and dilated which led me to order a toxicology screen. The results just came back. She had digoxin, that's known as Digitalis, in her system. It's a medicine used to control congestive heart failure among other things."

"Did she die of an overdose?" Pete asked.

"That, Sheriff, is not clear. Most substance abusers have multiple indications of drug use on their bodies—needle tracks, aggravated insult to the nasal passages or throat, etc. She had none of those. In fact, it doesn't look to me like she ever smoked, drank or took street drugs. I am reserving the cause of death until I do more tests."

"How long after she took the drugs would Carly have died?" Pete asked.

"It couldn't have been much more than an hour, an hour and a half at most. Are you ready to see her?" The pathologist was looking at him with the critical eyes of an irritated seagull.

Pete nodded. He knew it was a test. In the case of a violent or suspicious death it was expected that law enforcement would view the autopsy. He took a deep breath, squared his shoulders and followed the doctor into the morgue, dreading the grisly sight of the young woman's dead body.

The room had tall ceilings and metal flooring. It was filled with the coppery scent of blood and the pungent odor of formaldehyde. Carly Yellowwood's naked body lay on a stainless-steel table partially covered with a white sheet. He took a shaky breath, envisioning the young woman struggling to breathe before her car struck the tree.

"Would hers have been a painful death, doctor?" he asked.

"Probably not. Still, it's a shame, a young life snuffed out and she was a mother. I could tell from my examination that she'd given birth."

"Is this all you have for me?" Pete was feeling desperate to leave. He'd managed not to pass out or throw up, but he could feel his stomach churning.

"No, that is definitely not all, Officer," the coroner said, frowning. "Miss Yellowwood had sexual intercourse a day or two before she died."

"Was it assault?" he asked.

"No, the sex was consensual."

"Could you get DNA from the semen?" Pete asked. He was thinking it was likely to be the man Carly had sex with who gave her the drugs.

"Probably not. Unfortunately, the man used a prophylactic," the coroner said and Pete's heart sank.

Trudging out of the hospital through the swirling blizzard to where he'd parked his patrol car, Pete Manstead felt overwhelmed. The situation was made much more complicated by what he'd just learned from Dr. Winter. Carly Yellowwood was in an intimate relationship with someone. Because she was divorced, she was unlikely to be sleeping with her ex-husband, which made him automatically a suspect. In the case of a spousal, or ex-spousal death, the partner was always the first to be questioned.

Joe Yellowwood was Native American and lived on the small Indian reservation in Evelyn Township. Envisioning the township map in his mind, he remembered it was pretty close to Carly's address. Pete felt a twist of frustration, knowing he had no jurisdiction on their land. Native Americans were a separate nation and even entering the reservation sometimes required permission.

He'd interrogated some young Native Americans boys several years ago with respect to a robbery. They refused to answer. Didn't even claim the 5th or say, "No comment." He could see shutters closing over their eyes at his every question. While he could interview Native Americans who lived *off* the reservation, he wasn't even permitted to bring those who lived *on* the reservation into the station for questioning without their consent. That fact was going to make investigating this situation far more difficult.

Given the doctor's description of Carly's body and his assertion that she'd never smoked, drank or used illicit drugs, it was starting to look like a crime. *If Carly was forced to take those drugs, it might even have been manslaughter,* Pete thought. *Or attempted murder.* Taking a deep breath, he dialed the sheriff's number.

"Sheriff Dodgson."

"Hello, sir. I talked with the pathologist just now and he's unwilling to specify a cause of death for Carly Yellowwood without doing more tests, except to say it wasn't the car crash that killed her. He found Digitalis in her system, but didn't see any evidence that she used drugs. In his professional opinion, she was unlikely to have taken the drug voluntarily. I've been thinking about this and we could have a case of attempted murder or manslaughter here."

"Are you sure you aren't jumping to conclusions, Pete? Maybe it was a suicide attempt."

"I doubt the woman would have planned to kill both herself and her little daughter, sir. Her child was in the back seat."

"You're probably right, but suicide will have to be checked out. If she didn't intend to kill herself, then you're thinking someone forced her to take the drugs."

"That's exactly what I think, sir, and if so it's premeditated."

There was silence on the other end of the line. They both knew there hadn't been a murder in Charlevoix County in fifteen years, ever since an East Jordan man was convicted of murdering his brother. That trial was complex and lengthy because the body of the murdered man was never discovered. And although it had been almost thirty years, both of them still vividly recalled listening to family conversations during their childhoods about the death of Jon Benet Ramsey. She had won a child beauty pageant in Charlevoix and while she died in Colorado, the town became a flashpoint for hordes of reporters and photographers for weeks thereafter.

"I'd head home now, but I promised my wife we'd stay here for a week after the conference and she's arriving shortly. Do you want me to request a detective from Traverse City, or make a call to the state police?"

"Not yet. I think I can handle the first stage which is just information gathering."

"You better call in our deputies from the two sub-stations. They can do the door-to-door and talk to her neighbors."

"Charlie came in already and he's here with me now. I'll call Ben," Pete said.

"What do you think happened?"

"I think the woman was fleeing an assailant, probably the person who made her take those drugs, and died while driving away."

"Are you sure you don't want me to come back, Pete? I will, if you want me to. My wife will be pissed, but it wouldn't be the first time."

"No, I assume it's just putting together a picture of the victim and her movements on the morning she perished. It's a pretty tight window of time. It was 10:00 a.m. when the paramedics stopped resuscitation and declared Carly dead."

"Okay. In the worst case this is attempted or even premeditated murder, let me give you a little advice. When I was going through my training, I rotated through the serious crimes unit and learned something I've always remembered. You have to find out everything you can about the victim—her financial situation, her social media presence, her workplace colleagues, friends and especially the name of her husband or boyfriend. Young women keep their whole lives on their phones, so it's critical to find it. Dig deep and it will give you her killer. One other thing. Do you know the first question to ask in a murder investigation?"

"Did the victim have enemies?"

"That's a critically important question, although most people deny that the victim had any enemies. The next question is, *who benefits*? Following that line of inquiry will lead you to the perpetrator every time. If you can get by without me for the week, I'll step in then. I must admit it would smooth the matrimonial waters to take this vacation," Sheriff Dodgson said.

"Okay," Pete said. He wished the sheriff would have talked a little slower, especially when he was listing all the things he should find out about the victim. "I'll let you know as soon as possible about the child's condition, sir."

"Thank you."

FIVE

Returning to the ER from the library, Victoria asked the intake clerk the whereabouts of her little foundling. "The patient's last name is Yellowwood. The ER physician referred her to their social worker for an assessment."

"Just a minute," the clerk focused her attention on her computer and then said, "Okay, the assessment was done and the child was admitted to Pediatrics. The room number is 207 B."

"Can I see her?" Victoria asked?

"No problem, take the elevator to the second floor and then go right through the swinging doors."

When Victoria located Chenoa's room, she was wearing a tiny hospital gown, a diaper and lying in a crib. She was curled on her side, sucking her thumb and sound asleep. Obviously, the horrific events of the morning had worn the little one out. She stepped outside into the hall to call her husband.

"What's going on this morning?" Matt asked when he answered. "I called the office and when they said you weren't there yet, I checked your location on the Find My Friends app. It shows you in the hospital. Are you okay, sweetheart?"

"I'm fine, but I witnessed an accident on my way to work. It was a bad one. The driver didn't make it, but there was a small child alive in the back seat. The EMT and I took the little girl to the hospital and I'm going to stay with her the rest of today and tonight. I don't want her to be alone."

"Why did you go that way in the first place? It's not the route you usually take."

"You're right, I usually go through East Jordan, but for some reason I decided to take side roads today."

"If you hadn't, you might not have seen the car off the road," Matt said quietly. "It sounds to me like you might have saved her life."

"I believe I did, honey. It could have been hours before someone else came down the road and found them. Ever since I first set eyes on the child, I've been thinking about this situation and we should talk."

"What does that mean?" Matt said. He hated it when Victoria used that phrase. It always meant he had done something wrong.

"Since her mother's dead and I discovered that her father's had problems with the law, the child, her full name is Chenoa Kai Yellowwood, might have to be adopted. You remember we were talking a while ago about having a third baby. You know how much I'd love to have a daughter."

"And you know I was not in favor of a third child. We just got the boys in school full-time and I want to get a trained hunting dog for my guiding business."

Not the damn hunting dog again, Victoria thought and gritted her teeth. Trained pointers went for upwards of $15,000. Matt's guiding business had only brought in that much the previous year.

"Did you say the child's last name was Yellowwood?"

"That's right. Her father's Native American and her mother was Caucasian which makes her half Native."

"And you were thinking because I'm one-quarter Chippewa that I could be talked into this." He sounded mildly amused.

"I hoped you would at least consider the idea. We already have two sons and you come from a family of all boys, as does your father. My guess is if I got pregnant again, it would be another boy. I'd really like a little girl, Matt."

"Even if you could convince me, Victoria, we wouldn't be approved. I have the necessary blood quantum, but am three-quarters white. My paternal grandfather was First Nations, but he died when I was ten and I wasn't raised on the reservation. I remember him well, though, and he told me a lot about the history of the tribes. Did you know for over a century that thousands of Native children were systematically removed from their families—often without evidence of abuse or neglect that would be considered legal grounds for taking such an action? During that time, they were placed in boarding schools where they were forced to cut off their hair, beaten if they spoke their languages and often abused."

"That's horrible. I didn't know that," Victoria said. "We've talked a lot about your tribal background, but I don't think you ever told me about the schools." She felt deeply sobered by the information and awful about what the authorities had done that to those children and their parents.

"Even when the era of the boarding schools came to an end, a third of Native children continued to be taken and were invariably placed with Caucasian parents. The clear intent was to deprive them of their culture. It wasn't until 1978 that the Indian Child Welfare Act was passed which states that Native children are to be placed with tribal families whenever possible. The Supreme Court just reinforced the law's constitutionality. I'm certain the social workers will find that this child has a family."

"She does, but it's complicated because in addition to her mother having died, her father was convicted of assault and battery a few years ago. It was a bar fight and he served two years."

"Is he out now?"

"Yes, and living with his mother."

"So the child has a father and a grandmother. I'm telling you, sweetheart, they will get custody."

There was a significant pause before Victoria said, "Well, maybe we could be her foster parents until custody is legally determined. Would you be all right with me talking to the social workers about that?"

"It's up to you, Victoria, but even if they agree we can have her for a short while, it might be pretty hard on you when she leaves. I really don't think this is a good idea," Matt said gently.

"Tell the boys I love them and that I'll be home tomorrow," Victoria said crisply and clicked off the call. She hadn't added the usual, "love you" that she always said. Matt frowned as he hung up.

Walking back to Chenoa's room, Victoria pulled up a chair beside her hospital crib, and took the tyke's warm little hand in hers. With Joe Yellowwood's history of violence, she thought it was possible her husband could be wrong and the court might let them adopt her. Thinking the child might be comforted by a stuffed animal toy, she used her cell phone to order a pink teddy bear from Amazon.

DR. KIM, THE SOLE HOSPITALIST AT the Charlevoix hospital whose position required him to cover both adult and pediatric patients, had pushed open the door to Chenoa Yellowwood's room late that afternoon when he paused at the sound of a woman singing. Through the partly-open door, he could see a woman sitting on the edge of a hospital bed beside the patient's crib and heard the words of an old lullaby. The woman stopped singing when she heard the door swish open.

"Hello, I'm Dr. Kim," he said with a smile.

"I'm Victoria Treadwell. Thank you for coming."

"It's nice to meet you. I see in my records that the doctor who saw her in the ER was concerned that she wasn't talking. He had our social worker do an assessment because she was unresponsive on admission. I have the report right here," Dr. Kim said, looking at his tablet. "The social worker thought she would emerge from her lethargy naturally in time."

"I wanted to go with her for the assessment, but the ER physician said because I am not her mother, I couldn't be present. I worried that Chenoa would be scared."

"Our social worker has hit on a technique to help ease children's anxiety. She blows bubbles in the air and lets her small patients burst them. Then she walks around the office blowing bubbles in a trail behind her. The children follow her like she's the Pied Piper," Dr. Kim said with a smile. Then he pulled his stethoscope from around his neck and listened carefully to Chenoa's heart and lungs, entering his findings on a tablet. He palpated her belly, looked into her ears and checked her head and neck.

"Excuse me, Doctor, I want you to know that Chenoa tightened her fingers on mine earlier," Victoria said.

"Well, it could just be unconscious movement, but hopefully it was intentional. If so, it's a good sign. Everything you can do to stimulate her awareness is helpful. You can read to her, rub her back, and go back to your singing. You have a fine voice."

"Thank you. I used to sing in a church choir. I intend to do everything I can for this little one. Did they note on the record that her mother died?"

"Yes, I saw that," he paused. "It's apparent to me that you have feelings for this child. Do you wish to maintain a relationship with her after she leaves the hospital?"

"My husband and I have two sons, but we had been discussing having a third child. We would be open to adopting her, if there are no other family members who can raise her." With a brief self-conscious smile Victoria added, "I know it's silly, but I feel as if the universe nudged me to take a different route to work this morning and find her."

Dr. Kim smiled and in a gentle voice said, "In the East, there are two schools of thought about saving a life. One insists that the person who was saved owes a debt that can never be repaid. Others believe the person who saved someone has a duty to continue to care for them their whole lives. I am a Buddhist, Mrs. Treadwell, and you wanting to be involved in this little person's life sounds like karma to me."

TO VICTORIA TREADWELL'S IMMENSE RELIEF JUST as the sun came up the next morning, Chenoa emerged from her lethargy and sat up in her crib.

"Hello, Chenoa," Victoria said feeling a burst of joy explode in her core. "I'm so happy to see you're awake."

"I want my Mommy. Ouchy," Chenoa said and touched the site where her IV was inserted.

"And you're talking in sentences! I'm going to get the nurse and have her remove that ouchy thing. I'll be right back."

Standing up and walking from the room, Victoria's feet felt like they hardly touched the ground. *Thank you God*, she thought, almost floating down the tiled corridor.

"That's wonderful," the nurse said when Victoria told her the news. "I'll get some food ordered and check to see if her IV can be removed. The family has been notified that Chenoa is in the hospital. They contacted the grandmother, but she's got a bad case of the flu and can't come in today. She is going to tell her son that his daughter is here. I also heard from child services that Mrs. Robbins and her associate Sharon Tucker will be here this afternoon. They'll probably be putting Chenoa in foster care as there is some question about her guardianship."

"Did they tell Mrs. Yellowwood that Chenoa's mother died?" Victoria asked.

"No. Informing the family of an unnatural death is the job of law enforcement," the nurse said firmly.

"Thank you," Victoria said and pulled her cell phone from her pocket. She would have to remind Pete to tell Joe Yellowwood about Carly's death. And after that, she and Matt had some serious talking to do.

SIX

Tuesday

Pete practically blew into the station the next morning, pursued by a wild gust of wind that disarranged several papers on his red-headed dispatcher's desk. To his surprise, since she had texted him that she was staying with the little Yellowwood girl in the hospital, he saw Victoria at her station. He caught his breath, removed his coat and hung it on the hooks inside the door.

"How come you're here?" he asked.

"Chenoa is doing much better. Since my sons are in school full-time, I asked my husband to stay with her in the hospital today while I came in to work." The idea had come to her when the nurse said the social workers were coming to put the child in foster care. She thought Matt might take to the idea of adoption once he saw and interacted with little Chenoa. She also thought he'd probably represent them better with the social workers. She knew she might come across a bit prickly.

"Our deputies are both coming in to the post this morning," Pete said. "Please send them down to my office as soon as they get here." Then, nodding politely to the two people in the waiting area, he walked down the hall.

Their deputies arrived within the hour. Charlie had been with Pete when they found Carly Yellowwood, but Deputy Ben Wilcox had only been informed that they had an unnatural death. Ben was a good-looking guy in his twenties, tall with a receding hairline and a ribald sense of humor. He and Charlie were constantly engaged in practical jokes and friendly rivalry. They stomped the snow off their boots, removed their coats and talked briefly about the second surge of snow and icy rain that was headed their way.

Walking down the hall to the conference room, Ben asked Charlie what he knew about the situation.

"I was with Pete when we found her," Charlie said quietly. "Poor woman died. Her name was Carly Yellowwood."

"Yellowwood... sounds like an Indian name," Ben said, shooting him a glance.

"First Nations," Charlie said.

"Was she... First Nations?" Ben asked.

"She looked Caucasian to me, but the boss will bring us up to date."

"THANK YOU FOR COMING," PETE GREETED Ben and Charlie when they walked in. "I wanted to give you an update on the situation. Victoria was on her way into the office yesterday morning when she spotted a car lurching across the road behind her. The car swerved off the road and ran into a tree. I did CPR on the driver, and when the ambulance arrived they used the shock paddles, but we were too late. She couldn't be resuscitated. The woman had her young daughter with her in the car. Victoria and the EMT took the child to the hospital."

"Was the crash the cause of Carly's death?" Charlie asked.

"The pathologist is still doing tests, but apparently not. He found evidence of drugs in her system on the toxicology screen, but said she wasn't a user. He didn't believe it was an overdose either. It looks like Carly was drugged deliberately. If I'm right, what we have here, gentlemen, is an attempted or even a premeditated murder case."

The deputies looked at each other in stunned disbelief.

"What can we do to help?" Ben asked after a moment of silence.

"I have Carly Yellowwood's address. It's a small cottage on Phelps Road. I've requested a warrant to search the place."

"Want us to do the house-to-house in the meantime? See if anyone saw anything yesterday morning?" Charlie asked.

"Yes. There are only a couple of other houses on Phelps and the road probably hasn't been plowed," Pete said and then added, "If you talk to any of her neighbors, see if they know who Carly was dating."

"Because?" Charlie asked, raising his eyebrows.

"Because she was in a sexual relationship with someone who may have forced her to take those drugs. Since she was divorced, she probably wasn't having sex with her ex-husband. His name is Joe Yellowwood and I have to inform him about the situation. I want to keep Carly's death confidential at this point. Until we know more, she is officially a missing person. We're looking into her disappearance."

The men nodded, picked up their empty coffee cups and tossed them silently in the wastebasket.

By mid-morning, Pete was standing in front of the reception desk at the Charlevoix County Building on State Street. He had gone there to pick up a search warrant for Carly Yellowwood's home. The receptionist was on the phone with what seemed like a personal call. He was trying to be patient, but felt time ticking away. He knew the first days in a criminal investigation were critical and it was already the day after Carly had succumbed to the drugs in her system. Whoever drugged her could already be long gone.

"How can I help you, sir?" the receptionist asked, having concluded her call.

"I'm Undersheriff Manstead and I'm picking up a search warrant for a property on Phelps Road."

"Just a moment while I check with the Judge," she said and departed through a door behind her desk. She returned, after a significant delay (just as he was mentally ready to pull his hair out in frustration) and asked for his identification. He opened his coat, showed her his badge and pulled out his ID. She looked carefully at his name and the name on the envelope before handing him the warrant.

He was making his way back to the patrol car in rising wind when his phone rang. He pulled it out of his pocket seeing that the caller was Dr. Max Winter.

"Hello, Doctor."

"I have some more information for you."

"Hang on just a second, please." Pete said. He was standing outside his car in the parking lot and having a hard time hearing over the keening wind. He opened his car door and got in. "Go ahead," he said.

"Did you hear me, Officer?"

"No, I missed your last sentence. Sorry."

"I wondered if Ms. Yellowwood could have been injected with the drugs, rather than swallowing them. But there were no needle marks or residue of patches—which are sometimes used to infuse drugs—on her body. The bottom line is that Carly swallowed those drugs. But, since I suspect she didn't take them voluntarily, I also checked every inch of her body with a magnifying glass and found a trace of saliva on Miss Yellowwood's upper lip. It wasn't hers."

How could she get saliva on her lips from someone else? Pete wondered briefly, before realizing that someone must have kissed Carly on the morning she died.

"Go on," he said.

"The saliva was from a male. He was tall, blue-eyed and of Northern European ethnicity."

"Good to know. How could someone have forced Carly to take those drugs?"

There was a significant pause before the somewhat long-suffering voice of the pathologist said, "My job is to tell you what the physical findings *are*, Sheriff. Figuring out what happened and whether there was a *crime*, is why the taxpayers pay your salary. I'll be finishing my report today and will fax it to your office. I suggest you read it in its entirety," he said dismissively.

Driving back to the office, Pete thought through the scenario. Nothing about the situation was making sense. As Sheriff Dodgson had said, Carly either took those drugs to kill herself, which he thought highly unlikely, or someone forced her to take them. And why would Carly have taken the drugs at all, much less early on a Monday morning? If she had taken them the night before, by drinking a spiked beverage at a bar or a club, it would have made more sense—but the pathologist was certain if that had been the case, she wouldn't have lived long enough to see the light of day. Who could she have visited that morning? Was it the same guy who kissed her? Was having sex with? He shook his head.

SEVEN

The wind grabbed the station door and Pete struggled to pull it closed when he got back to the office.

"Have Charlie or Ben called in yet?"

"They are headed back now," Victoria said.

Victoria and her husband were a local family, bee-keepers in their spare time, who sold honey from a roadside stand in the summer. She kept a large flower garden and put cut flowers in disposable containers by their mailbox, free for anyone who drove by. Pete had been part of the search committee when she was hired and had voted in her favor. He respected her and they worked well together.

"I'll go down to the conference room and wait for them."

Fifteen minutes later, Charlie and Ben walked into the room. They were accompanied by Victoria. Pete frowned. As a dispatcher, she wasn't part of the investigative team, but he didn't really know how to exclude her, especially since she'd been the person who found Carly Yellowwood's car and stayed with the child in the hospital. A few minutes later, he heard voices in the front office and tilted his head meaningfully toward the door, whereupon his dispatcher left the room.

"Have a seat, guys. Were you able to talk to Carly's neighbors?"

"As you said, Boss, the road was unplowed so it was quite a slog. There are three houses on the road, but nobody was home at two of them. We found one family virtually snowed-in. We talked to the young mother with two preschoolers. All three of them had a bad case of cabin fever. The kids were running around and shrieking like crazy. She was pretty glad to see us," Ben said.

"Her husband works on Beaver Island for the power company and hasn't been home since the storm. The names are," Charlie stopped speaking and pulled out his notes. "Mike and Sherry Mills. They told me Carly Yellowwood sees two gentlemen at her home from time to time. One is a guy they said was her ex, Joe Yellowwood. The second guy is a . . ."

"A tall white guy," Pete said with a slow self-deprecating grin. "Turns out the person Carly's was in a relationship with is ethnically Northern European."

"How the heck did you find that out?" Charlie asked.

"Dr. Winter found some saliva on Carly's upper lip and did a DNA test. It's amazing what it can tell us these days. Did Mrs. Mills know the name of the second man?"

"Unfortunately, no, but she remembered his car. It was a navy-blue Chevy Blazer."

Just then Victoria re-entered the room. "I have something to contribute to the investigation," she said in a bright tone of voice. She was rising up and down on the balls of her feet.

"Go ahead," Pete said. He knew she was only trying to help, but she would have to back off. Finding the killer (and he was feeling more and more certain Carly had been deliberately slain) was his job. It was going to be hard enough without Victoria wanting to be part of the team.

Following proper procedure in this investigation was going to be critical. If they were to convict the perpetrator, all the evidence had to be uncovered by law enforcement. The problem was that his dispatcher, although keen to help and very intelligent, was a civilian. If she found information from her computer searches, which were part of her job responsibilities, such material could be used in building a case. If she found evidence outside her assigned tasks however, he decided he'd double-check with the sheriff as to whether it could be used.

"I found out where Carly worked. She was employed as a waitress at the White Swan, that's the fancy new restaurant on the marsh in East Jordan. It's just over the bridge on the south side, directly across from the Foundry."

"The owner of that restaurant is a tall white guy named Pat O'Connor," Ben said.

"I know Pat. He's married and is known as a bit of a womanizer," Charlie added with a tight grin.

"So, Pat O'Connor could be the new man in Carly's life," Victoria said, looking intently at Pete.

"What's next, Boss?" Charlie asked.

"I'd like you and Ben to have lunch at the White Swan. Since Carly worked there, you should be able to get some information from the wait staff about whether she and Pat were in a relationship. Victoria, I want you to try to find Carly's parents phone number."

"When I find it, should I call and tell them about Carly?"

"Absolutely not. That's my job." He was definitely not looking forward to it, but there was no choice. It was his duty as an officer of the law.

All three of them, Victoria, Ben and Charlie, were looking at him, waiting for his direction. He'd never had to lead a murder investigation before and felt the crushing weight of getting justice for this young woman. He swallowed, knowing he couldn't make a single misstep.

"Okay, you two guys head over to the White Swan. I have some calls to return and I want to write up what we have for the sheriff before I head out to Carly's place with the search warrant."

"Sounds good," Charlie said and Ben nodded. Victoria followed them out the door.

After they left, Pete took a few moments to review what they knew. One of those two men, either Joe Yellowwood or Pat O'Connor, who owned the White Swan, was most likely the perpetrator. He'd never dealt with a murder case before and had heard for years about how hard they were to crack. Murder detectives were considered the smartest on the force and he knew he was a plodder. Even his last name, Manstead, told the story. He was a steady man, slow to reach conclusions but smart enough to nail the perpetrator—given enough time.

His torturous thought processes weren't going to be a problem in this case, though, he told himself, feeling a bit more cheerful. Carly Yellowwood was a beautiful young woman who was involved with two men. She'd married and had a child with one guy and was in a sexual relationship with another. *What else could it possibly be except a crime of passion?*

HER CELL PHONE WAS RINGING WHEN Victoria got back to her desk. It was her husband, Matt.

"Hi, hon. How are things going?" she asked.

"There was a bit of a problem earlier this morning. Chenoa's father, Joe, came to see her. He wasn't very happy when he saw me here."

"Oh dear. What happened?"

"I told him you were the dispatcher for the sheriff's office and that you stayed with Chenoa last night because the hospital hadn't reached his mother until today. He asked why I was in the room and I said it was because you were at work and we didn't want her to be alone."

"Did that calm him down?"

"A bit."

"Does he know yet that Carly's dead?"

"It didn't come up and I sure as heck wasn't going to tell him. He stayed a while, played with the little one and then left. Hang on a minute . . ."

Victoria could hear Matt talking to a woman.

"The social workers are here to take Chenoa into care," he said when he came back on the line.

"Did you tell them that we'd like to be her foster parents?"

"Yes, but they already have someone in mind."

"Let me talk to Mrs. Robbins," Victoria said firmly. There was a brief delay before she heard the woman's voice.

"Hello."

"Hi. I'm Victoria Treadwell, the person who brought Chenoa to the hospital. My husband, Matt, tells me you want to take her to foster care."

"Yes, that's correct. There is some question about her guardianship, so until that's settled, she will be in foster care," Mrs. Robbins said firmly.

"Are you aware that Chenoa's First Nations? Given the recent Supreme Court decision that reinforced the constitutionality of the Indian Child Welfare Act, you should probably place her with a tribal foster family. My husband and I are prepared to act as foster parents for her until the situation has been clarified. Matt's one quarter Chippewa and has the blood quantum necessary to qualify. He's enrolled in the tribe and speaks the language. Are the foster family you have in mind First Nations?"

"No, Caucasian, I believe."

"Would placing her with a white family be legal?" Victoria asked, realizing she was coming across as challenging the woman.

"I'm going to check with my supervisor about this matter," Mrs. Robbins said.

"Just wouldn't want you to face any kind of repercussions because you put her in a non-tribal household," Victoria said. "We are willing to help."

"I'll get back to you about this," the social worker said.

EIGHT

When Sheriff's deputies, Charlie and Ben, arrived at the White Swan restaurant they were shown to a table beside a large window that looked out on the frozen cattails and tan reeds surrounding the marsh. The water was mostly encased in ice, but there was a pond-sized patch of electric blue in the middle where miniature ice bergs were blown around on its surface by the wind. Swimming in the area of open water were a pair of immaculate white swans. For some reason, probably due to the case they were investigating, Charlie thought they looked malevolent.

"Good afternoon, my name's Louise," the dark-haired waitress said when she walked up. "I'll be taking care of you two gentlemen today. Can I get you something to drink?" She was about forty with brown eyes, wire-rimmed glasses and a fair complexion.

"Just coffee, please," Ben said.

"And for you, sir?"

"The same."

When Louise returned with their coffees, Charlie asked her if she had a moment. She looked around. No other customers had arrived and at their invitation, she joined them at the table.

"How can I be of help to the forces of law and order today?" she asked, noticing both men were in uniform.

"We're looking into the disappearance of Carly Yellowwood. I understand she works here." Before they left for the restaurant, Pete reminded them to say Carly was missing and not to admit she was dead.

"Carly's missing? That's odd. She worked her shift Saturday night but was supposed to be here today," Louise said with a slight frown.

"So, the last time you saw her was on Saturday night? What time was that?" Ben asked.

"We closed up together around nine. What with the storm on its way, we didn't have any customers. We checked with Pat and he said we could lock up. Carly was worried about getting Chenoa from the baby-sitter and whether she'd be able to get down her road if the snow got too deep."

"Do you know the baby-sitter's name?" Charlie asked, pulling out a little notebook pad.

"It's Rose Applebee. She lives on Bridge Street. Her house is a few blocks past the center of town."

"Thanks. We've heard your boss has the reputation of coming on a bit strong with the waitresses here. Do you think Carly could have been in a relationship with him?"

"No way. That's actually funny," she shook her head with a grin. "Pat is totally harmless. He is a terrible flirt and a hugger, but if any woman actually said she'd see him outside of work, he'd probably faint. He's married, they're expecting baby number two and his wife, Gina, has him on a very short leash."

Ben and Charlie looked at each other briefly. This wasn't panning out.

"Could Carly have stopped by here yesterday morning between eight and ten a.m.?"

"No, Pat and I were here doing inventory. We would have seen her."

"What kind of a car does Pat drive?" Ben asked, remembering the information they'd received from Carly's neighbor.

"It's a green Subaru, pretty new model I think. Now, do you gentlemen want to order?"

STANDING OUTSIDE CARLY YELLOWWOOD'S CABIN IN two feet of snow, Undersheriff Pete Manstead was having a hard time catching his breath. Although the snow had stopped falling temporarily, a relentless wind was whipping it into high drifts. With the warrant in his gloved hand, he walked up onto Carly's front porch and banged on the door. He was prepared to crack a window, or even break the door down if necessary, but when he grabbed the door handle, to his surprise the door swung open. The house wasn't locked. When his deputies were there earlier, they reported the place had been locked up tight. Someone was inside, or had been, and that person had a key.

He looked around for tracks from a vehicle or even footprints, but the high wind had erased any evidence of the recent visitor. Pulling his gun from his shoulder holster, he opened the door, stepped inside and called, "Hello. Anybody here? Armed Police." Nobody answered. He clicked on the light switch near the kitchen table. Nothing happened. The power was still out pretty much across the county.

He walked through the small place with his heart racing. Fearing the killer might be hiding in a closet or under a bed, he used his cell phone light to illuminate all the places anyone could hide. He checked every closet and under both the small child's bed and the bed in the master bedroom. The full-sized bed had been made, but remembering that Carly was sleeping with someone, he pulled the sheets back. The sheets had been recently changed and the clean scent of bleach rose in the air. Walking into the small bathroom, he opened the medicine cabinet. It was nearly empty except for vitamins, Ibuprophen, Tylenol, and baby aspirin. Pulling on a pair of plastic gloves, Pete scooped the bottles into an evidence bag. The meds would have to be checked to be sure they were what the label read and analyzed for fingerprints.

Walking from the bedrooms toward the front of the house, he noticed the kitchen was immaculate; there weren't even any dishes in the sink except for one insulated blue thermos. He was pretty sure if Carly Yellowwood had been drugged in her home, there would have been signs of a struggle. This was not their crime scene. She had left her house to meet someone on Monday morning and whoever she met had given her those drugs.

A cold fury burned in his core knowing that someone had drugged Carly which led to her death. When he'd tried to get a pulse by touching her neck and realized she wasn't breathing, he'd made a promise to himself that he would find the monster who killed her if it was the last thing he did. Walking back outside, he battled his way back through the drifts to the connecting road where he'd left his patrol car.

BOTH PETE'S DEPUTIES HAD RETURNED TO the station when he got back from searching Carly's house. The lobby was filled with citizens from town—mostly reporting fender-benders or paying for tickets.

"Come down to the conference room, guys. I want to hear what you learned," he said quietly.

Once seated at the conference table, Pete asked for their reports.

"I'm afraid you're going to be pretty disappointed, Boss," Charlie said. "We had a delicious and expensive lunch at the White Swan, thank you very much. We gave the receipt to Victoria. We talked with Louise, the waitress who works with Carly and told her we were investigating Ms. Yellowwood as a missing person because you said you didn't want anyone to know she was dead. Louise last saw her on Saturday night. We asked if Carly had stopped there on Monday morning. She hadn't. Louise and Pat O'Connor were doing inventory and would have seen her. We asked her how Pat behaved around Carly, and I'm afraid that's also a bust. She said he is a flirt, but didn't think there was even the faintest possibility he and Carly were in a relationship. Apparently, his wife keeps him on a pretty short tether."

"Well, horn dogs have been known to slip their leashes," Pete said dryly.

"True, but he drives a green Subaru," Ben said. "And you said the man was Northern European. Pat's Irish."

"Damn. Looks like a dead end then. But Carly was in an intimate relationship with some white guy, we know that from the pathologist who found evidence she'd had sex recently. Are there any other men working in the restaurant?"

"Only the cook and the bartender. The cook's wife is the dishwasher so he's under her supervision. The bartender's gay and has a male partner," Charlie said.

"One other thing. Louise told us Carly's baby-sitter was a woman named Rose Applebee. She lives in East Jordan and so we drove over there and talked with her as well," Ben said.

"Good initiative. Did you learn anything helpful?"

"Carly picked up her daughter Saturday night after work. She told Mrs. Applebee that her next shift was today. Rose was surprised she hadn't heard from her. We asked her whether Carly was worried or upset lately. She said the opposite was the case. Carly told her she had someone new in her life and it was going well, but she hadn't told Mrs. Applebee the man's name."

"Unfortunate, but still good information," Pete said.

What did you find?" Charlie asked.

"I searched Carly's place and there was one odd thing. The front door was unlocked and that wasn't the case when you were there. The house hadn't been broken into, so whoever was there has a key. My guess is that they were looking for something that could tie them to the murder, possibly the drugs. The house was clean as a whistle, no evidence of a scuffle. I brought all her meds from her medicine cabinet back here for analysis, in case someone tampered with them, or there are fingerprints on the bottles other than hers."

"So what do we assume happened at this point?" Ben asked.

"Carly must have left her house Monday morning to visit someone and was drugged by that individual before fleeing in her car with her daughter and ending up dead."

"Where do we go from here, Boss?" Charlie asked.

The case that had seemed so simple in the beginning was starting to look deeply impenetrable. Of the two men Pete considered to be his prime suspects, Joe Yellowwood was living with his mother on the reservation, which meant he'd be difficult to interrogate, and at the moment they had no idea at all who Carly was sleeping with. If he could only find her cell phone, he thought, it would give him a lead.

NINE

THE FRONT DESK CONTINUED TO BE busy for a couple of hours, but by late afternoon when the lobby emptied, Victoria put on her parka and walked outside to the parking area. Riley from Inman's plowing had towed Carly Yellowwood's car to their lot. The victim's purse had been brought into the station and gone over, but no one had found her cell phone. Pete told her the sheriff had mentioned the importance of the phone when they talked. Climbing inside the vehicle, Victoria pulled her own phone from her pocket. She'd gotten Carly's number by calling the White Swan. When she dialed, a faint buzzing sound could be heard and by twisting herself in knots she managed to look under both front seats with her cell phone light.

Seeing nothing, she opened the car door, got out and crouched down shivering in the snow. Wishing she had worn pants instead of a skirt, Victoria knelt and pulled up the floor mats. Yes, there it was, blinking under the driver's seat. She grabbed the phone and was about to close the car door when she saw a single dark hair lying on the driver's seat. She picked it up carefully with her gloved hand. Then closing her fist tightly on the hair and stuffing Carly's phone in her pocket, she dashed back into to the office. She took off her coat, caught her breath and sat down at her desk.

After slipping the hair into an evidence envelope, she turned her attention to Carly's phone. It was an old one, a version 6S. Like a lot of early generation iPhones, it had a little circular button at its base. Those phones opened only to the fingerprint of the owner or an exact number combination. It was too much of a risk to try a combination because after three failed attempts the phone locked, but Victoria had an inspiration. She walked down the corridor, collared their jail Sergeant, basically bribed him to sit at the front desk for a bit and headed to Pete's office.

"What?" he asked in a gloomy tone of voice when she knocked.

She opened the door and walked inside. Pete was slumped in his chair. He was doodling on a pad of paper and didn't even look up.

"You know how you wanted to find Carly's phone?"

Pete raised his head, a hint of hope in his eyes.

"I found it." She held it up with a wide smile.

"That's great news!" he said. But his elation was quickly replaced with gloom when she handed him the phone. "You know we can't get combinations for iPhones. The providers won't unlock them. They won't even release passwords to the FBI or the CIA."

"I've had an idea of how Carly herself can open the phone," Victoria said. Her merry eyes were dancing.

"You do remember she'd dead," Pete said, giving her an annoyed look.

"But her body is still in the Morgue, right? She hasn't been cremated?"

"No, we have to locate her next of kin first. Since Carly and Joe were divorced, he can't make that decision. I told you earlier to find her parents. You haven't done that yet, by the way."

"I'll get on that today, but I also wanted to tell you I found a long black hair on the driver's seat of Carly's car. Don't worry, I picked it up wearing gloves and put it right into an evidence envelope. It's not Carly's hair, hers was curly and blonde. I thought it might be helpful to the investigation."

"I doubt Carly was drugged in her car," Pete said in an irritable tone of voice. "But we better keep it in evidence just in case."

"I will. Do you know about the home button on these old iPhones?"

"I know the phone requires the fingerprint of the owner," he said.

"I could be wrong here, but if we took the phone to the morgue, I think we could press Carly's finger on the button and her fingerprint might still open it."

"I doubt it will work."

"Why not?"

"Because when a person dies, the human body loses its mild electrical charge and that buzz is what's required for the phone to recognize the fingerprint. Still, it's worth a try." He stood up and grabbed for the keys on his desk.

"If you think you are going to the morgue without me, Boss, you have another think coming," Victoria said grinning and flipping her heavy red braid over her shoulder.

"What about the front desk?"

"We don't have any prisoners in the jail and I've assigned Sergeant Craig to man the phones."

"How did you convince him to do that? He hates answering the phones."

"Promised to make him chocolate chip cookies," she said giving him a cheeky grin.

"Better grab some fingerprint dusting material and a pair of thin plastic gloves," Pete said.

TWENTY MINUTES LATER, PETE AND VICTORIA were standing in the coroner's office, explaining their idea to Dr. Winter. Looking dubious, he nonetheless took them down to the basement. Exiting from the elevator, they walked down the hall to the morgue. Once inside, Dr. Winter slid open the silver-fronted drawer containing Carly's body.

"We know it's a long shot, doctor, but do you think it might be possible to transfer a fingerprint from Carly's finger to the plastic glove Victoria's wearing?" Pete asked.

"I'm doubtful, but I'll give it a try," Dr. Winter said. "I've got some dental putty. If anything works it would be that." He proceeded to copy the dead woman's fingerprints onto the dental putty he took from a cabinet and then using the fingerprint dusting material carefully transferred Carly's fingerprints to the thin plastic glove Victoria was wearing. "I presume your theory is that the mild electrical charge from a living person will come through the gloves and trick the phone," Dr. Winter said.

"That's what we hope. Go ahead and try your thumb on the home button," Pete said.

Victoria took a deep breath and pressed the home button. It didn't work. She looked at the men.

"Use your first finger this time and hold it down a little longer," Pete said.

She tried again and to her amazement the phone actually opened. Rapidly clicking on the multi-colored pinwheel icon for photos, Victoria immediately found what they had been looking for. The picture showed the happy couple standing in front of a beautifully decorated Christmas tree. The tall blue-eyed Caucasian man with his arm around a smiling Carly was wearing a Santa hat. In the background they could see a window, a snowy landscape, blue water and two spotless white swans.

"Now about that raise I've been asking for," she said.

"You'll have it, if I can get the sheriff on board," Pete said.

As the door to the morgue closed behind them, Dr. Winter shook his head, saying, "Now I've seen it all."

BACK IN THE PATROL CAR, PETE pulled out onto the street. "I really appreciate you coming up with the idea to open the phone,

Victoria. I'm just going to drop you off at the office and go back to the White Swan. Someone there is going to recognize our Mr. X." He was feeling better, back on track. The case was about to be cracked wide open.

"I have an errand to do before returning to my desk which our Sergeant Craig has probably destroyed by now anyway. Oh, one other thing," she said with a grin, she was practically bouncing in her seat. "I've located Joe Yellowwood."

"At his mother's place?" Pete asked.

"No. You said you could interrogate him if he was off the reservation, right? Anyway, he works in town."

"Where?"

"At ACE hardware in East Jordan. So, after you find the identity of our Mr. X from the employees at the White Swan, you can walk across the street and nab Chenoa's father."

"I owe you big time," Pete said. "Excellent find."

"Don't forget that raise I've been asking for and I'm expecting it to be substantial," she said. "Cheer up, will you, Boss? You're going to solve this one."

"Once Joe's in custody, I just might," he said and felt his mood lighten.

Driving to the White Swan in deepening twilight, Pete recalled his conversation with the sheriff about whether they could use the evidence Victoria found. Luckily, in this case, there was no problem. His dispatcher had found Carly's phone in her car which had been towed to their parking lot. In essence, the phone was already on their property when Victoria retrieved it, as was the hair.

He'd decided not to take Carly's phone with him and left it with Victoria. He was afraid he might inadvertently shut it off, and she wanted to look at it in more detail. She'd forwarded him the Christmas photo of the man they thought might be Carly's lover.

"Good afternoon, sir. Any more people in your party?" the

hostess asked when he walked in. She wore a black apron with a white blouse and a long black skirt. Her name tag read Jacquie.

"I'm Undersheriff Manstead from Charlevoix," he said opening his coat so she could see his badge. "I would like some information and hope you can help me."

"I'm happy to try," she said.

"Take a look at this photo please. Do you know the man in the picture?"

Jacquie reached for his phone and used her fingers to enlarge the photo. "That's Mr. Webster. He comes in from time to time, almost always with his wife. This picture was taken at our Christmas party. It was quite the bash." She handed his phone back with a smile.

"Thank you. Do you know where Webster works? Or lives?"

"I'm pretty certain he works right here in East Jordan. He's a city employee. Hang on. Let me ask Louise if she knows where his office is."

After Jacquie left to get her co-worker, Pete considered what she'd said. Webster was married and usually came to the restaurant with his wife. It seemed unlikely he'd have had an opportunity to be see Carly and force her to take those drugs so early on a Monday morning. It wasn't looking hopeful, but the photo was the only thing they had.

Jacquie returned minutes later with the dark-haired waitress who said her name was Louise.

"I think you were the person who spoke with my deputies. They were asking for information about Carly Yellowwood. Can you identify the man in this picture?" he said, holding the phone out to her.

"That's Dave Webster, he's the City Attorney for East Jordan," Louise said. "Have you found Carly yet? After your deputies were here, I called her multiple times, but she didn't answer," Louise said. Her eyes looked worried.

"You will have to make some other arrangements for her shift. Carly Yellowwood isn't going to be able to come in," he said.

"Why? Have you found her? What about her daughter?"

"Please keep this to yourself, but Chenoa Yellowwood is in the hospital. She's doing well and will probably be discharged soon."

"To Carly?" she asked and when Pete shook his head added, "To her father then?"

"I'm going to talk to him later. One last question. Do you know where Mr. Webster's office is?"

She did.

Walking outside the restaurant, Pete struggled through the raging snowstorm to his car. It was very dark, there was near-zero visibility and a temperature in the teens. Checking his phone, he saw it was after six p.m. The city offices would be closed, as would Ace Hardware. Knowing he was exhausted and not thinking well, he started his car and headed for home.

THE SNOW WAS BLOWING HORIZONTALLY OUTSIDE Pete's kitchen window when he arrived at his cabin on the Jordan River. The wildly tumbling flakes were lit by the motion light that came on. The lights had been triggered by a large white-tailed deer walking slowly through the snow-filled back yard of his property. The phone rang as he took a beer from the refrigerator. He glanced at the call seeing the Sheriff's phone number.

"Hello, sir."

"How are you coming on the case, Pete? Can you give me an update?"

"Certainly. We've had a bit of a breakthrough. Victoria found Carly's phone and had an idea of how to get it open. She suggested using our victim's fingers and Dr. Winter copied her fingerprints on to her glove. Unbelievably, it worked, and we found a picture of Carly with a guy by the name of Dave Webster."

"Webster, isn't he the guy who is the attorney for East Jordan?"

"That's correct and I'm going to interview him first thing tomorrow morning."

"Tread carefully. He's an important person around here. What about the question of suicide? Any progress there?"

"Victoria is going through all of Carly's texts thinking she'll find some evidence of depression or plans to kill herself, if that was what she was intending, but we both believe it's highly unlikely that she would have decided to end her life with her little girl in the car."

"Probably right, but you have to rule it out. I've been thinking about the drugs Dr. Winter found in her body. Traditionally poison is a woman's weapon, but drugs have become a male *modus operandi* of late."

"That's what I think too, sir. I believe we have a crime of passion. Carly was divorced from her husband, Joe Yellowwood. He's Native and lives on the local reservation with his mother. I was worried about how I was going to be able to interview him, but Victoria found out he works at Ace Hardware. I'm planning on picking him up and bringing him into the station after I talk with Webster."

"I agree that Joe has to be ruled out, but I think he's likely to be a dead end. If he was angry that Carly had started seeing a new man, given his history, which I remember as I was the arresting officer, I think he would have been more likely to beat her up, not drug her."

"Well, like you said, sir, we have to rule him out."

"It sounds to me like Victoria is the person who had been the most helpful so far," his voice was dry. "She got the victim's phone open, identified Dave Webster as our victim's potential lover, found out where Joe Yellowwood works and is looking for evidence ruling out suicide. What have you and the deputies been doing?"

After a moment's hesitation, Pete said, "I got a warrant to search Carly's home and sent the deputies to do the house to house." He realized it sounded pretty minimal.

"You already texted me that you found nothing at the victim's home and the deputies learned from her neighbors that Carly was seeing two men, right?"

"Correct."

"You should have realized that from the start, Pete. Our victim is a divorced mother, so naturally she had contact with the father of her child. And Dr. Winter told you she had sex recently, which tells you there was another man in her life. I hope you get something out of Webster tomorrow, but if you don't have anyone in custody by Monday when I get back, I'm taking over. I dislike putting more pressure on you, but this has to be handled perfectly or it could all blow back into our faces," he said and clicked off the call.

Pete sat down on his couch facing the fireplace and took a long pull on his beer. There was no cheerful flickering of flames and the black firebox looked back at him reproachfully. What had he accomplished on the case? Not very damn much, he thought gloomily as he finished the beer and walked off to bed.

TEN

Wednesday

PETE DROVE INTO THE VILLAGE OF East Jordan at seven-thirty the next morning. It was still dark and the wind was blowing hard. He knew city offices didn't open until eight. Finding a gas station that was open, he filled up his car. Driving across the bridge and turning left on Main Street, he arrived at the building that housed the offices for city employees. The old brick structure had been extensively renovated. New windows and a glass door edged in black metal were banded by wide sections of split fieldstone. He parked at a meter and waited while he thought.

Webster was an attorney. If he was having an affair with Carly and she was pushing him to divorce his wife, he might have a motive to want her dead, but why would he have drugged her? Getting ahold of those drugs was risky—especially for a lawyer—and unless he had a prescription for that medication, having it in his possession would be illegal. And why would Carly have agreed to take those drugs? The woman wasn't a drug user. Nothing about this case was making any sense to him.

Watching the building, he spotted a woman walking up to the door. When she opened the door with her key, Pete got out of his car and followed her inside. Beside the elevator was a list of offices for city hall employees. City attorney, David Webster, JD, LLM's office was on the third floor.

When he got off the elevator at the top of the building, the view from the windows was impressive. From there, Pete could see all of East Jordan, the empty snow-filled marina and multiple ice-fishing shanties that had been erected on Lake Charlevoix. A lone street light illuminated a narrow tongue of black water where the Jordan River entered the lake. Irregularly shaped plates of ice had been deposited on the beach by the waves. He knocked on Webster's office door.

"Come in," the voice said.

Opening the door, Pete saw a tall good-looking guy in his forties. He wore glasses and was dressed in black slacks and an open-collared striped shirt.

"Dave Webster," the man said, standing up, walking over and holding out his hand.

"Pete Manstead," he said and they shook hands.

"Good to meet you, Pete. I know your boss, Sheriff Dodgson, but haven't met you before. Want some coffee?" He gestured to a small sideboard with a coffee pot. He'd obviously just made it as the enticing scent of ground coffee beans permeated the air.

Offering him a cup of coffee could have been meant as a distraction, but Pete hadn't taken his eyes off Webster since he opened the door. The man had a frank countenance with no hint of dismay at finding an officer of the law in uniform standing at his door. So far, Webster wasn't looking like a killer.

"Coffee would be good. It's still very cold out there," he said.

Webster poured him a cup, asking about cream and sugar, before offering him a seat in a chair in front of his desk. "What can I do for you this morning, Officer?"

"I'm looking into a disappearance. Do you know Carly Yellowwood?" Pete's attention was riveted on the man.

"Carly? Yes, of course I do. She's our favorite waitress at the White Swan. Did you say she's disappeared?"

"I'd like to ask you to look at a picture, if you would. Do you recall this photo?" He held up his phone.

"I recall that day, of course. It was taken at the Christmas party at the restaurant. Very nice affair, as I recall. Now that I see this, I remember Carly asking Louise to take our picture. I don't believe you answered my question, sir. Has she disappeared?"

"This is confidential, so please do not share what I'm about to tell you. We found Carly Yellowwood dead on Monday morning. She perished in a car crash," Pete said. His eyes were glued to Webster's face.

"My God, that's awful," he looked stunned.

"It gets worse. Dr. Winter did an autopsy and someone kissed Carly the morning she died. He did a DNA analysis of the saliva on her upper lip. The saliva came from a man who is tall, blue-eyed and Northern European. Were you having an affair with Carly, Mr. Webster?" Pete asked.

"I certainly was not," Webster said, in a shocked tone of voice. "I'm a happily married man, sir. As you can see from the pictures in my office, I have four children. This is just terrible news. My wife, Deb, loves Carly. She will be devastated."

"Look at this picture again. You have your arm around Carly and it looks to me like you two were very close, possibly intimate."

"Intimate? No way! It's true that my right arm is around Carly, but my left arm was around my wife when that picture was taken. She just doesn't show in the photo. Deb and I are both very fond of Carly and her little daughter, Chenoa. We've had her bring the child over to play with my kids several times. If you thought I was sleeping with her, Sheriff, you are way off base." Webster was clearly irritated and his blue eyes snapped.

"Would you be willing to stop by the office and give us a DNA sample to exclude you from our investigation?"

"Absolutely. No problem," he said firmly.

"What kind of a car do you drive?" Pete asked, feeling a groundswell of discouragement. Although the man met the pathologist's description, being tall, blue-eyed and looking Nordic, Webster wasn't sounding in the least like Carly Yellowwood's killer.

"No idea why you are asking, but I drive a red Ford Escort."

"Please keep what I've just told you confidential," Pete reminded him and departed.

AT TEN O'CLOCK, VICTORIA GRABBED HER tote bag and walked down the hall to the breakroom. Although Pete hadn't seemed very open to her helping with the investigation, she was determined to help him get justice for Carly. She had dreamed the previous night of the beautiful woman and her final ride in that terrible storm with her little girl. *Nobody should get away with killing a young mother*, she thought, realizing how closely she identified with Carly.

She set her bag on the table and made a pot of coffee. While it brewed, she munched on a banana and scrolled through Carly's texts on her phone. There were only four people that she texted regularly: Louise and Jacquie from the White Swan, her ex-husband, Joe, and Rose Applebee, the woman who was her daughter's baby-sitter. It did seem odd that there were no texts to Carly's new boyfriend (whoever he was), or her parents, but they probably preferred phone calls. She checked the Recent Calls list and saw only unidentified numbers. It would a tough job to sort through those.

Most of Carly's texts to her co-workers were about her work schedules, but going back several weeks, she hit upon something interesting. Carly had requested a week off in April to go visit her parents. It wasn't specifically stated, but reading between the lines, Victoria could tell that Carly's parents were elderly and that her mother was quite ill. "I can't put off a visit much longer. Mom has to see Chenoa again . . . before it's too late," she'd written before adding, "It will be nice to see them both and bask in the Florida sunshine."

Going back still further in the string, Victoria found a text to Louise saying she'd been accepted to Northwestern Michigan College in Traverse City. The message was followed by smiley faces and exclamation points. Carly would be starting an elementary education program in the fall.

Victoria sat back in her chair with a sense of accomplishment. Sheriff Dodgson had told Pete that Carly's phone would tell them if she had intended to commit suicide and she'd just found the evidence. Carly wasn't depressed. In fact, she was making plans for the future, looking forward to seeing her parents in Florida in April, and starting a college degree program in the fall. She hadn't taken those drugs to commit suicide. Although it was an appalling thought, it was clear to her that Carly Yellowwood had been murdered.

Then further inspiration struck. Carly's calendar had to be on her phone. It was one aspect of the device she hadn't pursued thoroughly. She checked and discovered Carly's work schedule and a handful of other appointments going back a full year. Once she'd gone through the calendar and found who Carly was meeting with, Pete would have to make her officially part of the investigative team. She smiled at the thought.

AFTER HIS TALK WITH THE CITY attorney, Pete walked in a high wind that took his breath away to the Ace Hardware store across the street from the White Swan. He was in search of Joe Yellowwood. As her ex-husband, Joe was unlikely to be the man who kissed Carly on Monday morning, but he had to inform him that his former wife was dead.

Ace Hardware was a modern emporium with aisles that optimistically showcased spring gardening utensils, lawn care products, and a multitude of other items. Taking a quick glance at the check-out desk, he spotted his target. Joe Yellowwood was tall and thin, had the reddish skin usual in Native Americans, dark eyes, and a firm chin. He watched while Joe checked out two people, noticing he didn't make small-talk with the customers.

Before he cornered him, Pete checked his likely escape routes. The guilty ones always ran. There was the front door he'd come in through. By meandering through the aisles to the back of the store, he spotted a back exit. If Yellowwood took off toward the rear, he would be hard-pressed to stop his escape. He had to take him directly to the station if at all possible to avoid him returning to the reservation.

Making a purchase would provide the opportunity to study Joe close-up, he decided, and strolled around the store a while longer before spotting the battery shelf and picking up a package of batteries. He walked to the check-out register and put them down on the counter.

"Is that it, sir?"

"This will do it," Pete said, reaching for his wallet. "I see on your name badge that your name's Joe Yellowwood. Any relation to Carly?"

"Yes," he hesitated, "she's my wife. I mean . . . my ex-wife."

"We've been trying to reach you, Joe. I wonder if there is somewhere private where we can talk."

Joe looked somewhat anxious, but nodded. "Nobody in the store but me. I can take a break and we can go back to the office." He put a small "register closed" sign on the counter and led the way to the back of the store.

"What is it, Sheriff?" he asked when they were in the private room.

"I think you better sit down, Joe." Pete was dreading what he had to say.

Joe took a seat. He was looking increasingly nervous. "If this is about Chenoa being in the hospital, Sheriff. I already know that. The hospital contacted my mother yesterday. She couldn't go because she's got a bad case of the flu, but I went to visit."

"I'm not sure what the hospital told your mother, but Carly was in a car accident," Pete said. "She died, Joe."

"What? No! Carly's not dead," Joe said. His eyes were huge and he was visibly shocked. "You're wrong, Sheriff. Carly's alive. I just talked to her Monday morning."

It was something Pete had seen before. The first reaction of a family member, when told of the sudden death of a loved one, was invariably disbelief. It seemed almost impossible to comprehend that someone they had just spoken with could possibly have passed away.

"I'm so sorry, Joe, but she's gone."

When Joe's shock turned to sorrow and he lowered his head on the table weeping, Pete decided it was time to leave. He would have to officially interview the man soon, but it could wait until he got control of himself. "I'm sorry to give you such awful news," he added and departed. On his way through the store, he picked up the small paper bag containing his purchase and walked outside in below-zero temperatures to his car.

Assuming Joe Yellowwood would be working all day, Pete drove back to the station, hoping either Charlie or Ben would be there. He wanted back-up to bring him into the station. Pulling in, he saw Webster, the city attorney for East Jordan, arriving in his red Ford. Both men got out of their cars at the same time.

"Come on into the office," Pete yelled over the wind as they walked in together.

"Victoria, could you come to my office when the lobby is clear and bring the DNA kit?" Pete asked. She nodded. "Want some coffee, Dave?" he asked.

The two men grabbed cups of coffee as they walked to Pete's office.

Victoria appeared shortly thereafter with the kit.

"Victoria, I'd like you to meet David Webster," Pete said. "He's the city attorney for East Jordan." Casting a quick meaningful look at her he added, "Mr. Webster's come in of his own volition for a DNA test to *exclude* him from our investigation."

Victoria managed to control her suspicious reaction to seeing the tall, blue-eyed man and said, "Nice to meet you, Mr. Webster. Now, I will take two samples, one swab on the inside of your cheek and one at your gum line. Just open your mouth for me, please."

With the test was completed, Webster shook hands with Pete, bid Victoria good-bye and left the office.

"I take it, he's not our guy," Victoria said in a flat tone.

"Well, the test will tell us for sure, but I didn't get the sense it was him," Pete said. "Are either Ben or Charlie around? You were right about Joe Yellowwood working at Ace Hardware in East Jordan. Thanks for finding that out. I want to bring him in, but one of the deputies has to come with me and stand by the back door of the store, in case he takes off."

"Ben's chatting with Sergeant Craig down by the jail. I'll roust him out for you." She practically ran down the hall. The woman was draining to be around. He wondered how her husband coped.

ELEVEN

Victoria had received a call from Mrs. Robbins, Chenoa's social worker, just as she was leaving the office the previous day. To her dismay, the social worker said there were no legal objections to putting Chenoa in foster care with a white family because she would be with Rose Applebee, her regular baby-sitter, where she had been cared for when her mother was working at the White Swan. They thought a familiar place would help Chenoa adjust. It was discouraging, but Victoria reminded herself the Applebees would be ineligible to adopt her, which meant there was still hope she and Matt could do so. All she had to do was convince him.

After hours of discussion late into the night, she and Matt reached a compromise. He agreed to support an attempt to adopt Chenoa, even though he thought it was a long shot. Before filing a petition with the court, however, her husband insisted on a trip to the reservation where Joe and Mrs. Yellowwood lived. The purpose of the visit was to find out if they were planning to take custody of Chenoa. Because her husband had been willing to go forward with the adoption, Victoria reluctantly agreed he could buy his trained hunting dog.

Matt picked her up from work late that afternoon and the couple headed toward the southwest area of Evelyn Township. Although the storm had been in full-force earlier in the day, by the time they left the sheriff's office the wind had died. It was beautifully still as they drove along the south arm of Lake Charlevoix. Despite the fact that Matt had never visited the reservation before, he seemed calm and relaxed, but Victoria was nervous about meeting Chenoa's grandmother, certain the woman would resent them visiting.

"Are you sure we have to meet Mrs. Yellowwood?" she asked Matt.

"Yes, we do. You have been driving yourself crazy worrying about Chenoa ever since she went into foster care. I happen to know you even drove by Mrs. Applebee's house yesterday," Matt said with a frown.

"How do you know that?"

"You took the boys, and those little blabbermouths can't keep a secret. I contacted the chairman of the tribe yesterday and he got us an appointment. Doris Yellowwood is expecting us.

"What exactly do you think talking to Joe's mother is going to accomplish?" Victoria asked.

"It's traditional to express condolences on the loss of a family member. As far as the rest goes, I'm still working it out in my head," Matt said. "Leave it to me."

ONE OF THE COUNTY SNOWPLOWS WAS parked on the side of the road on the outskirts of East Jordan and Matt pulled over beside the vehicle. He rolled down his window and gestured to the driver to do the same. They were very close to the edge of the lake there and a small patch of open water showed clearly against the white snow. A few Canada geese were paddling in an unfrozen spot near the shore, ducking down to pull grasses and snails from the water.

"Good afternoon. Do you go out to the local tribal reservation with the plows?"

"Yes, we plow the roads and the parking lot of the social services building. The tribe owns a tractor with a plow for the driveways and they were working to clear the snow when I was out that way yesterday. The women had lined up some of the kids with shovels and were having them clear the porches of the old folks. It's a tightly-knit group that supports its elders. Better than we do, I think," he said with a rueful shake of his head.

"Thanks, great information. What road do I take to get there?"

"The reservation's on Raney Road. When you arrive, you will see a sign that says Grand Traverse Band of Ottawa and Chippewa Indians."

"Thanks again," he said and continued toward their destination.

Reaching the reservation, they parked in the lot of the social services building. Victoria donned her gloves, pulled up her hood and getting out of the car, took her husband's hand.

"I'm familiar with how one approaches a visit to a Native family after a death. It's important that we express our sympathy," Matt said as they walked down the hilly road with modular homes on either side.

"After that will you ask her about us adopting Chenoa?" Victoria asked.

"Not right away. Just don't forget your part of the bargain," he said.

"I won't," she said, rolling her eyes in exasperation. She still felt the dog was an awfully pricey luxury.

As they walked down the only road in the reservation, Victoria took deep breaths of the painfully sharp zero-degree air, feeling its cleansing power burn into her lungs. The sky was cobalt blue and cloudless. Five minutes later they came upon a gaggle of small children throwing snowballs at each other. When Matt called out to them, they stopped their fight and assembled into a shiny-eyed fascinated pack.

"I'm trying to find the home of Mrs. Yellowwood. Do you know where she lives?" he asked.

The little band moved closer. They were intrigued but wary, seeing two people that didn't belong on the reservation and had invaded their territory during what was obviously a major battle.

"Why do you want her?" the tallest boy asked in a bravely challenging tone. Victoria tried hard not to smile, the kid couldn't have been older than eight.

"She has a granddaughter, Chenoa, who's in the hospital. We've come to talk to Mrs. Yellowwood about her," Matt said.

"Last house at the end of the street. She might not let you in, though," the youngster cautioned.

"Why is that?" Victoria asked.

They looked at her as if she was too dumb to live and ran off giggling to resume the snowball combat.

When they knocked on Mrs. Yellowwood's door, Matt introduced himself saying, "*Mino Gigizeb*, grandmother of Chenoa. My name is Matt, this is my wife, Victoria. We have come to visit you this morning and to offer our sympathy for the loss of your daughter-in-law, Carly. A limb has fallen from the family tree," he said.

"I brought you some banana bread I baked," Victoria said, handing the woman the loaf wrapped in silver foil.

Joe's mother invited them inside, told them to have a seat on the couch and offered them coffee. Doris Yellowwood was a short stocky woman with dark hair sprinkled with silver. She was dressed in a long skirt, a blue denim shirt and a Petoskey stone necklace.

"I hope you are feeling better today," Victoria said. She'd been told by the nurses that the woman was ill. It was the reason she hadn't come to visit Chenoa.

"I am getting over the flu, but am very sad today. I had grown to love Carly deeply. She tried hard to become part of our way of life."

"Her loss was a terrible tragedy for you, Joe and her daughter. In addition to our condolences for your loss, we would like to ask you if you plan to pursue custody of Chenoa."

"What is your interest in this family matter?" Doris Yellowwood asked, with a little warning note in her voice.

"I am the person who took Chenoa to the hospital after the accident," Victoria said. "My husband and I stayed with her because we didn't want her to be alone. I don't know if the hospital told you, but Chenoa is being placed in foster care until her custody can be legally established."

Mrs. Yellowwood clenched her fists, obviously trying to control her resentment. "They had no right," she said furiously.

"Matt and I would like . . ." Victoria's voice trailed off when her husband touched her arm to make her stop talking.

"My wife and I are wondering if you plan to keep Chenoa with the tribe," Matt asked and added, "It is not idle curiosity that causes me to ask this, Grandmother. I have a reason for my question."

"Of course we do," Mrs. Yellowwood said, nodding with a sharp downward head movement. The Petoskey stone necklace she wore rose up and down on her ample bosom with her rapid breathing.

"It causes me pain to say this, but I fear your claim could be denied by the white man's court because of your son's time in prison."

"My son got in trouble because of the drink. He doesn't drink now. He's been sober for three years. And the knife belonged to the man in the bar, not my Joe. He just fought back."

Mrs. Yellowwood's impassive face had assumed a severe expression and Victoria's stomach tightened. The visit wasn't going well.

"I was raised by white parents, but had a Chippewa grandfather who taught me much about our people. I respect your ways and what you have suffered. My wife is a white woman, but like Carly, she has a large heart. It is big enough for three children."

"I see your wife noticing my oxygen machine. She is thinking I wouldn't be up to a toddler. Perhaps she thinks I would die before Chenoa grew up." Her black eyes glistened.

"My wife only wishes you to consider whether, by saving Chenoa after her mother died, she may have an ongoing part to play in her life."

"I will think on this, grandson of our tribe. You may ask me again when they find the evil one who took Carly from us," Mrs. Yellowwood said and rose from her chair to escort them from her home.

"Thank you very much for seeing us today," Matt said as they were leaving.

"Yes, we appreciate you giving us the time," Victoria added.

Walking back down the main street of the hilly reservation with its modular homes on either side of the road as the brilliant sky clouded over, she recalled the fable about King Solomon who was approached by two women—both of whom claimed to be the mother of the same child. When the King ordered the child cut in half, so each woman could have a part, the woman who gave up her claim was revealed as the rightful parent.

By the time she reached their car with the wind rising and tiny shards of ice clinging to her eyebrows and lashes, Victoria was struggling to decide whether pursuing the adoption of Chenoa would be in line with their values as a couple and ethically the right thing to do.

Due to handling a series of phone calls and other issues, it was almost six o'clock in the evening when Pete and Deputy Ben Wilcox left the sheriff's office to bring Joe Yellowwood into the station. They parked the patrol car in the lot in front of Ace Hardware and waited until the last customers left the store.

"I hate to ask you in this weather, Ben, but can you stand by the back door of the store, in case he makes a run for it?"

"No problem, but it looks like it's not going to be necessary. Our guy's coming out the front door now."

Both men got out of the car. The street lights had come on and helped illuminate the dark parking lot bounded by twelve-foot-high walls of snow. The two lawmen headed directly for Joe Yellowwood who looked at them in surprise.

"I'm Undersheriff Manstead, this is Deputy Ben Wilcox. You have to come with us to the station," Pete said.

"Am I under arrest?" Joe asked, looking nervous.

"No, but we want to talk with you with respect to the death of Carly Yellowwood. You're coming with us," Pete said. He took Joe by one arm.

Ben grabbed his other arm and they propelled him toward the vehicle. Pete opened the back door to the patrol car and told him to climb in. He laid his hand on Joe's head so he wouldn't bump it getting into the car. He hadn't resisted, and indeed had seemed devastated when he learned of Carly's death, but they were taking no chances.

Once back at the sheriff's office, they turned Joe over to their custody sergeant. A night in the cells often softened the most recalcitrant and closed-mouthed of criminals. He would wait until morning to interrogate Joe Yellowwood.

TWELVE

Thursday

When Pete arrived at the office the following morning, having navigated through drifts that floated like white-capped waves across the road, he was surprised to see the front desk unmanned. But spotting Victoria's red parka, he knew she was there. It was just as well. He wanted to have some time to think through his strategy for the interrogation, and his dispatcher was definitely not relaxing. She'd been galvanized by the murder case and, although he had to admit she'd come up with a number of good ideas, he didn't find it easy to think in her busy bee presence.

The previous night he hadn't answered any of Joe Yellowwood's questions, except to tell him he wasn't under arrest. They were just holding him for twenty-four hours. Not getting answers to their questions made it easier to penetrate suspects' defenses and often led to a confession. That was what he was going for. He was well aware that he had nothing else.

He knew Carly hadn't been drugged at home. If she'd been forced to take the drugs in her house, he would have seen evidence of a struggle. If she had gone to Joe's place on the reservation Monday morning and was drugged there, he would be blocked from obtaining any forensic evidence from the scene. Mrs. Yellowwood simply wouldn't let him inside, and he had no jurisdiction to demand she do so. All he could do was batter Joe over and over again with the fact that Carly had been in a sexual relationship with another man. That would eat at him and his previous conviction for assault gave Pete further ammunition pointing to him as the culprit. Feeling like his strategy was pretty well thought out, he headed down the hall for coffee.

VICTORIA HAD TAKEN CARLY'S PHONE WITH her to the breakroom. The DNA results on Dave Webster had come back and what they suspected had been borne out. Webster wasn't the man who kissed Carly good-bye the morning she died. In addition, he was in the office by eight o'clock that morning, something his secretary confirmed. With Webster eliminated, she worried Pete would say she didn't deserve a raise for her idea of using the victim's fingerprints to open her phone. It was critical to find more evidence. Standing at the counter, she dumped yesterday's coffee out in the sink and made a new pot. Then she sat down to look through Carly's phone in more detail.

"So this is where you're hiding," Pete said when he came upon Victoria.

"In going through everything on Carly's phone, I found nothing indicating she was depressed or thinking of ending her life. In fact, I saw the reverse. She had been admitted to college in the fall, was excited about it and was planning a trip to see her folks who live in Florida. I still haven't gotten a phone number for them, but I will as soon as possible," Victoria sat back in the chair with satisfaction. She thought Pete would be pleased, but he looked just plain grumpy. When he motioned for her to go on, she continued saying, "In looking for the man Carly was having an affair with, I found one other photo that might help."

"Let me see."

Victoria held out the phone and Pete took it from her hand. The photo showed Carly in an orange bathing suit wearing a straw hat and smiling. The vast blue sheet of water behind her was indisputably Lake Michigan. No other large body of water had water that exact shade. A tall man in the background was skipping stones into the water.

"We won't be able to identify that guy. He's too far away."

"Gee whiz, Pete, I thought you would be pretty pleased with what I have found so far," Victoria said feeling frustrated. "Actually, I did have one other thought . . ."

"Sorry, Victoria. I don't have time to hear your ideas now, but we can talk more later. Please have Sergeant Craig bring Joe into interrogation."

She cast him a long reproachful look before leaving the room.

PLACING A HAND ON HIS UPPER arm, Sergeant Craig escorted Joe Yellowwood down the hall from the jail to the interview room.

"Are they going to let me go pretty soon?" he asked. "I'm supposed to be working a shift at the store today."

"Sorry, no idea. I presume it depends on what the Undersheriff learns in your interview."

"Well, I haven't done anything wrong, so I have nothing to tell him. I consider this a breach of my rights. I'm not sure he even has the power to keep me here. Shouldn't I have gotten a phone call?" Joe asked. He was obviously feeling frustrated and put-upon.

When they arrived at the room, Pete was sitting at the table. Deputy Ben Wilcox was standing in the corner to observe the interview.

"Thanks for bringing him, Todd. Come on in, Joe. Take a seat."

"I have rights, you know," he said, sitting at the table. "I didn't get a phone call last night."

Pete glanced quickly at Sgt. Craig who said, "You didn't ask for one."

"Well, I want one now. I want to call my mother."

"Tell you what, I'll have our dispatcher, Victoria, call your mother and tell her you're here with us. How's that? Please have her take care of that, Sergeant. Now, I have some questions for you."

"What do you want to know?" Joe's voice was sulky.

Pete flicked on the video recording equipment and said, "Joe Yellowwood is being interviewed by Undersheriff Manstead and observed by Deputy Wilcox regarding his whereabouts at the time someone forced his ex-wife Carly Yellowwood to take drugs which caused her death."

Joe's livid expression vanished and anguish spread across his ruddy features. "Someone forced her to take drugs? You didn't tell me that before. When Carly saw the devastation drugs wreaked on the tribe, she made a pledge never to drink or smoke. The only drugs she ever took were over-the-counter or prescribed for her." He swallowed hard, shook his head and rubbed his hands across his face. Then he lowered his head on his crossed arms and Pete heard hard sobbing.

Joe had been told the previous day that Carly was dead, but until now he'd not been privy to the information that she'd been murdered. The man was so clearly suffering, Pete was starting to doubt he was their guy. That level of emotional pain just couldn't be faked. He waited until the man got control of himself and said, "Are you okay now? Sorry, but I have to ask where you were on Monday morning?"

Joe blew his nose on a tissue and nodded. Then he cleared his throat and said, "I woke up around 7:30 and had breakfast with my mother. I'm living with her at the moment. After that I drove into town for my AA meeting."

Pete gave his deputy, Ben Wilcox, a quick oblique glance. AA meetings were totally confidential. There was no way to confirm anyone's attendance. "What time did your AA meeting start?"

"Nine o'clock."

"Was the meeting in in Charlevoix? Or in East Jordan?"

"East Jordan."

"The town's only about a twenty-minute drive from the reservation. When did you leave for the meeting?"

"Because of the storm, I left early. It was just after eight."

"What route did you take?" Pete asked.

"A lot of the roads were blocked with snow, so I had to work my way over to M-66. Can't remember which side roads I took."

"Did you take Miles?" Pete's light blue eyes were focused tightly on the man. In his mind he saw Carly's black vehicle shoved to the side of the road and thought of her losing control of her car and driving into the tree. Had she cried out in anguish when she died? Had little Chenoa heard her dying words?

"I don't think so."

"But, there's no way to confirm this, Joe, and nobody will vouch for your attendance at an AA meeting, so it's not much of an alibi. Did you stop for anything on your way? Coffee? Gas?"

"Now that you mention it, I did stop at the 4-corners in East Jordan. There's a BP gas station on the corner and I filled up."

"Did you pay at the pump, Joe? Go inside the store for anything?"

"Paid at the pump and left. Didn't go into the store. I didn't want to be late for the meeting and the drive had taken longer than I thought."

"The problem I have, Joe, is that there's no way to check your story. I think what really happened is that you saw Carly's car on your drive to the meeting. You probably stopped to talk to her and things got out of hand when she told you she had a new boyfriend."

"What? Is that true?" he asked, torment clearly evident in his dark eyes.

"Yes."

"Are you sure?"

"We know she was having sex from the autopsy," Pete said and Joe flinched. "My guess is you stopped to see Carly before you went to your AA meeting and forced her to take those drugs."

Joe was shaking his head and his naturally reddish complexion blanched. "I would never have hurt Carly. I love her, Sheriff, I always have, ever since we were fourteen-year-old kids. Plus, she's Chenoa's mom."

Pete frowned and decided to take another tack. "If you don't mind telling me, why did your marriage break up?"

Joe took a deep breath and said, "It was because of a stupid bar fight. The other guy started it and took a swipe at me with his knife. I got the knife away from him, but in the scuffle, I cut him. I didn't mean to. When I went to court, I pleaded guilty and the Judge gave me a sentence of two years. Carly was pregnant by then. By the time I got out, Chenoa was a toddler. I wanted us to get back together, but my wife couldn't forgive me for not being there with her during the pregnancy and at our daughter's birth."

Pete nodded.

"I have paid child support every two weeks since I got out of the slammer. It's taken right from my paycheck and put into Carly's bank account. I haven't had a drink in almost three years, and it was alcohol that got me into that bar fight. I would have done anything to get my beautiful wife to take me back," it was obvious the man was struggling not to break down again.

"But, all I have is your word, Joe," Pete told him gently. "There's nobody who can confirm where you were that morning."

"Wait, wait. I just remembered something, Sheriff. Let me check my wallet." Joe pulled it from his back pocket and flipping through the compartments, retrieved a receipt. "Here's my receipt for the petrol I got in East Jordan. It's probably got the time stamped on it. And there's something else. While I was pumping gas, my parole officer pulled up. He reminded me that my appointment with him was right after my AA meeting. He was going to wait until afterwards and we were going to talk then." More scrambling through the wallet, and Joe produced the business card.

Pete looked gloomily at the gas receipt. The time listed was 8:35. He checked the parole officer's card, handing it to his deputy. The two lawmen glanced at one another in silence. The timeline didn't work. Carly didn't die until 10:00 Monday morning, but she would have been drugged at virtually the same moment Joe Yellowwood was filling up his car. He wasn't their killer.

"Well, I'll verify this with your parole officer, but for now you can go. Just don't leave town and make yourself available if we have to talk to you again. Got it?"

"I understand," he said. "I'm going to the hospital to see my daughter."

"I'm sorry, Joe, but the social workers already put her in foster care. Until her guardianship is established legally, I'd steer clear."

"I'm her father. I'm entitled to custody," Joe said, clenching his teeth.

"Like I said, there's an ongoing process, so do yourself a favor and wait until this is legally settled. You might lose her otherwise."

"I'm going to talk with my mother. If they won't let me have custody because of my record, I'm certain they will let her have custody, and that way she'll know her people and heritage," Joe said, grabbing his jacket and stormed from the room.

THIRTEEN

After his discouraging interrogation of Joe Yellowwood, Pete left the office and drove into town. He wanted to take a break from obsessing about the case and stopped to get a sandwich from the Subway shop on Bridge Street. Sitting in the booth next to the window, he looked gloomily out at Round Lake. It was roofed with a thick layer of snow. The lake emptied into a channel that ran under the drawbridge, past the red lighthouse and out into Lake Michigan. In the summer, the park next to the lake was filled with cheerful tourists, the bandstand hosted concerts and happy shoppers walked in and out of the stores. Today, the wind-swept streets were empty. Checking his phone, he saw his boss had called. As soon as the sheriff heard that Pat O'Connor, Dave Webster and Joe Yellowwood had been removed as suspects, he would call in the state cops, or at a minimum a detective from Traverse City.

Carly's case had been his one big chance to prove himself, to show the sheriff and the community that he was up to the job of finding her killer. He knew he was considered a plodder, that he lacked the flashy brilliance of the highly verbal types. The contribution he made to ferreting out thieves and tracking down druggies always resulted from his seemingly constitutional inability to give up. That trait wasn't much help now though, as the sheriff had only given him a week. He dreaded the moment he knew was coming when he would be shunted aside. His paltry efforts would be disparaged, and he would feel his self-confidence plummet to the floor.

It was probably only a matter of a day or two before the information leaked about Carly's death. Once the news was out, the office would be swarmed by the locusts of the press. He crossed his fingers that by some far-fetched chance the killer would learn of her death and would come in and confess. *Unlikely in the extreme, dumbass,* he told himself. He grabbed his coat and left the restaurant where he'd been the only patron. Walking out to his car, he shuddered at the cold. He cracked open his car door when a sudden idea struck him. Could he use the press to help find Carly's killer? Not without the sheriff's permission, but at last he had a possible direction he could discuss with his supervisor.

"I'VE GOTTEN PERMISSION FROM THE SHERIFF to do a TV appeal for information about Carly's murder," Pete told Victoria proudly when he got back to the office.

"Wow, that's big. We've never done anything like that before, have we?"

"Nope, but it's been three days since Carly died, and the sheriff only gave me a week. I haven't got much time before the case gets taken away, so I called the television station in Traverse City. They are going to tape it here today at six o'clock. I've left word for our deputies to be on the panel with me."

"What about me?" Victoria asked, pouting. "Can't I be on the panel?"

"I am indebted to you for the fingerprint idea that opened Carly's phone, and finding out she wasn't suicidal." Pete's voice trailed off as he hung up his coat. "Tell you what, if you agree not to speak, you can be on the panel."

"Thank you, Boss," Victoria said, trying not to sound resentful. It wasn't much of a concession. Getting to be considered one of the team had been a struggle, but she wasn't giving up.

"The deputies aren't going to speak either, Victoria," Pete said, seeing the look on her face. "Sorry, but the TV people made the decision."

"Okay. I called the high school and got Carly's parents' local address from when she was a student. I know they don't live here anymore, but I thought I'd go out there and talk to the neighbors. I can drive there and back before the appeal is taped. Somebody has to have contact information for them."

"While you do that, I'm going to work on my presentation for the news report. I want it to sound professional. If this leads to our killer soon enough, I won't have to give the case away," his voice trailed off.

Looking at her boss, Victoria was moved by how important it was to Pete to succeed and felt a twinge of concern for him. She knew he'd been working almost twenty-four/seven since that awful day she found Carly Yellowwood dead and he learned from the Coroner that she'd perished from being drugged. There were dark circles under his eyes and he'd lost weight.

I've been working just as hard and haven't lost an ounce, she thought resentfully. *There's no justice.* She suppressed a giggle, recognizing the irony. She was, after all, working in the justice business.

"The TV people want to hear from Joe Yellowwood as a part of the appeal, so please ask one of the deputies to pick him up and bring him to the station. They want all the photos you can find of Carly, Chenoa and Joe," Pete said.

"No problem, Boss," Victoria said, patting him on the shoulder.

HAVING MANAGED TO CONVINCE SERGEANT CRAIG to get the phones by promising him more homemade chocolate chip cookies, Victoria left the office. The temperature had fallen to zero and she virtually ran to her car, jumped in and turned the key in the ignition. She was heading to the address where Carly's folks had lived when they were still Charlevoix residents.

The Lynley's former neighborhood sat on a peninsula of lake-frontage at the bottom of the hill below M-66, the highway located on the high backbone of land paralleling Lake Charlevoix. A half-dozen expensive homes sat on the flat peninsula that stuck out like a tongue into the iced-over lake. Although mansion-like, many of the homes were used as summer cottages and Victoria doubted they would be occupied in the winter.

She wondered if the County had plowed the roads for the subdivision and whether driving down the steep ridge on the access road would result in her not being able to get back up to the main road again. Slowing down, Victoria spotted the house where Carly's parents had lived. The driveway of their former home hadn't been plowed, but the driveway next door had been. She considered leaving her car on the side of M-66, but the shoulders were piled high with snow and there was no space to pull off. She'd have to risk driving straight down the hill to reach the lakeside neighborhood.

Taking a deep breath, she turned left and inched down the icy trail. It was a relief to see the lights on in the house next door to the Lynley's former home, a hopeful sight as many homes still lacked power. Driving onto the cement apron at the neighbors' home and turning her car around, Victoria got out and walked to the front door. She rang the doorbell above a little camera which showed an image of the person on the porch to the homeowners. It was only moments before the door opened.

"Hello, sir. My name is Victoria Treadwell. I'm the dispatcher for the sheriff's office in Charlevoix. I'm wondering if you remember Mr. and Mrs. Lynley and their daughter Carly who used to live next door. We're trying to locate them."

"Come on in," the white-haired elderly man said, opening the door wider. He was stooped and wore a knitted cap. Wisps of his hair stuck straight out from under his hat. Victoria commiserated, her own hair being similarly out of control.

They passed through a front entry into an enormous, vaulted room with a picture window that looked out on the mostly-frozen lake. A center strip of open water could be seen about thirty feet from shore. The steel blue water in the cleft had been stirred into white caps by the high wind. "Thank you for inviting me in. May I have your name, sir?"

"I'm George Hunt. Just a minute and I'll get my wife." Both members of the couple returned a few minutes later. Mrs. Hunt was wearing a hand-knitted sweater, thick pants and gloves.

"I'm happy to see you folks have power," Victoria said, smiling at the elderly couple.

"Just came back on. It takes a while for the house to heat up," Mrs. Hunt said. "Take off your hat, George. You look ridiculous. Now, how can we help?"

"Until about five years ago, I believe a Mr. and Mrs. Lynley and their daughter, Carly lived next door to you. We're trying to find them and hoped you had an address."

"I always get a Christmas card. Hang on a minute, and I'll go get it."

"Is this about Carly?" Mr. Hunt asked in a low voice when his wife left the room.

"Yes, it is. She's a missing person and we want to speak to her parents in case they know something that could help," Victoria said, reluctantly towing the company line. She hated lying to members of the public.

Mr. Hunt looked at her sadly. "I heard she died," he said in near-whisper.

"I was just about to put the Christmas cards into the fireplace," Mrs. Hunt said as she bustled back into the living room. "Lucky you came when you did." She handed Victoria the card and its envelope. There was a return address in the upper left-hand corner.

"Thank you so much. Do you mind giving me their phone number?"

"Of course, it's no problem," Mrs. Hunt said and grabbing a pen, wrote down the number.

"I sure hope you two are able to get out to get groceries," Victoria said. "Hate to think of you folks not having enough to eat."

"We have a deep freeze in the garage with enough food to last a Russian Army through the winter. My wife freezes and cans just about everything," George said with a grin. "I'll walk outside with you and help you get started up the hill." He donned his Mackintosh and pulled his knitted cap back on. They walked out together.

"I didn't want Suzanne to hear, but Carly's dead isn't she?" he asked in a voice as forlorn as the winter wind. The outdoor lights motion flicked on. The snow swirled around them making white drifts in the air.

"I'm sorry to have lied to you, sir. You're right, Carly's dead. We're going to be doing a TV spot asking for information later today. You can tell your wife, but please don't tell anyone else, especially not the Lynleys. The sheriff is going to call them after the appeal is taped and before the broadcast. We're hoping that somebody saw something or heard something that will help us find out what happened."

"Don't worry. I won't say a thing. Such a beautiful girl, Carly. It always bothered the Missus and me that the parents moved away so soon after the wedding. She didn't seem grown up enough to be married. Now who will raise little Chenoa?"

"Possibly her grandparents," Victoria said.

"I doubt Carly's parents will be able to help. Michelle Lynley is dying of lung cancer. She was a lifetime smoker. And Jerry wouldn't be up to a toddler. He's close to seventy. They married late and he has health problems of his own. Carly was their only child and finding out she's dead will probably kill her mother. We saw her grow up you see, lived next door to the family for over twenty years." There was an ache in his voice.

"Had you seen Carly recently?"

"She came for a visit over at the holidays with some Christmas cookies. Brought the child with her. Our kids are all grown and flown. We're lucky if they come for a week in the summer. It was a treat to see them both."

"How did you know she was dead?" Victoria said looking at him intently.

"The waitress at the White Swan told me. Louise, I think her name was. Now, you can make it up the hill if you keep your car in low. Don't touch the brakes, just gun it."

Getting into her car and backing up as far as she could before tackling the acute slope, Victoria waved good-bye at the old man. She'd gotten the Lynley's contact information and more. Louise, Carly's co-worker at the White Swan, had kept vital information from the Sheriff's deputies.

FOURTEEN

Pete Manstead, his two deputies, Ben Wilcox, Charlie Pierce and Victoria, their dispatcher, were seated at a table in front of a large map showing the two-arms of Lake Charlevoix. The village of East Jordan was at the south end of the map and the town of Charlevoix was at the north where the channel flowed under the drawbridge and out into Lake Michigan. The Director and his crew had arrived an hour earlier and the production lights for the TV taping were set up and turned on. The cameraman was in position and the sound had been checked.

"Ready everyone?" the Director asked. "Okay. I'm going to count backwards from three to one. When I say one, you can start your presentation, Sheriff. Three . . . two . . . one."

Pete looked directly at the camera and said, "Twenty-three-year-old Carly Yellowwood was found dead this past Monday morning." He stopped speaking for a moment and it was obvious he was struggling to keep his emotions in check. After clearing his throat, he said, "She had been assaulted but managed to drive from her house until she lost control of her car, ran off the road and died." He took a deep breath and the camera went in tight on his face. "The Sheriff's office is asking anyone who saw or heard anything about the attack that caused Carly Yellowwood's death to call our tip line. It will be set up and ready to receive calls at 8:00 am tomorrow morning." The phone number appeared over and over in a continuous loop at the bottom of the screen as the camera pulled back from its close-up.

"Cut," the Director said. "That was just fine, Sheriff. Now we are going to add a spot with Carly's ex-husband, Joe and some photos of Carly and their daughter."

"I have the photos on a flash drive," Victoria told him and handed the little blue device to the cameraman who inserted it into a laptop linked to a projector and screen.

"Joe Yellowwood is waiting in our outer office," Pete said. "By the way, he's been cleared of her assault."

"Glad to hear it," the Director said, looking startled. It obviously hadn't occurred to him to think of Joe as a suspect.

"I'll get him," Victoria said and left the conference room. She returned with Joe who was dressed in a plaid flannel shirt and jeans. Already thin, it looked to her like he had lost more weight since learning of Carly's death.

"Thank you for joining us, Joe," the Director said and they shook hands. "Please take a seat next to the sheriff at the table there. We're going to ask you to say a few words about Carly and Chenoa. It's important that you look directly into the camera and that you convey your loss. Got that?"

Joe nodded. He was obviously finding it hard to cope with the situation. Victoria wondered if he could even speak without breaking down.

He took his seat, and after several preliminary "takes," the Director said they were ready. He asked Pete to start by introducing Joe and then counted down "Three . . . two . . . one."

"This is Joe Yellowwood, Carly's ex-husband and their daughter Chenoa's father. He's doing an extremely courageous thing in speaking to us today. Go ahead, Joe," Pete said.

The cameraman moved in for a close-up. Joe cleared his throat and began, "I have lost my beautiful Carly. We were high school sweethearts who got married right after graduation. Although we divorced three years later, I never stopped loving her," he stopped and gritted his teeth. "Someone out there saw something, or heard something about what happened on Monday morning. If that's you, call the tip-line at the Sheriff's office. Nobody should get away with taking Carly from me and our little daughter, Chenoa, who will now have to grow up without a mother." His eyes filled with tears and he turned quickly away.

There was silence for a few minutes as the photos Victoria collected played over and over again. The pictures showed Carly and Joe at their senior prom, walking down the aisle of the local church after their wedding, Carly nursing an infant Chenoa, and the couple sitting on the edge of the lake holding hands. All told the poignant tale of a young life cut short.

The Director made a 'cut' gesture with his hand and said, "That's a wrap. This segment will be broadcast tonight on the ten o'clock local news. Thank you everyone. We're out of here." Then turning to Pete, he said "I hope this helps you solve the case, Sheriff, but I know from previous experience that these appeals bring out a lot of crazies. In small towns you only have to run your tip line for around four hours. After that, it's just the people who are looking for attention who call."

"Thank you," Pete said in the disheartened voice of a man who recognizes the inevitable result of appealing to the public.

The TV people packed up their gear and left the office.

Pete caught Victoria as she was putting on her parka and boots. "Did you find out anything by talking to the people who live near Carly's parents' old house?"

"Carly's folks have moved to Florida and I got the address from their previous neighbors and their phone number, too. I left the return call slip on your desk. The mother is very ill. She's got stage four lung cancer and it sounds like the dad isn't in good health either."

Pete nodded.

"One other thing, the neighbor I spoke to already knew Carly was dead."

"How the hell did they find out?" Pete asked with an angry grimace.

"Mr. Hunt learned about her death from Louise at the White Swan. You'll have to talk with her again and don't forget that you have to call Carly's parents before you leave tonight. They can't find out their daughter has passed away from someone who sees the appeal and contacts them after the broadcast."

Pete nodded, his jaw was locked in a grim line.

IT WAS EIGHT O'CLOCK IN THE evening and totally dark outside when Pete found himself alone in the office. He walked down the hall to the jail cells, hoping Sergeant Craig was still around, but they had no one in custody and the jailer had gone home. He returned to his desk and sat looking at the phone slips for the calls he had to return and the note reminding him to contact Louise, the waitress at the White Swan. None of them were going to be easy. He drummed his fingers on the desk, trying to think of some way to avoid making the calls and decided to call his girlfriend, Ashley. He always felt better after talking to her.

"Hi, Pete," she said when she answered.

There was a very long pause.

"Could you come up here for the weekend?" he asked in a voice thick with emotion.

"Why? What's going on?"

"There's been a murder here," he said and fell silent. After a few silent moments, he added, "I'm heading up the investigation."

It was horrific news. Homicide in Northern Michigan was virtually non-existent. This rare and terrible crime seemed to have made her boyfriend all but mute. It took her only a moment's thought before she said. "Of course I'll come. We only have a half day tomorrow. I should be there around twelve-thirty. Love you."

"Love you, too," Pete said and clicked off the call.

Then taking a deep breath he dialed Sheriff Dodgson's private number. When, his boss didn't answer, he left a message saying, "The appeal to the public for information about Carly is going to be broadcast on the ten o'clock news tonight. We are set up to receive the tips starting at eight a.m. tomorrow morning. We asked for anyone who knew where Carly went the morning she died to call us. I didn't say on the video appeal that Carly had been murdered, just that she was assaulted. I'll call you again tomorrow."

Pete clicked off the call and rubbed his hands across his face. Fatigue washed over him. He knew he should get on the road. His house was south of East Jordan on the river and the driving conditions in the basin were treacherous. Crumpling up the message reminding him to call his boss, he tossed it into the wastebasket and looked at the note with the phone number for Louise, the waitress at the White Swan. He decided he'd wait on that one, doubting it would lead anywhere.

Then he looked at the Lynleys' number. He had never had to tell a parent that their child was dead before, much less that she had been murdered. The news about a death was always supposed to be given in person, but Carly's parents were in Florida and they had to know before the appeal was broadcast. Reluctantly, he punched in the number. It rang for a long time and he was about to give up when he heard the man's voice.

"Hello." It was a thin scratchy voice of an old man.

"Mr. Lynley, this is Undersheriff Manstead from Charlevoix, Michigan. I have some bad news. I'm sorry, sir, but I think you might want to sit down for this."

"It's about Carly, isn't it," the man said and his thin voice was filled with apprehension.

"That's right, sir. I'm sorry to tell you that your daughter has died."

"Oh, my God," the old man said and Pete could hear him calling for his wife.

FIFTEEN

Friday

Four separate phones had been connected and set up on tables in the lobby of the sheriff's office. The entire staff, with the sole exception of their jailer, were ready to respond to calls. Sergeant Craig, scowling resentfully, was seated at the front desk. He hated taking calls and dealing with walk-ins. Victoria had her lap-top computer in front of her and the men, who were not particularly keyboard-adept, had paper and pens to write down the names and numbers of people who called. It was 8:15 and there had been no calls so far.

"Now remember, whoever calls be sure to get a name and phone number. It's possible some people will want to leave anonymous messages, but push them hard to tell you their names. Take your time with each call. Write down whatever they tell you, even if it seems unimportant. And don't tell any of the callers exactly how Carly died. We're keeping that quiet for now." Pete stopped for a moment before adding, "The boss will be back soon. If we have nobody in custody by the time he gets here, Sheriff Dodgson is going to take over the case himself, or turn it over to the state police." He felt the pressure of time bearing down on him and forced his rapid breathing to slow.

Then the first call came in and Ben picked it up. "Sheriff's Office," he said and there was silence as all of them turned to listen. Then two other phones rang simultaneously. The expected mayhem had begun. They were bombarded with callers until shortly before noon when the phones fell silent.

"Let's take a break, people. I want to hear what all of you have learned. Victoria, you first," Pete said.

"A lot of people called in saying they had seen Carly at the grocery store, dropping Chenoa off or picking her up from the baby-sitter, going in to work at the White Swan, stopping by the pediatrician's office, the pharmacy or the public library. I wrote down the dates but nothing stood out as important, until the last person called. It was a women named Julie who waits table at the Bridge Street Tap Room. She remembers seeing Carly sitting in a lakeside booth a couple of weeks ago. When Julie approached the table to take their drink orders, they waved her away. It's pretty loud in that pub, but she thought she heard Carly say something about not needing the money now."

"What description did she give you of the man Carly was with?" Pete asked. His eyes bored into hers, his face alight with expectation.

"She wasn't with a man. It was a woman." Victoria paused seeing Pete's discouraged expression. "I asked her if she knew the woman's name and she did. Her name is Nancy Barnes, she's a local attorney. When I checked Carly's calendar on her phone, I saw she had written the initials N.B. on the date of their appointment. I had some time between calls to look her up and she does family law."

"Well now, that is interesting," Pete said. "What about the rest of you? Anything pertinent?"

"I had one caller, a woman who insisted on remaining anonymous, who said she'd seen Carly talking to a guy named Walter Sorenson on Saturday afternoon. They were standing in front of the library and he was gripping her by the arm. The caller said they looked like they were arguing," Charlie said.

"Do any of you know this guy?"

"I know him," Ben said. "He's a well-to-do businessman and a local employer."

"Is he married?" Pete asked.

"Very much so. He's a devoted Catholic, passes out the collection plates at St. Mary's at Sunday services and has six kids."

"Sounds like we have two promising leads," Pete said, feeling a sense of relief.

Receiving no further calls, Pete shut off the tip line. As soon he left the lobby, Victoria called the phone number for Nancy Barnes. Not only had the attorney been identified as talking with Carly just a short time before her untimely death, but she was in family law and therefore could answer a few questions about their chances of adopting Chenoa. When the office secretary answered, she said there was a half hour opening in the lawyer's schedule at twelve-thirty.

"Thank you. That time will work for me."

"May I tell Ms. Barnes the reason for the consultation?"

Yes, I'm Victoria Treadwell, the dispatcher for the sheriff's office and wish to consult her about a crime we are investigating."

"I saw the news last night. I presume this is about Carly Yellowwood."

"I'll see you shortly," Victoria said, ending the call. She switched the phones to the setting that sent any calls to the station directly to her cell phone and left the office. The temperature was hovering around fifteen degrees and the wind was gusting. Getting into her car she turned the key hearing the sluggish engine struggle to start. It finally caught and she reached the office of Nancy Barnes a few minutes later.

The attorney's office was on the second floor of the building at the very end of Bridge Street. It was the last building before the drawbridge. At street level the building housed retail establishments, but the upper level had been made into office space.

She opened the door with the name plate for Nancy Barnes, J.D., LLC. The secretary for the practice greeted her and offered her coffee, gesturing to a sideboard. It was just minutes before the secretary heard a buzz on her phone and said, "Miss Barnes will see you now."

Nancy Barnes stood up from her desk and greeted Victoria when she walked in. The attorney's office had a spectacular view of the channel that ran from Round Lake to the end of the pier where the square red lighthouse could be seen at the edge of the Lake Michigan. The waterway was one of the few bodies of water that hadn't completely frozen. The ice on the edges had formed into bumpy shapes that resembled the armored plates on the back of a stegosaurus. Victoria smiled to herself, thinking of her sons. They were at the stage in which dinosaurs were a constant subject of discussion.

"Please have a seat and tell me what I can do for you," the young attorney said. She was whippet-thin with straight black hair and intimidating steel-rimmed glasses.

"As I'm sure you know, the sheriff's office has asked the public for help in identifying anyone Carly Yellowwood saw on Monday morning before she died. The segment was on the ten o'clock news last night. Your name was mentioned as a person who met with Carly at the Bridge Street Pub a couple of weeks ago."

"I did meet with Carly about two weeks ago, but can't share the contents of our consultation. As I'm sure you know, Mrs. Treadwell, all attorney-client conversations are privileged." Nancy Barnes eyes narrowed.

"I believe there are exceptions to the rule," Victoria said.

"There are. If someone came seeking my help in carrying out a crime, I could inform the authorities. Or, if I believed disclosure of client information was necessary to prevent death or bodily harm I could. Those are the only two reasons to break confidentiality."

"As you know, Carly Yellowwood is now deceased. Perhaps if you had gone to the authorities with the information about your consultation in December, her death could have been prevented," Victoria said looking directly at the woman.

Nancy Barnes frowned, looking discomfited. "I resent your assertion Mrs. Treadwell. I can't tell you what we talked about in consultation, but since we went out to dinner afterwards and chatted in a social setting, I can say that Carly's ex-husband owed her back support from the time he was in prison and she was prepared to forgive his debt. I asked her if she would be okay financially without his money and she told me there was someone new in her life who wanted to help her. That's all I'm prepared to say and I doubt very much whether a question about child support had anything to do with her death."

Feeling she'd gotten about as much as she could have out of the tight-lipped attorney, Victoria thanked her and said she had another issue she wanted to consult her about. "My husband and I are hoping to adopt Chenoa Yellowwood, Carly's daughter."

"Isn't she First Nations by birth?" Nancy Barnes asked.

"Yes, and I know her family has first priority, but the situation is complex because, as you know, her mother is deceased and her father was recently released from jail after serving time for a violent offense. The social workers have put Chenoa into foster care until her guardianship can be legally determined."

"What about other family members, aunts, uncles or grandparents for example?"

"Both Joe and Carly were only children. Carly's parents are elderly and ill, plus they are Caucasian and live in Florida. Joe's father is deceased, but his mother resides on the local reservation. He lives with her and it seemed to me that the family court judge would be concerned about having the child in a home with her father, given his criminal record."

"The law states that when the state cannot return a foster child to their birth home due to concerns about her safety, the goal is to place children into adoptive homes as quickly as possible after parental rights have been terminated," Nancy Barnes said.

"Wait, are you saying that she couldn't be adopted unless her father surrendered his rights?"

"That's correct, or if a judge terminated them, which rarely happens. Plus, the recent Supreme Court decision reaffirming the constitutionality of ICWA would make it highly unlikely that you could adopt her."

"What I haven't mentioned is that my husband is one quarter Native. He has the necessary blood quantum to qualify as tribal," Victoria said.

"That would definitely help your case, but as I said, parental rights have to be terminated before an application could be acted upon. In addition to any living relatives, the tribe itself would have to agree to Chenoa leaving the reservation. Suing for adoption could involve many years of litigation, Mrs. Treadwell," Nancy Barnes said and added, "not to mention the considerable expense."

Having had her hopes pretty thoroughly dashed, Victoria left the lawyer's office and walked back to her car. She knew Pete wouldn't be happy she'd met with Nancy Barnes. There had to be a way to tell him what she'd learned without having him completely scrub her from the investigation. At least, she'd discovered why Carly Yellowwood had consulted the attorney, but it didn't help find the man she was having an affair with. Victoria wasn't sure Pete was right about the motive for the crime anyway. All along, she'd doubted it was male jealousy. Carly's death, she thought, had been spurred by a different motive, something deeper and more complex.

SIXTEEN

Unusually for her, Pete's girlfriend, Ashley Hamilton, was having a trying day with her first graders. It was Friday and students were going home at noon, but just before the bell rang, Billy Phillips had pulled little April Johnson's braids again. It was his third offense. Although she rarely did so, she sent him to the Principal's office and asked that Billy's parents be called. Mr. and Mrs. Phillips were waiting in the hall with their tow-headed son when she ushered the rest of the kids out to the pick-up line, handing them to the assistant who took them to the cars or walked them to the big yellow school buses.

"I'll be back in a minute," she told the Phillips family as she walked by. "You can wait in my classroom."

When she returned, Mrs. Phillips said, "Was there a behavioral problem with my sweet Billy today?" She sounded like she couldn't believe it of her little angel.

Ashley looked down at the little miscreant and said, "Why don't you tell your parents what you did today?"

The tyke gave her an evil look and said, "I only pulled April's hair. She's a big whiny baby. It didn't hurt her."

"And?" Ashley asked. "What else did you do?"

He looked askance at her and said, "I got really mad and kicked Miss Ashley's desk. I really hurt my toe, Mom. You should kiss it better." He started to take off his shoe.

"You kicked Miss Ashley's desk?" Mrs. Phillips asked. She sounded shocked.

At that point, Mr. Phillips joined the conversation. "There will be no more pulling hair or kicking desks in school. You will do exactly what Miss Ashley tells you from now on or you will be in serious trouble with me. Do you hear me?" Then taking Billy by the arm, he started roughly propelling him from the room. Looking over his shoulder, Mr. Phillips said, "If you have any further problems with my son, Miss Hamilton, you don't have to have Principal Adams involved, just call me directly. I left my card on your desk."

It had been a long time since Ashley had gotten such unconditional support from a parent and although she deplored Mr. Wilcox's 'tough love' approach, she couldn't help stifling a grin. The tearful Mrs. Phillips managed, after dithering around a bit, to say that they probably shouldn't take Stinky home with them for the week-end. Ashley agreed, saying having the class pet was a privilege and ushering the woman from the room. She tidied up her classroom, fed Stinky, the class hamster, some extra rations so he'd have food over the week-end and walked out in a howling wind to her car

ONCE ON THE ROAD, ASHLEY MADE better time than she had anticipated. When she was ten miles from East Jordan, she called Victoria. In the four years she and Pete had been dating, the two women had become good friends.

When Victoria answered, she said, "Pete called me last night and asked me to come up. He said there had been a murder in Charlevoix. I was shocked. We so rarely have violent crime in Northern Michigan. Can you tell me who died?"

"This is all confidential information so you have to keep this to yourself. A woman named Carly Yellowwood was killed this past Monday morning. She was divorced and has a two-year-old daughter by her ex-husband, Joe. He's in the clear because he was on his way to an AA meeting and in then a meeting with his parole officer around the time she died. Sheriff Dodgson is out of town so Pete is in charge of the investigation. He believes this is a *crime of passion*, but I don't. To me it's something else, something more complicated. I've been trying hard to contribute to the investigation, but it's been all uphill."

"Well, I hope he's listening to you. Can you have lunch with me? I should be there in about half an hour."

"Sure can. Let's meet at the Bridge Street Tap room."

Clicking off the call, Ashley thought about Pete, what a slow thoughtful man he was, and the pain in his voice when he'd called the night before. It had produced a surge of compassion in her that flowed outward toward her troubled boyfriend. She was nearly six feet tall, and had always felt self-conscious about her height until they started dating. Pete was six foot five and built like a football player. He made her feel positively diminutive. They had been seeing each other for a month before they made love. Afterwards, sitting side by side in bed, she asked him why he'd waited so long. He admitted he'd been afraid he would hurt her.

"You're so delicate," he'd said. She'd turned her head away quickly, hiding her face in the pillow to squash her giggles. Although they weren't able to live together, due to their jobs keeping them in separate cities, over the four years they'd been dating, they had fallen deeply in love.

ASHLEY AND VICTORIA MET FOR LUNCH at the Bridge Street Tap Room. They were seated in a booth overlooking frozen Round Lake with its empty marina. Victoria ordered coffee and Ashley asked for a coke.

"I have serious hair envy," Victoria said looking at her friend's beautiful ash-blonde curls that always seemed to be under perfect control. Even having just pulled off her knitted hat, Ashley's hair settled instantly into a cloud of loveliness. It wasn't fair.

"Don't be silly," Ashley said. "You have red hair. Apparently, all men think redheads are wildly hot." Victoria chuckled. "Pete didn't tell me much when he called. Can you bring me up to date?"

"Yes, but remember everything I tell you is confidential." Ashley nodded and Victoria continued in a near whisper, "Carly was having an affair and Pete thinks the man she was sleeping with was the person who drugged her and caused her death."

"So Carly died from an overdose?"

"Yes, but she didn't take those drugs voluntarily. We know from Dr. Winter, the coroner, that a tall man with Nordic ancestry kissed her good-bye on Monday morning. We were clutching at straws until," She paused for a dramatic effect and then added with a twinkle, "I got Carly's I-phone to open."

"How the heck did you do that?" Ashley asked looking at Victoria in amazement.

"I was pretty darn proud of myself. The coroner managed to transfer Carly's fingerprints to the plastic glove I was wearing and to my astonishment when I pushed on the home button, the phone opened."

"You should get a big fat raise for that."

"Exactly my thinking, girlfriend, but Pete keeps saying he has to ask Sheriff Dodgson. Unfortunately, the man we identified from Carly's photos was later eliminated on the basis of DNA."

"Bummer," Ashley said. "Still there's a lot of information on most people's phones. You can probably get more. Changing the subject, I saw you did a request for information on the evening news. Did it give you anything?"

"One of the people who called in on the tip line said that she'd seen Mr. Walter Sorenson standing outside the library with Carly the Saturday before she died. He was holding on to her arm and they were arguing."

"What do you know about this Sorenson guy?"

"He's a local businessman, married with six kids. Pete sent our deputy Charlie out to see him at home last night and asked him to come into the station today. I'm afraid it's not Sorenson though, because he told Charlie he was at a meeting to raise funds for an addition to the church on Monday morning. He said the priest would confirm that he was there."

"I can certainly see why Pete is struggling," Ashley said. "Did you get anything else from the tip line?"

"One of the calls was from Julie, a waitress who works here. She saw Carly having dinner here one evening a couple of weeks before the accident with a local woman who's a family attorney. I just met with her. Pete's going to kill me when he finds out. He keeps reminding me that I'm not part of the investigation."

"I would think he would be happy for any help at this point. What did you learn from the attorney?"

"She agreed to tell me a few things since she and Carly had an informal conversation over dinner. Carly's ex-husband owed her back child support from the time he was in prison and she was prepared to forgive the total amount."

"That's interesting. Maybe the guy Carly was sleeping with is wealthy and wants to help her financially. I don't think you mentioned where Carly was drugged. Was it at her house?"

"No. Pete got a warrant for her place just in case. It wasn't the crime scene. However, there was something odd he noticed when he was there. The house was unlocked. Our deputies were there earlier and the house was locked then, so we're assuming someone besides Carly has a key."

"It's taken me three years to get a key to Pete's place," Ashley said, rolling her eyes. "He keeps teasing me, saying we aren't family . . . yet. My guess is that it would have been Carly's ex-husband, Joe, who has a key."

"That makes sense. But the question is why he would have been there in the first place, especially during that storm," Victoria said.

"Perhaps he went out to see his daughter."

"Maybe," Victoria said, but she looked dubious.

"You're destroying all my ideas this morning," Ashley said and to her annoyance found herself on the precipice of tears.

"For goodness sakes, my friend. I didn't mean to hurt your feelings," Victoria said looking concerned.

"You didn't. I'm just a hot mess at the moment."

"I understand, I get weepy once a month, too," Victoria said. "I do think you are on to something about Joe having a key to Carly's place. I'll tell Pete and we'll bring him in again. Maybe we should order. We're getting looks from the wait staff." She gestured for the waitress who walked over.

"Hello. My name's Julie and I'll be taking care of you today," the waitress said and asked them what they wanted to eat.

Victoria ordered fish and chips and Ashley asked for a grilled cheese sandwich. When the waitress left, Ashley asked, "Isn't Julie the name of the woman who called in on the tip line saying she saw Carly in here with that attorney?"

"That's right."

"When she comes back with our food, could you ask her if she knows Walt Sorenson? I can't ask, but you are the dispatcher for the sheriff's office."

"I'm just clerical, not an officer of the law," Victoria said, frowning. She was well aware that her status as a civilian had been the main obstacle to being considered part of the team investigating Carly's murder. It was a sore point.

"Still, worth a try, don't you think? Pete's getting pretty desperate."

Despite her hesitation, when Julie returned with their orders, Victoria asked, "Do you know the Sorensons?"

"Sure do. They come in all the time. Such a nice family. In fact, last October the whole family, grandmas and grandpas included, came in for their oldest son Leo's 21st birthday. Tammy Fowler, Leo's fiancé, was with the group. They rented our private room overlooking the lake and had a lovely dinner for everyone. We all sang happy birthday for the boy. He's studying business in college."

"That's nice. Most kids just want to hit the bars with friends for their twenty-first," Victoria said, looking keenly at their waitress.

"He did that, too. Mr. Sorenson booked a private suite for Leo and his friends at the Turtle Creek casino for later that evening. They were driven over there in a limo. He told me that way the boys could stay up all night, try their luck at the tables and he and his wife wouldn't worry about them driving. He'd hired a waitress to keep the drinks coming. I overheard Tammy being a bit put out that it was a *no girlfriends allowed* event," Julie grinned.

"When is the wedding?" Victoria asked.

"I am not sure. It was originally going to be in June, but I've heard whispers that there's been recent trouble in the relationship. Tammy was in here last week with a friend. She looked like she'd been crying. Poor thing."

"Do you by chance know the name of the waitress who served the birthday boy at Turtle Creek last October?" Victoria asked.

"No, but I can probably find out."

"Thanks. If you do, could you please call me? Here's my phone number," Victoria said and handed Julie her card.

"Do you two want anything else?"

"We're fine, thank you," Ashley said. Setting a napkin down, she said she had to visit the ladies.

When she returned to the table, Victoria was on the phone. She quickly ended the call saying, "It was Pete at the office. I have to get back. Sorry."

"No big deal. I've got the check," Ashley said.

"Good ideas earlier, especially about Joe having a key to Carly's place," Victoria said.

AFTER LEAVING THE RESTAURANT, ASHLEY DROVE to the Charlevoix library. Unbeknownst to Pete, she had been looking into teaching jobs closer to where he worked. They had been dating for four years and she felt it was time he asked her to move in with him.

While she could have checked her email on her phone to confirm the appointment, as a first-grade teacher, Ashley was a firm believer in the importance of libraries, and wanted to see the children's reading area. She was immediately impressed with the size of the building. Once she went inside, she saw that the remodeling of what had once been a middle school had been superbly done in the Arts and Crafts style from the early part of the nineteenth century. She took a seat in the large open area where there were computers available to patrons and read her email. "Your interview with Principal Harris is confirmed for 4:00 p.m. today at the East Jordan Elementary school," the message read.

SEVENTEEN

Pete walked heavily down the hall to the front desk. He'd been thinking obsessively about Carly's murder and growing more and more frustrated. He wanted someone to bounce ideas off and neither of his deputies were around. Unwilling to call Sheriff Dodgson and admit that he hadn't found the perpetrator, he decided to pick Victoria's brain. Checking the reception area, he was irked to see that his dispatcher wasn't at her desk. He glanced at the clock. She was late coming back from lunch. Just then the phone rang and Pete picked it up.

"Sheriff's Office," he said.

"It's Dave Webster calling, Sheriff, and I owe you an apology. The day after we met, I went to the White Swan for lunch and Louise basically cross-examined me about Carly. She knew you and I had talked because she and Jacquie identified me in the photo you showed them. She kept on me for information until I caved and told her Carly was dead, but I made her swear not to share the information. I hope that isn't going to be a problem."

"I don't think so, but please don't tell anyone else. This is an active murder investigation and we have to control the information about the crime."

"I won't," he said. "Again, I'm sorry I let the information slip."

Disgruntled, Pete stomped back to his office and dialed Victoria's cell number.

"You are supposed to be at the office," he said in an annoyed voice.

"Coming," she said and cut off the call.

Pete, you are losing it, he chided himself. Calling Victoria when she had been working so hard and was having lunch with his girlfriend to boot was *not* how he usually operated. His inability to get anywhere with this seemingly impenetrable case was making him unbearable. All he was used to handling were citizens who were frustrated about parking tickets, lost bicycles, mild domestic disputes, and smash 'n grab cases where young thugs made off with tourist's purses.

If I only had some spotty teen-ager in the jail at the moment, I could browbeat him into confessing to something, he thought. It would make him feel better, but the jail cells were empty. It was surprising, but some of those teen-age delinquents became good cops when they reached adulthood. He often told them that he'd tangled with the law once when he was a kid. It led to increased trust in the police, but it wasn't true. He'd never been in any serious trouble as a youth (he didn't count helping himself to watermelons from the neighbor's patch). The truth was that he'd been too afraid of his mother to step very far out of line.

He smiled to himself, thinking about his parents who lived in a small town in Michigan's Upper Peninsula. They were in their late seventies and still in love. They held hands even when shopping in the grocery store. He envisioned the small house where he grew up and wished he could take some time to visit. His mother would fuss over him, cook his favorite foods and then take him aside and tell him what he should do with his life.

Mary Margaret Manstead might be only four feet, eleven inches tall, but she was a force to be reckoned with. She looked sweet, but when her temper was roused, the woman was downright terrifying. Once when he was eight years-old, she'd caught him in a lie and made him go out into the yard and pick a switch off the willow tree. She threatened to whip him with it. It didn't happen, but he never forgot that threat.

The Almighty, with whom Mary Margaret was in near-constant communication, had told her that if Pete didn't ask Ashley to marry him, he was going to lose the woman . . . and since they were sleeping together while unmarried (something Pete had reluctantly confessed to his mother under close questioning), he'd be going straight to hell. Ashley's love for him and her willingness to drive in blizzard conditions to be with him had given him back a measure of self-confidence. She was his soul mate and he knew he was lucky to have her.

Trying to organize his thoughts, Pete decided to make a list. Sitting down at his desk, he pulled out a pen and wrote;

Carly was having sex with a tall, blue-eyed man of northern European ancestry.

She'd been intimate with the man on the weekend before she died.

Her lover kissed her good-bye on Monday morning.

She was drugged that morning and died at 10:00 a.m.

Carly hadn't taken the drugs voluntarily and was not suicidal.

Her death was attempted or premeditated murder.

This was a crime of passion.

He stopped, drew a line across the page and started a list of suspects.

Prime suspect: Carly's unknown sexual partner.

Joe Yellowwood: eliminated, alibied by parole officer.

Dave Webster: eliminated, alibied by DNA.

Pat O'Connor: eliminated, alibied by waitress doing inventory.

Walt Sorenson: eliminated, alibied by Father Jake.

All my suspects are out of the picture, he thought gloomily.

DRIVING BACK TO THE SHERIFF'S OFFICE after their lunch at the Bridge Street Pub, Victoria mentally reviewed Ashley's ideas. Her thought that Joe Yellowwood's having a key to Carly's place was genius. He hadn't revealed that little fact in his interrogation and it could be critical. Pete would definitely have to bring him back in. Pursuing Mr. Sorenson any further, however, was just plain ridiculous. The man told them he was at a meeting at the church at the time Carly died, something Fr. Jake had confirmed. He could be dismissed as a suspect.

Parking her car in the sheriff's office lot, Victoria mentally patted herself on the back for what she'd already contributed to the case, especially getting Carly's phone open. *Still feeling pretty proud of myself for that idea,* she thought. But the phone hadn't given them much help, which was unusual. As Ashley said, most young women's whole lives were on their phones.

Then it dawned on her—what was weird about Carly's phone. When a woman started a new relationship, her phone was invariably loaded with texts to him, pictures of him, plans to meet him, calls, etc. There hadn't been any texts in Carly's phone except to Joe, her colleagues at the White Swan, and her baby-sitter. Almost all her photos were of Chenoa, the lake, or local wildlife. Even the one picture that showed Carly in an orange bathing suit with a man skipping stones in the background had been eliminated. Victoria was crestfallen when she showed her husband the photo and he recognized the guy as one of his friends who had been visiting the day the photograph was taken.

What kind of relationship was it where a woman didn't want to show off her new man? Maybe he was married, or had asked her to keep it a secret. But, there might another reason. Right from the beginning, she thought this crime was less about sexual jealousy than about an unknown and elusive motive.

Victoria decided she would mention her insights, and Ashley's, to Pete. Although he was an unreconstructed male chauvinist (who would have been shocked to be told he was one), she'd been making progress on getting him to give her some credit as a member of the team. He had been impressed with her idea about Carly's phone and let her be on the panel for the appeal to the public, although she wasn't allowed to speak which still irked. The problem was that none of her ideas had helped identify the person Carly was sleeping with. *Not nearly enough to justify a raise,* she thought gloomily. She got out of her car, scrunched across the snow-covered parking lot and walked into the building.

Hearing Victoria's voice speaking to Sgt. Craig in the lobby, Pete waited. When he heard the expected knock on his door, he said, "Come in."

"I'm back," she said. "I had a nice lunch with Ashley. We got caught up on stuff."

"What did you talk about?" he asked, feeling uneasy. Women were not known for keeping information confidential. They always told their best friends everything and Victoria and Ashley were close.

"The case, of course, but I told her to keep everything to herself. Anyway, Ashley came up with something that might be important. Remember when you went out to Carly's place with the warrant? It was after your deputies were there and you found her place unlocked?"

He nodded, but in fact he'd almost forgotten about that little oddity in the blizzard of clues that had blown in with the storm to seemingly wrap an invisibility cloak around Carly's killer.

"Ashley thinks Joe is the person who has a key. Assuming Carly was going to meet someone on the day she died, maybe she asked Joe to go out to her house and wait for her. As I recall, he said absolutely nothing about this to you in his interview."

"Good thinking," he said, feeling like they'd finally gotten a break. "Let's get him back in here."

"Already called him," Victoria said smugly. "He'll be here in by five. There's something else I wanted to mention. I was going to tell you before, but we were busy getting ready to interview Joe Yellowwood, and you brushed me off," she frowned at him severely.

Sometimes when Victoria was irritated with him, the look in her eyes reminded him of his mother. "Go ahead," he said.

"You recall that I've spent a lot of time going through Carly's phone, right?"

He nodded.

"Well, when a woman starts a relationship with a new man, she can't wait to tell everyone she knows about it. She texts him a dozen times a day. He texts her back. They call each other constantly. She takes pictures of him and writes, 'in a relationship with so and so' on her social media pages. Carly did none of those things."

"What does this tell you?" Pete asked, feeling mystified.

"It tells me either the guy was married and didn't want her to reveal the relationship, or there was something else going on."

Pete didn't respond. He was thinking.

Glancing out the window, Victoria could tell the storm had died down. The trees had stopped thrashing and there was a discernable penumbra of light around the shrouded sun. When Pete remained silent, she said, "There's something else I have to tell you, Boss. I had an appointment with Nancy Barnes." Seeing his angry expression, she quickly added, "It was to ask her about Matt and me adopting Chenoa, but I also found out why she saw Carly at the pub."

"Why," he was scowling.

"Carly wanted to forgive the back child-support Joe owed her. That's why she had gone to meet with the attorney. She intended to legally stop the child support agency from going after him for the money. It was a lot, Pete. He owed her $7,000."

"First off, you had absolutely no business talking to Ms. Barnes about the case. You aren't a cop, Victoria." He shook his head.

"I know," she said.

Seeing her hurt expression, he added, "I'm sorry, Victoria. You have done some excellent work on this crime, and I appreciate it. Frankly, it's my first big case and I'm at my wit's end trying to solve it. Also, I wasn't sure initially if I could use anything you found. I've checked with the sheriff though, and we can."

"I did learn one other thing that might be relevant."

"Go ahead."

"Carly told Nancy Barnes that money wasn't going to be problem for her going forward."

"Which means the guy she's sleeping with is rich and since you saw nothing on her phone about him, he wanted her . . . or was paying her, to keep the relationship a secret," Pete said.

"Exactly what I thought," Victoria said and left the room.

EIGHTEEN

When Joe Yellowwood appeared at the sheriff's office at five o'clock that afternoon he was directed to the interview room where Pete was waiting to question him. Sgt. Craig was present to observe the interaction.

"Thanks for coming in, Joe," Pete said, standing up and shaking him by the hand. He pushed the button to begin the video recording saying, "Undersheriff Pete Manstead interviewing Joe Yellowwood regarding the murder of his ex-wife Carly Yellowwood."

"I thought we were done with all this, Sheriff. Don't know why you called me in again," Joe said. He was trying to sound confident, but his eyes shifted and he looked uneasy.

"Because we've discovered that you lied to us," Pete said.

"I didn't give Carly those drugs," Joe said.

"We know you couldn't have, but there's still something you're keeping back. Do you have a key to your ex-wife's home?"

Joe hesitated. He hadn't seen this one coming. Or didn't want to go there. He swallowed and in a quiet voice said, "Yes, I do."

"Were you out there the morning Carly died? Monday morning?"

"Yes." Joe's forehead was shiny with sweat. "I went to her place after I met with my Parole officer. It was about 10:30 when I got there."

Pete could sense the man's anxiety rising. "Tell me why you went."

"Because Carly called and asked me to come over," he said.

Pete's patience with the man was at an end. He smacked his hands down on the table. The noise was so loud and startling that Joe actually jumped. "Why would Carly ask you to come out to her place in that white-out, and don't you dare lie to me." He knew he was getting red in the face.

"She had something to show me that meant I didn't have to give her the back child support I owed."

Give me strength, Pete thought. It was like pulling teeth getting the man to tell him what he knew. "What was it?" he asked, forcing himself to lower his voice.

"It was a receipt for a bank deposit. She told me she put it in her cookie jar. It's made out of pottery and looks like a big apple. I checked, but didn't find it."

"You didn't think to tell me this when we talked before?" Pete asked in a menacing tone of voice. "Jesus, Joe, don't you want me to find the bastard who killed Carly?"

"Of course I do," he said and swallowed. "I'm sorry."

Pete struggled to compose himself before saying, "Todd, get him out of here before I totally lose it."

His custody sergeant came forward and took Joe, looking shell-shocked, from the room. After they left, Pete shook his head, feeling baffled. He knew from Victoria's report about her conversation with Nancy Barnes, that Carly was prepared to forgive the back child support Joe owed her. The receipt was proof that with her new boyfriend's money, she didn't require his. With respect to her murder though, the information didn't seem to help at all. He could have howled in frustration. Just then he heard a tap on his door and yelled, "Come in."

"You have to call Ashley right now, Pete," Victoria said. "She's at your place, terrified and crying. Somebody stuck a threatening letter to your door. She sent me a picture of it."

Holding out her phone, Victoria showed him an image with bold letters cut from magazines or newspapers. The message read: "Carly's killer is still at large. He could kill again. Relinquish the case to someone who can solve it." At the bottom of the page there was a carefully drawn image of a street sign for the corner of Miles and Detour.

"Get Joe back right now before he leaves," he barked and Victoria ran.

Heading home later, Pete struggled to keep his car from being blown off the road. The wind that had died earlier had risen again with a vengeance. It drove the heavy snow in squalls and his vehicle was difficult to keep under control. Before he left, he'd put Joe back in the cells telling Sgt. Craig to be sure to give him his phone call. Then he called Ben, who had returned to Boyne City, and asked him to go out to Carly's place first thing in the morning.

"I want you to find every damn receipt in her house. Go through all the pockets in every one of her jackets or coats and all her wastebaskets. Check under her cookie jar too. I don't care if the receipts are for McDonalds, get me *all* of them!"

Once he reached the stoplight at the turn to E. Jordan, Pete forced himself to settle down. Ashley had been frightened by the note and he wanted to be there for her, but it was obvious to him the letter wasn't a threat. The writer had said, "Carly's killer is still at large . . ."

They had kept virtually all the information about Carly's case in house. The only person they had talked to in detail was Joe Yellowwood, which meant that the message was from the tribe. Joe, of course, had denied any knowledge of the note's author. It was probably one of the elders who still remembered the days when the white man didn't meddle in tribal crimes who wrote the note. Or else they wanted to call in the tribal cops from Traverse City. He thought for a bit, realizing there was one other option he had to consider.

Could Carly have been drugged on the reservation? It was possible, but that irksome sovereign nation issue would keep him from investigating. He felt stymied. The rest of the way home, he was unable to do anything except manage to keep the car on the road.

ASHLEY WAS LOOKING OUT THE STORM door window when he pulled in. Even through the icy sleet that had been plastered on the glass, he could tell she was frightened. He walked to the house, opened the door and gave her a huge hug.

"It was so scary," she said. She was shaking.

"It's going to be okay, sweetheart. I came as soon as I could," he said. Then standing back and looking at her, he noticed she was dressed in a business suit. Her hourglass figure looked good in suits. He wondered why she was professionally dressed... another little mystery, but not one he had to unravel at the moment.

He grabbed a beer from the fridge, took it to the couch and they sat down together in front of the cheerful, flickering fireplace. He took a long pull on the bottle. "Don't you want something?" he asked. Her pale hair shone in the firelight and she smelled like apple blossoms.

"Just to be with you," she said. "What do you make of the letter?"

"I think it's a misdirection sent from the tribe. I'm sure they would rather I kept my hands off this case or hand it over to the tribal police. That's not going to happen, though, because even if Carly was drugged on the reservation, she died in my jurisdiction. On another matter, Victoria told me you were the one who figured out that Joe Yellowwood had a key to her place."

"Was I right?"

"He admitted it. According to him, Carly told him to come out to her place the day she died. She wanted to talk to him about Chenoa's child support and told him to find a receipt for something. The dimwit didn't find the receipt and of course poor Carly never came back."

"That's so sad," she said.

"I am still finding it hard to accept. Carly had her whole life ahead of her. This should never have happened, and especially on my watch. This damn case is like a one of those oriental puzzles that would take a year to solve. And I only have a couple more days before the sheriff comes back," he said. "Why don't you get into something more comfortable?"

"Now there's a good idea," Ashley said smiling at him.

NINETEEN

Saturday

Pete hated leaving Ashley the following morning and delayed long enough to make a pot of coffee. "Wish I could stay here with you today, but I have to talk to Joe Yellowwood this morning and see what Ben found in the way of receipts at Carly's place."

"I'm fine here by myself," she said. "I have some paperwork to do."

"Come give me a kiss," Pete said and she did.

"Love you," she told him.

"Love you more," he said.

Driving north on M-66, Pete pulled out his phone and dialed his parents' number. They still had a landline, just about the only people he knew who did. Their old black phone didn't even have a mobile headset. He knew the day would come when he would hear the voice of a woman coming to the end of her life, (his mom had beaten breast cancer several years earlier) but that day was not today.

"Hello, Son," she said, sounding just as staunch as ever.

"Hi, Mom. I'm on my way to work but thought I'd call. How are you and dad?"

"Snowed in, but your father drove the tractor all the way into town yesterday and got some groceries. We're fine."

"I have some news for you. I've decided I'm going to ask Ashley to move in with me."

"It's about time. She's a fine woman. Proposing would be even better."

"We'll get up to see you soon, both of us," he said before adding, "Love to you and dad," and clicking off the call.

"Morning, Pete," Victoria greeted him when he arrived. "Ben put all the receipts on the conference room table and Joe is agitating to get out of here."

"He can just sit tight. Did you look at them yet?"

"Of course. I couldn't sit around here doing nothing or snuggling for hours with my hubby, which is no doubt what you did with Ashley last night," she said with a grin.

"Guilty as charged," he said smiling.

Walking into the conference room and seeing the paper receipts on the table, Pete had the strongest sense that Carly was helping him find her killer. That receipt was the critical piece of evidence he required. He felt his confidence take an upturn thinking he'd have a suspect in custody by the time the sheriff returned. Everything, including his personal life, seemed to be going his way.

All eight of the paper receipts had been placed in a line on the table. Sitting down, he looked at them carefully, one by one. Two of them were for local restaurants, one was for the dry-cleaners, two were from the grocery store, one was from the gas station and one was a bank deposit slip. Pete looked at that one for a bit, noticing it was for a large amount of money credited to Carly's account. It could be the reason she didn't need Joe's child support, but getting information from banks about customer accounts was an uphill battle even for law enforcement. Looking at the last receipt, however, he felt a quickening of excitement. It was from the Turtle Creek Casino. Standing up, he opened the door to the hall and yelled for his dispatcher.

Hearing him, Victoria raised her eyes to the heavens. She had to break him of the habit of yelling for her. The glass ceiling was clearly still in place in law enforcement and it was time for it to be shattered. She rose and strolled slowly to the conference room.

"From the look on your face, I gather you spotted the receipt from Turtle Creek."

"I sure did. All we have to do now is find out who Carly was with on October 28th at the resort and we'll have the creep dead to rights. Can you call the casino hotel and find out who paid for that room?"

"Hold your horses just a minute, Boss. When Ashley and I were at lunch yesterday, we asked our waitress, Julie, if she knew the Sorenson family. Remember she was the person who called in on the tip line."

"I remember," Pete said. He had no idea why she would bring Mr. Sorenson up and no time to listen to women's gossip. He drummed his fingers impatiently.

"There was a birthday family dinner at Bridge Street pub for Leo the night of his 21st birthday, but knowing his son would want to go out with his friends afterwards, Mr. Sorenson rented a suite at the Turtle Creek resort."

Pete brightened up considerably. "Go on," he said.

"Anyway, Leo's dad paid for all six of them to stay in the hotel, so they wouldn't be drinking and driving. And he hired a waitress to serve drinks," Victoria could hardly contain her grin. "Julie just called me. The waitress was Carly."

A huge smile broke out on Pete's face. "Then the guy she's sleeping with has got to be one of those six boys. And given that the person who called in on the tip line saw Mr. Sorenson arguing with Carly two days before she died, it's most likely his son, Leo."

"Or maybe it's one of the others, Pete, because Leo's engaged. The wedding was supposed to be in June, but I've heard there's been trouble in Paradise lately. Julie said she'd seen Leo's fiancé in the pub and there were tears on her face."

"Regardless, I have to talk to Leo Sorenson. Can you find out where he goes to college?"

"I'll get on it. Meanwhile, you were going to talk to Joe again."

"Okay, I will, but interrupt us as soon as you have the information."

WHEN SGT. CRAIG BROUGHT JOE YELLOWWOOD into the interview room, he parked himself at the table, so frustrated he was practically steaming.

Pete pushed the letter with the ink drawing of the street sign across the table. "Yesterday you denied writing this letter which someone left stuck in my storm door. We know the person who delivered wasn't you, because you were here at the time. However, you could have asked someone to take it to my house. You practically scared my girlfriend to death, by the way."

Joe flushed, looking down at the table.

"I know the letter came from the tribe. It's not a crime to write a letter, but if Carly was drugged on the reservation, I have to know."

Joe took a deep breath and Pete waited. From the times he'd gotten someone to confess, mostly to trivial infractions, he knew the signs. Unless they were psychopaths, and Joe wasn't, people who were guilty could only hold out so long before they caved in. Before him was a man standing on the bank of a whitewater river. He'd reached the point of no return.

Joe took a deep breath and said, "None of my people would have drugged Carly. She was treasured on the reservation. Ever since we started dating as teenagers, she wanted to participate in all our ceremonies. And Chenoa was . . . beloved."

"That's what I thought, but it's a crime to withhold information from the police. I can make sure you are sent to prison for a very long time if you don't tell me everything you know."

Joe swallowed. His forehead was slick with sweat. "That letter was from some of the elders who want to find Carly's killer themselves and subject him to tribal justice."

"I don't even want to know what 'tribal justice' means in this case. Was Carly on the reservation the morning she died? Could she have been drugged there?"

"No. She hadn't been out to see my mother much since last fall."

"Okay. Now, we talked about you being at Carly's place on Monday morning. Were you there when my deputies showed up?"

Joe hesitated before saying, "Yes, I was inside the house when they banged on the door."

"Why didn't you answer?" Pete asked, frowning.

"I panicked, Sheriff. With my history and being on parole, I was afraid they'd think I broken into Carly's house to steal something. As soon as they left, I ran."

"And forgot to lock the door."

Joe nodded. "I realized that when I got to my truck, but I didn't dare go back."

"Is there anything else you haven't told me?" Pete asked. His eyes bored into Joe's although mentally he was already done with the man. He'd gotten what Joe knew and was already moving on. He had the strongest feeling it was Leo Sorenson that Carly was sleeping with and further that he was responsible for her death.

"That's all," Joe said.

"Okay, you can go. If you think of anything else pertinent though, anything at all, you have to call me. Understood?" Joe nodded.

As soon as Joe left, Pete walked rapidly to the front desk. His adrenaline was so high, he could hardly keep himself stationary. "Where does the Sorenson creep go to school?" he growled.

"Central Michigan University in Mount Pleasant. He's in a fraternity, Sigma Chi. The frat house is at 390 Main Street."

Pete grabbed his coat off its hook.

"Hang on a minute. It's almost a hundred and fifty miles to CMU and in this weather you would be on the road all day. Plus, if you're planning to arrest Leo Sorenson, you better call Sheriff Dodgson first. Sorry, but you really should."

"Dammit," Pete said, but pulled his phone from his pocket and called the number.

"Dodgson," the sheriff answered.

"Good morning, Sheriff. I've finally gotten a break-through. Looks like the perpetrator is one Leo Sorenson. He turned twenty-one in October and his father rented a suite of rooms at the Turtle Creek Casino for him and some friends. Carly Yellowwood was hired to serve the drinks. The date was October 28th, and I have the receipt for her room. I believe that Leo and Carly started having an affair that night. He's engaged and she was probably putting pressure on him to break the engagement. That's the motive for the crime."

There was a fairly long pause before the sheriff said, "That's it?"

Pete was taken aback. It was so clear to him that Leo was their guy. "We originally brought Leo's father, Walt Sorenson, in for questioning because one of the reports we received from the tip line was from a caller who saw him holding Carly by the arm in front of the Charlevoix Library the Saturday before she died. They were arguing. But Sorenson was in in a meeting about an addition to St. Mary's church on Monday morning. His attendance was confirmed by Father Jake. He's not our guy."

"Did you get Mr. Sorenson's DNA?"

"No, we didn't. His alibi was gold-plated," he said, feeling irritated with himself that he'd missed a chance to collect what could have been a vital piece of evidence.

"I see how you got to the Sorenson's son, but if you think Judge Hartley is going to give you a warrant to arrest the kid on circumstantial evidence alone, you're dead wrong. I know Angela, she's a stickler."

"I got a warrant to search Carly's place from her," Pete said in his defense.

"That was a bit different. Carly was dead, you were looking for evidence. This is about arresting the son of one of our prominent citizens. Have you gone to Turtle Creek and spoken to the staff?"

"No. I will do that today."

"It's driving me crazy to be stuck here where I can't help. I'm only trying to be sure we have covered all the bases. You've done some good work, Pete, and you're getting close. Your next step is to find out if they have CCTV in the halls at Turtle Creek. If so, and if you see Leo going into Carly's room, note the time. If you have evidence he was with her, you can bring him in and question him. Possibly he will give you his DNA, but you can't force the issue. His father is a wealthy local businessman, and my guess is that the boy, who will be represented by counsel, won't give you permission. And that's the only way, barring a confession, you will be able to get a judge to give you a warrant to arrest him."

"Yes, sir," Pete said, agreeing with the sheriff's assessment.

"One other thing, Monique and I went skiing yesterday. She took a fall, injured her ankle and tore some tendons. I'm going to be stuck here for a bit longer before she can travel. Call me every day," Sheriff Dodgson said and broke the connection.

"What did the sheriff say?" Victoria asked when Pete hung up the call.

"That everything I have is circumstantial. There were six young guys there that night. Any one of them could be the guy Carly was having an affair with. And even if all of them give us permission to get their DNA, it hardly narrows it down in a town full of tall white guys with Northern European ancestry and blue eyes."

"Including you, by the way," Victoria said with a grin.

"That's not even remotely funny," he told her.

TWENTY

Undersheriff Pete Manstead drove beneath the hundred-foot-long glass bridge that stretched high in the air across the driveway of the Turtle Creek Casino that afternoon. He had never been a gambler and hadn't visited the place. It was an impressive facility. Locating the parking lot, he left his patrol car in an area reserved for police. Entering the enormous and beautifully decorated lobby, he saw three reception desks. Choosing one at random, Pete asked the woman with shining dark hair and an ivory complexion if he could speak to the manager.

"We have multiple managers. Which one are you looking for?" she said.

"Someone with access to your CCTV," Pete said.

"Could I see your identification, please, Officer?"

"Yes, ma'am," he said and showed her his I.D.

She wrote his name on a piece of paper and said, "Have a seat anywhere in the lobby. I'll page you when I've located the head of security."

Fifteen minutes later, he heard, "Will Sheriff Manstead please report to lobby reception west?"

Walking in that direction, Pete saw a burly white guy with a shaved head standing with the erect posture of a soldier. Near him was a shorter man wearing the uniform of the tribal police. The tribal police officer was slender, with dark eyes and a wispy moustache.

"Jason Sturbridge, Head of Casino Security," the guy with the shaved head said, holding his hand out to shake Pete's.

"Thanks for meeting me. I'm Undersheriff Manstead from Charlevoix."

"Will Leonard," the second man said. "Traverse Band Tribal Police."

"Pleased to meet you," Pete said and they shook hands. "I'm investigating a crime and looking for some CCTV footage I think will help."

"Follow me, we're going upstairs to the Eye in the Sky," Jason Sturbridge said.

They traversed the lobby and walked to a private elevator that Jason opened with a key. The three men were the only people in the silver box that rose silently through the floors.

"Are you looking for a particular date, Sheriff?" Jason asked.

"Yes, October 28th last year. Mr. Walter Sorenson booked a suite of rooms that night for his son's 21st birthday party. He hired a woman named Carly Yellowwood to serve drinks. She was found dead this past Monday from a drug overdose, and I'm interested in who may have entered her hotel room after the party broke up." Pete added nothing more, trying to avoid giving out too much information. He was nervous that the tribal police officer would want to take over the investigation.

When the small party exited the elevator, Will Leonard stopped. "Hold on a minute, I have some questions."

"If you are thinking this is a tribal matter, Officer, I can assure you that the murder falls under my jurisdiction. Carly died in Eveline Township," Pete said.

"What caused her death?" Officer Leonard asked.

"Someone forced her to take a fatal drug overdose. My theory of the crime is that one of the boys with the Sorenson party had sex with Carly the night of October 28th and has been seeing her since. We believe that man is our killer."

"Could the assault have happened on reservation land?" the tribal police officer asked, looking at the Undersheriff with cool penetrating eyes.

Pete took a deep breath, stalling on answering the question. He was certain if he could only view the CCTV from October 28th, he would see Leo Sorenson entering Carly's hotel room. With that evidence, the judge would give him his warrant and he could interrogate him until he confessed.

"In answer to your question, I believe the assault happened closer to where she died. The coroner said she would only have lived a short time after she took the drugs," Pete said.

"Could she have made it from the reservation to where she died in that time?"

"Possibly," Pete admitted, feeling beleaguered. "Someone stuck a message to the door of my cabin yesterday telling me to relinquish this case. I interviewed Carly's ex-husband Joe Yellowwood about it. He confirmed the message came from the local Chippewa/Ottawa band. They want this matter left to them, but the woman died in my jurisdiction."

"But, you don't have any real evidence of that do you," Will Leonard said.

"No, but I don't believe Carly could have driven from the reservation to the site of the accident before she died. I'm operating under the assumption that the man who drugged Carly is the son of the man who booked the party last October. His name is Leo Sorenson. He's engaged to be married. I think he snapped when Carly wanted him to break his engagement."

"If it turns out that Ms. Yellowwood was killed on tribal land, you will be relinquishing the case to me," the tribal officer said, fixing him with an unwavering gaze.

Pete nodded. If he didn't have a suspect in custody by the time

Sheriff Dodgson returned, his boss would take over the case or turn it over to the state police anyway. This had to work.

They walked down a minimally lighted hall adjoining a huge glassed-in room filled with banks of computers. They were humming and little lights were blinking red and green.

SEVERAL HOURS LATER, PETE HAD HIS evidence. On the night in question, Leo Sorenson had entered Carly Yellowwood's hotel room at 1:39 a.m. He left two hours later. There was no doubt about the identification of the young man because in all the earlier footage from that night, Leo was wearing a ball cap from the Northern Michigan Dune Bears team and a red sweater. He was wearing that same sweater and cap when he entered Carly's room. The CCTV showed Carly was dressed in pajamas. She was smiling when she opened the door.

Driving back to town with the sun setting behind silhouetted trees that looked like they'd been drawn in black ink on a white canvas, Pete was conscious that everything from this point on had to be done just right, or the oldest son and scion of the wealthy Sorenson family wouldn't be convicted. There were still unanswered questions. While there was no doubt Leo Sorenson was with Carly at Turtle Creek Casino the night of his birthday, he could have an alibi for the morning she died.

Once he got back to town, he'd call Sheriff Dodgson, tell him about the evidence and ask for his advice on how this should be handled. He felt sorry about the sheriff's wife's sprained ankle, but her skiing injuries had given him another day or two to solve the crime. Brushing aside his doubts, he told himself he had Carly's killer in his sights and the CCTV would be enough to get a warrant for Leo's arrest.

Pulling into the grocery store parking lot, Pete decided he'd buy some white roses for Ashley. *Maybe a nice bottle of wine, too*, he thought. Envisioning the beautiful woman who was the love of his life, he smiled.

THEY WERE FINISHING DINNER, A PIZZA Ashley had picked up, and Pete was on his second beer when she asked, "Where are you now on Carly's case?"

"I've now removed Walter Sorenson as a suspect, but I didn't let him off lightly. I accused him of being Carly's lover and claimed she had threatened to tell his wife about the affair when they were spotted arguing outside the Library."

"What did he say in answer to your questions?"

"That he had been faithful to his wife since they married and had only been urging Carly to come back to church. Father Jake said he hadn't seen her at mass since last fall."

"Hmmm. That must have been when she started having the affair. If so, Fr. Jake would have been the last person she would talk to," Ashley said, shaking her head at men in general and Mr. Sorenson's bad timing.

"In addition, Walter Sorenson has an impeccable alibi. He was in a meeting at St. Mary's Church on Monday morning when Carly was drugged. Father Jake came into the office to confirm his attendance. But, I caught a break today," he said and his whole demeanor changed. "It was partly because of you and Victoria talking with Julie at the pub. Turns out that Carly was the waitress who was hired to serve drinks at Leo Sorenson's 21st birthday. I went to the Turtle Creek casino today and got the CCTV that shows Leo entering Carly's room after hours. They were together for a couple of hours. He's her lover and since he's engaged, she was probably pressuring him to break the engagement. That must have been the impetus for him to drug her. It's enough to get a warrant."

"That's just huge! You've got him before the sheriff got back," Ashley said.

Feeling the absolute correctness of his identification of Carly's killer, Pete leaned across the couch and kissed his girlfriend passionately. Having Ashley fall in love with him still seemed like a miracle.

TWENTY-ONE

Sunday

SUNLIGHT SLANTED THROUGH THE WOODEN VENETIAN blinds in the bedroom where Pete was lying next to Ashley. He opened his eyes and smiled, remembering their conversation from the night before. She'd told him about the job interview for the teaching position in East Jordan. While she hadn't gotten the job yet, she felt pretty confident it had gone well. He sat up and slid silently from the nest of colorful pieced quilts and padded barefoot out of the room. Closing the bedroom door, he walked into the kitchen, sat down at the table and called his boss.

"Sheriff Dodgson," the man answered.

"Good morning, Sheriff. How is your wife feeling?" Pete asked.

"Still in a lot of pain, but we hope to be back in town by Tuesday evening. What's happening?"

"I went to Turtle Creek yesterday and got the CCTV from October 28th. It shows Leo Sorenson entering and then leaving Carly's hotel room well after the party broke up. He was there for two hours and was the only person who entered her room. Leo is engaged to his long-time girlfriend, Tammy. She wasn't included in the casino party in October and was a bit pissed about it. The couple will be tying the knot this coming June. I assume at some point, Carly started putting pressure on Leo to break his engagement. He could see his whole future with Tammy going down the tubes and drugged Carly to keep her from talking. Do you think this is enough for me to get a warrant for an arrest?" Pete asked.

"Have you checked where Leo was when Carly was murdered?"

"Not yet," Pete admitted. "I just got the CCTV yesterday. It's Sunday and the Sorensons are church-goers. They'll be at St. Mary's for mass this morning. I thought it would be better to wait until tomorrow. You said I should be sensitive to their position in the community."

"Is Leo in college?"

"Yes, he goes to Central Michigan University. I know I'm going to have to get a warrant before I can go down there and pick him up. I didn't think the judge would be very amenable to a request for a warrant on a Sunday morning."

He heard a frustrated grunt before the sheriff said, "It's been a week since the woman died. Go over to St. Mary's Church this morning, wait until Mr. Sorenson comes out after the service and take him into the station. Leo could be home for the weekend. If he's at mass, you can nail both of them. I know how tough this investigation has been on you, Pete. I'm sorry that I'm not there to help, but if you don't have a suspect in custody by Tuesday night, I will have to take over the case."

Pete grimaced hearing the definitive click of the call being cut off. Once he told Ashley that he was going to have to leave, he knew she'd be crushed. He hated that he couldn't spend the day with her.

"I just talked to the Sheriff," he said walking back into the bedroom. Ashley's beautiful hair was tousled and her eyes were sleepy and warm. He sat down on the edge of the bed and had to force himself not to climb back in and lie down next to her.

"Did you tell him about the CCTV?" she asked.

"I did, but the sheriff says I should go to St. Mary's this morning and bring Mr. Sorenson into the station," he shook his head. "If I don't have Leo or his father in custody by Tuesday night, he's taking over." He felt the minutes clicking past faster than ever.

Ashley touched his hand and looked up at him sweetly, "Well, would that really be so bad, Pete? You have been killing yourself for a week. You have this figured out and the CCTV to prove it. I'm only here until this afternoon and then I've got to get on the road. I'd hoped you could spend the day with me. Can't you?"

Unable to speak, Pete just stood there looking at the woman he was failing. He thanked God that his steely-eyed mother wasn't there, because he knew exactly what she would say. He felt trapped between conflicting loyalties, caught on the horns of a dilemma. Then he saw the image of Carly's head bent over her steering wheel, little Chenoa in her car seat, and knew what he had to do. Standing up, he said, "I'm so sorry, Ashley, but this is my one chance to solve this case. I'm torn that I have to leave you."

"I may as well take off now then," Ashley said. She got out of bed and pulled her suitcase out of the closet. Caught between his mental promise to find Carly's killer, and the woman he wanted to spend his life with was tearing him apart.

"Please don't go, honey. This is only going to take a couple of hours."

She shook her head.

SITTING IN THE SQUAD CAR BEHIND St. Mary's in the mostly empty parking lot, Pete worried whether he'd made the right decision, but it was too late now. Checking the church website, he'd found they held two masses on Sunday morning. There was one at 8:00 a.m. and one at 10:00 a.m. He'd arrived just as the early mass was ending. Only a half dozen people came outside after the service, blinking at the bright blue sky, their breath making vapor trails in the frosty air. Neither Mr. Sorenson nor his son were among them.

Knowing he had some time before the people coming to the 10:00 a.m. mass arrived, he checked Ashley's location on his Find My Friends app. He hoped she'd changed her mind and was still at his cabin, but he could see her car on the road to Gaylord. When he dialed her phone, she didn't answer. He took a deep breath and shut his phone off knowing he couldn't be looking at his screen and miss seeing Walter Sorenson. It was critical to keep his eyes on the congregants who were pulling into the parking lot. He could only hope, once he'd succeeded in nailing Carly's killer, that Ashley would understand. They'd been a couple for four years and she was a warm and loving woman. Regardless of the weather, Pete decided he'd drive to Gaylord that evening so they could talk things over.

Watching each car that pulled into the parking lot, Pete didn't see either of the Sorenson's vehicles. When he heard the beautiful notes of the opening hymn float out to the parking lot, he felt his stomach clench. He'd chosen his job over his girlfriend's wishes to spend the day together and now he'd failed to nab the perpetrator. He put the car into gear and was backing out when he saw Walter Sorenson. He was almost running from his car toward the rear door of the sanctuary. Hitting the brakes and hearing them screech, Pete clicked off his ignition, opened the car door and called, "Walter Sorenson, we have to talk."

His target stopped and turned in his direction. Pete got out of his car and walking rapidly across the still-slippery parking lot, planted himself in front of the man.

"What is it, Officer? I'm late for church."

"We're going to the station," Pete said. He wasn't about to let this chance pass. The two men faced each other in silence as the wind rose. White eddies of snow swirled in the light wind around their booted feet.

"It this still about Carly Yellowwood?"

"I have evidence that your son, Leo, killed her," Pete said.

The blood drained from Sorenson's face. He looked like he was about to faint. Pete grabbed him by the arm and deposited him in the rear seat of the squad car.

TWENTY-TWO

THE STATION WASN'T OPEN TO THE public on Sundays, and Pete had to use his key to get in the building. Afraid his man might bolt, he kept a tight grip on Sorenson's upper arm as he took him through the door, led him down the hall and into the interrogation room. Seating Sorenson firmly at the table, he said, "I'm going to allow you one phone call and then I'm taking your phone for the time-being. Who do you want to call?"

Walter Sorenson took a deep breath and pulled his phone out of his coat pocket. Pete could see him trying to decide what number to pick as he scrolled through his contacts.

"I'm calling my lawyer," he said. The phone rang for a long time with no answer. "Can I try his house, please?" he asked, sounding timid. Pete nodded. The phone rang twice and he heard a male voice say, "Hello."

"Spence, it's Walt Sorenson. I'm at the sheriff's office in Charlevoix. He says he has evidence that Leo killed Carly Yellowwood. Can you come?"

"Leaving now," Pete heard the lawyer say and the call clicked off.

"I'm calling my sergeant to be an observer for our interview, and I would like my dispatcher here, too. It will take a while before everybody shows up. Give me your phone."

"My son did not kill Carly Yellowwood," Sorenson said, as he handed it to Pete.

"Was Leo in town the weekend of January 7th through the 9th?"

"Yes, but I'm telling you, my son didn't kill Carly."

"Then he has nothing to worry about," Pete said and left the room.

WALKING TO HIS OFFICE, HE CONSIDERED calling Sheriff Dodgson again, but thought better of it. The sheriff was far more experienced in investigating serious crimes, and talking with him made his own insecurities worse. He dialed Sergeant Craig's number instead.

"I know you're not on duty today, but can you come to the station? I've got Walter Sorenson here. His son killed the Yellowwood woman."

"On my way," Sgt. Craig said.

Pete then called his dispatcher. When Victoria's husband answered, he sounded exasperated, but said he'd get his wife.

"I'm really sorry to ask," he said when she came on the line, "But I have Mr. Walter Sorenson in the office and want to get his DNA. Can you come in?"

"I will have to bring my youngest son, but I'll be there in twenty minutes. Matt is taking our eldest ice-fishing, so he can't watch him."

The southern end of Lake Charlevoix was an ice-fisherman's paradise after the lake froze. Pete had seen fifty some fishing shanties when he drove past the previous night. There were even cars parked out on the ice, a hare-brained idea to his way of thinking. For just a moment, the night the snowmobile fell through the frozen surface into the water flashed into his consciousness.

When he forced himself to dive into the black opening, he dimly saw two bodies lying on the floor of the lake. He'd grabbed the smaller one and swam to the surface. Holding the little boy in his arms, he looked around, trying to gauge where the ice was thickest.

Then using all his strength, he pushed the child up onto the surface of the ice. Seeing people standing on the beach, he screamed for someone to help before he dove back down again. The fall-out from that day still stalked his nights and haunted his dreams. He realized that was why solving this case was so important to him. Whoever killed Carly had also put her child in jeopardy.

Taking a quick breath, he said. "No problem bringing him, Victoria, and thank you."

With his jail sergeant and dispatcher on their way, Pete walked out to the front desk. Standing by the window, he waited for Sorenson's attorney to arrive. Checking the location app on his phone, he saw that Ashley was about thirty miles from home.

VICTORIA PULLED IN TEN MINUTES LATER with her son, Max, in the car. Watching them walk across the parking lot, Pete felt a stab of pride. His dispatcher had stood by him throughout the investigation and had come up with several excellent ideas. He had grown to truly respect and count on her thinking. She was holding her little boy's hand and carrying a tote bag. He'd been so moved by Victoria's instantaneous willingness to help, he was afraid if he spoke, he might find himself in tears. He blinked rapidly.

"I'll take Max down to the breakroom," Victoria said when they came through the door. "I brought snacks and a puzzle. He'll be fine for an hour or so. I'll get the DNA kit."

Seeing Victoria walking down the hall with her son, the day he'd found another young mother's dead body hit his core. *Carly Yellowwood will never again have the privilege of holding her daughter's hand. My pledge to bring her killer to justice is all I can give her. I have to succeed. I've risked it all, including the love of the woman I want to be with forever for this.*

Sergeant Craig was the next to arrive. He was a big husky guy and a sound officer. "Thanks a lot for coming in. Sorenson's in interrogation. His son drugged the Yellowwood woman. All you have to do is observe."

"No problem, Boss," Todd said and Pete clapped him on the back.

Fifteen minutes later, Pete saw a black BMW pull in. When the driver opened the car door, he recognized him. It was Spencer Chastain, a well-known criminal attorney. Sorenson had brought in the best in the business.

Holding the door station open, he said, "I'm Undersheriff Manstead. Mr. Sorenson is in the interrogation room. I'll give you ten minutes alone with your client."

"Attorney Chastain," the lawyer said, but didn't extend a hand. "Which room is he in?"

"Second on the right," Pete said as Victoria came out of the staff room holding the sample kit.

PETE SAID HE'D GIVE THE ATTORNEY and his client ten minutes and kept checking his watch. When their time was up, he said, "Okay, Victoria, let's get his DNA now. As soon as you get the sample, call Dr. Winter and ask him how fast he can do the analysis. You'll have to take the swabs over to the hospital."

She nodded.

Pete opened the door to the interview room and flicked the switch on the video capture saying, "Interview commenced at 11:10. Undersheriff Pete Manstead, Sheriff's Dispatcher Victoria Treadwell, Sergeant Todd Craig, Attorney Spencer Chastain and suspect Walter Sorenson are present in the room."

The attorney frowned when he heard the word suspect.

"My dispatcher will be taking your DNA now, Mr. Sorenson," he said.

Walt Sorenson looked quickly at Chastain. They had a short, whispered conversation before the lawyer nodded.

"Open your mouth, please," Victoria said and expertly swabbed his gum line and upper palate.

"Thank you, sir," she said and left the room.

"Victoria Treadwell is leaving the room having obtained the suspect's DNA sample," Pete said for the tape.

"What evidence do you have on Mr. Sorenson's son?" Chastain's voice was challenging.

Pete summarized his theory of the case, concluding his presentation by saying, "Late yesterday, I obtained CCTV evidence from the Turtle Creek Casino that shows Leo Sorenson entering Carly Yellowwood's hotel room at 1:39 a.m. on October 28th. He left her room two hours later."

"There is no CCTV in the rooms, is there?" Chastain asked.

"No, sir. There is not. However, given that he had been drinking, and that Carly was wearing pajamas when she let him in, I'm certain they were having sex. Because Leo was engaged, Carly Yellowwood could use their sexual encounter to put pressure on him to break up with his fiancé. That's the motive for this crime."

"Are you prepared to show us the CCTV?"

Pete felt his hands get clammy and rubbed them on his pant legs. "No, I'm not going to share that information," he said. The truth was that he had no actual evidence that Leo Sorenson was the man Carly was sleeping with or that he gave her the drugs that killed her. Once again, he could hear the sheriff say, *it's all circumstantial.* He felt his self-assurance falter.

"What is my client accused of?" Chastain asked.

"Mr. Sorenson's suspected of failing to provide information about Carly's murder to protect his son, Leo, who is my prime suspect. He hasn't told me all he knows."

"What? No, you're wrong, Sheriff. Leo had nothing to do with Carly Yellowwood's death," Sorenson said.

"May I have another few minutes alone with my client?" Chastain asked and after a short uncomfortable silence, Pete reluctantly nodded. He and Sgt. Craig both left the room.

Victoria was waiting for them in the hall. "I'm on my way over to the hospital," she said. "Is that all you wanted from me today?"

"Yes, you can go home afterwards. Be sure to tell Dr. Winter I would like the results ASAP. I really appreciate you doing this."

Victoria nodded and headed down the hall. Her little boy darted after her.

RE-ENTERING THE INTERVIEW ROOM, PETE THOUGHT about Sorenson saying repeatedly that his son hadn't killed Carly. The man wouldn't insist that Leo wasn't the killer, unless he knew something he hadn't revealed. It was critical to get Sorenson to tell him what he had been holding back. He sat down at the table and said, "For the tape, Undersheriff Manstead has reentered the room interviewing Walter Sorenson. His attorney, Mr. Chastain, is present as is Sgt. Craig who is observing. Mr. Sorenson, if you've failed to tell me something that would lead to Carly Yellowwood's killer, I can arrest you for obstruction of justice. Now, why you are so certain your son didn't kill Carly Yellowwood?" he asked narrowing his eyes.

Walt Sorenson took a shaky breath. "Because on the Sunday night before Carly died, Leo told me that he'd ended his engagement with Tammy over a month ago. She refused to accept his decision and threatened to find out who he was seeing. She said that when she found out who it was, she'd kill her."

"She threatened to *kill* her?" Pete asked.

"Yes, but only in the way people use the term when they are especially upset. Leo asked for the engagement ring back, it was a family heirloom, but she refused. She told him when he came to his senses, he'd be on his knees, begging her to take him back. Tammy's father and I are good friends, and our families are close. When Leo told me his decision, I realized that we'd put pressure on him to marry her, assuming it was a foregone conclusion. They had been practically raised together, played in the same playpen from babyhood on, but I feel badly that we inadvertently forced the issue."

"Go on," Pete said.

"My son received an inheritance of $15,000 when his grandmother passed away last year and he wanted to give it to Carly.

He was twenty-one and, although I felt it was inappropriate, given how short a time they'd been involved, I couldn't prevent him from giving it to her. I'd invested the money in a short-term CD and said I had to speak with my friend Axel Fowler to get the money released. He's my investment broker."

"Did Leo see Carly on Monday morning?"

"I don't know, Sheriff. He was planning on returning to the University that morning, but he could have stopped by to see her. I do know Leo wouldn't have hurt Carly. My son is not a killer."

"Well, we will soon know whether Leo was with Carly on that Monday morning. Dr. Winter found a trace of saliva on Carly's upper lip. It was from a blue-eyed male. If it shows a familial match with your family's DNA, I'll have the evidence that she and Leo were together the morning she died. My theory is that Carly Yellowwood was blackmailing your son."

Walter Sorenson frowned, shaking his head.

"I already have the paperwork initiated to request a warrant for Leo's arrest, but I appreciate your candor and if you will bring your son into the station tomorrow morning, I'll hold off one day before I request the warrant."

"Thank you, Sheriff. I promise you he'll be here."

"Sergeant, you can process Mr. Sorenson and let him go. Give him back his cell phone."

Walking down the hall to his office and sitting down at his desk, Pete opened the application for a warrant on his computer and reviewed what he'd entered. He'd completed the information on the arrestee, Leo Sorenson, and the information on himself as arresting officer, when he stopped. He'd been thinking of taking the request to the judge as soon as he finished completing the form, despite it being a Sunday, but he'd told Mr. Sorenson he'd hold off. And when he got to the section requesting evidence, he knew it was inadequate.

Proving a case of murder required documentation that the killer had *means, motive and opportunity*. He had to know if Leo

Sorenson was with Carly Yellowwood the morning she died. If he confessed to seeing her, that would be his *opportunity*, but he had no evidence that Leo gave Carly the drugs that killed her. The drugs were the *means* of her death. Nor did he have any solid evidence of the *motive*. It wasn't enough. He saved the document, turned off his computer and left the building.

TWENTY-THREE

Pete arrived home in a dim gray twilight. He parked his car and walked in blowing snow to his front door. Once inside he took a shower, got dressed in a new shirt and trousers, a Christmas gift from his parents, and packed a small overnight bag. Ashley was still not answering his calls and he knew it was up to him to heal the rift between them.

It was about fifty miles from his house to hers. In the summer, he could make it in under an hour, but in the wildly drifting snow, he knew he'd be lucky to get there before eight o'clock. In most seasons of the year it was a pleasant drive, following winding country roads through hills and forests. Heading south on M-66, he crossed the Green River seeing a tiny ribbon of black water flowing between curved banks of white snow. A cluster of dark birds took flight as he drove over the culvert. They were cawing indignantly and he recalled hearing that a group of crows was called a murder.

How sadly appropriate, he thought.

Putting the car in low, he gunned the car up the enormous hill where the road cut through a gap in the pine forest before reaching a straight stretch leading out of Antrim Township. As he drove, he mentally rehearsed what he wanted to say to Ashley. Before they made any promises to each other, she had to understand that he'd already taken a vow at the closing ceremony of his police officer training. When he'd taken the Oath of Office, he'd pledged to protect and defend all the citizens under his protection.

"*Both the living and the dead,*" he thought, recalling the mental promise he'd made to Carly. If he failed in his duty as an officer of the law, what kind of partner would he make for Ashley? Would it even be right to ask her to move in with him if he failed? Snow started falling harder and Pete flicked on his windshield wipers, feeling a sense of despair. He knew there were cases that never got solved. This could be one of them.

He'd overheard two citizens talking in the front office the previous day. A confident male voice had said, "Sheriff Dodgson's a smart guy. He would have the killer in custody by now."

The other person responded in a cutting tone, "Manstead isn't the sharpest knife in the drawer."

Pete wanted to grab the speakers by their shoulders and say, "I've been working nearly twenty-four hours a day since we found Carly. I've hardly slept and when I do, I hear her voice pleading with me to find her murderer. The image of her little daughter crying for her mother haunts my every waking hour. I may not be as sharp as the sheriff, but I never ever give up.

"I had a little spotted dog as a kid. He ran away once and I searched for him for days, staying outside all night. My mother nearly lost her mind because I was only seven years-old. I finally found him shivering in a culvert with a broken leg. I'm still that same persistent bloodhound and I'm going to get Carly's killer if it takes me the rest of my life."

He shook his head, trying to silence the negative voices in his brain, telling himself he was getting close. When he'd questioned Mr. Sorenson, it was obvious the man was absolutely convinced that his son Leo wouldn't have drugged Carly. Thinking about it as he drove, a germ of an idea took root in Pete's mind. If Leo Sorenson stopped to see Carly the morning she died and they talked, she would have told him who she was going to see after he left. If he only knew who it was, he'd have his killer, the person who, in the words of Sheriff Dodgson, would *benefit* by Carly's death.

Approaching the outskirts of Gaylord, Pete turned his thoughts to Ashley. He hoped she would open the door to him and he would see her welcoming smile. The image made him feel better. He turned into her neighborhood and drove up her driveway. Leaving his overnight bag in the truck, in case their encounter didn't go well, he walked up to the porch and rang the doorbell. It was completely dark by then and the wind whipped past him, chasing little snowflake clusters sidewise into the night.

He heard her voice from inside call, "Hang on, I'm coming." Then she opened the front door. Standing there, looking at each other, both of them simultaneously said, "I'm sorry." Ashley opened the door wide and they fell into each other's arms.

Afterwards, Pete took off his coat and they walked hand-in-hand into the kitchen. He could smell something delicious simmering on the stove. Women had that unique talent to make their dwelling places into homes, he thought. His own place still looked like the hunting cabin it once was. Inside Ashley's warm comforting space, he felt himself start to relax, a gentle lassitude came over him and his breathing slowed. Touching his girlfriend on the arm, he said, "Sweetie, I have to tell you something."

"I want to say something, too."

"You first."

"I'm sorry I made you choose between spending time with me and your duty. You are a good man and I know how important it is to you to find Carly's killer. I just have to know that I'm equally important to you," her eyes were glistening with unshed tears.

"Ashley, you are the most important person in the world to me. I love you and . . . I've loved you for a long time. Most of my job is paperwork, you know, and serving as number two to Sheriff Dodgson. But the day I found Carly's body bent over the steering wheel in her car and saw her tiny daughter in the back seat, changed me in some profound way. I've always been a follower, a laid-back kind of a guy who was never the lead dog. This is my one chance to prove I'm more than just the number two man. I can't fail at this, Ashley, I just can't." He took a deep breath.

"You aren't going to," she said resolutely.

"I love you so much and once this is over, I promise to be there for you," he said. He could feel his own emotions rising and rubbed his eyes.

"I feel the same commitment to my job as you do to yours, you know. Teaching my students how to read is a crucial proficiency and I'm proud to be able to help them become competent readers. It's a skill that will make them successful in life."

"I know your job is important. Most of the time it's way more important than mine."

"I think both our jobs are important. Now, I have something else to tell you," Ashley's eyes were dancing. "I got the job teaching in East Jordan starting in September."

"That's terrific news. You are just amazing," Pete said. "Sweetheart, would you please consider moving in with me after the school year ends? I would do anything to have us together every day. I hope you feel the same."

"Of course, I'll move in with you, I was just waiting for you to ask. Took you long enough," she grinned. Can you stay over tonight?"

"Just in case, I packed an overnight bag," he said with a slightly shamefaced grin. "I didn't want to presume. I'll go out and get it. I love you so much."

"Lucky for you, Pete Manstead, it's mutual," she said smiling.

TWENTY-FOUR

Monday

By the time Pete got back to Charlevoix the next morning, after his wild skittering drive from Gaylord, it was almost ten o'clock.

"Sorry I'm late, Victoria," he told his dispatcher as he blew in.

"What took you so long? Leo Sorenson, his father and his attorney are waiting in interrogation. They've been here almost an hour already."

"Ashley is going to move in with me," Pete said and started to chuckle. Victoria shrieked and ran out from behind her desk to hug him.

"That's such wonderful news. When?"

"June," Pete couldn't wipe the smile off his face and Victoria embraced him again.

They were both grinning from ear to ear when Sergeant Craig came into the lobby. "What's going on?" he asked.

"Our very own Undersheriff's girlfriend, Miss Ashley Hamilton, is moving in with him," Victoria said.

"That's great, Boss, but we do have three frustrated gentlemen waiting to talk to you."

"Hang on a minute. What did you find out from the DNA test, Victoria?"

"We got him. The DNA report shows a familial relationship between Mr. Walter Sorenson and the saliva on Carly's lip. His son Leo's the man who kissed Carly on the morning she died."

"Excellent news," Pete said.

"I'M SORRY I WAS DELAYED THIS morning," he told the glowering Mr. Sorenson, his son, Leo, who looked utterly miserable, and their thousand-dollar-suit attorney, Spencer Chastain, when he walked into interrogation.

"Well, it's about damn time you showed up. I'm not used to being put on the back burner, Sheriff," Chastain said in a furious tone.

"I apologize, gentlemen. I was coming all the way from Gaylord this morning and the driving conditions were tough. Let's get started." Pete quickly flipped on the video capture equipment and said, "Leo Sorenson is being interviewed regarding the death of Carly Yellowwood. Present in the room are Leo's father, Mr. Walter Sorenson and their defense attorney, Mr. Spencer Chastain. Undersheriff Manstead is interrogating the suspect with Sergeant Craig observing. It is 10:15 a.m."

"Are you prepared to make an arrest today, Sheriff?" Chastain asked, drumming his fingers on the table.

"No, I am not. I just want to ask Leo some questions." He turned to the young man. "I know you are twenty-one, and therefore it's your choice as to whether you want your father and attorney present for the questioning. Do you?"

"Yes, sir," Leo said softly.

Leo Sorenson was a handsome kid. Tall with curly brown hair, he wore a navy sweater over a light blue collared shirt, a gray blazer and charcoal slacks. With those looks, strong family support and a top-notch attorney, he should have been confident, but he looked completely shattered to Pete. He suspected the young man had just learned about Carly's death.

"When was the last time you saw Carly Yellowwood?"

"It was a week ago today. I was headed back to CMU and stopped to see her before I left town." His voice was so quiet it was hard to hear the boy.

"What time was that?" Pete asked. The precise timeline was critical.

Leo quickly glanced at his father and then said, "It was early, about seven-thirty."

"How long were you there?"

"About half an hour. I left to return to Central Michigan's campus by eight."

"Do you have any proof of that, Leo?"

"I do, Sheriff," Walter Sorenson said. "My son texted me when he reached M-66. The time was ten minutes after eight and I can retrieve the text and link it to his vehicle's position on the Google maps, if necessary."

"What this tells me, Leo, is that you were the last person to see Carly alive. She was dead just two hours later." He hadn't asked a question and nobody responded. Pete looked intently at the three men. Mr. Sorenson looked exhausted. Being initially suspected of being Carly's killer and then having his son targeted as her murderer, had taken a heavy toll on the man. Attorney Chastain seemed irritated and slightly bored. Leo was breathing hard and looked on the verge of collapse.

"Please think carefully about your answer to my next question, Leo. Did you give Carly drugs that morning? Someone gave her a lethal dose of a prescription medication and that's what killed her."

Leo Sorenson looked totally shocked. For a moment, he was unable to speak. Then he swallowed and said, "No, sir. I would never have done such a thing. Carly was dead-set against drugs and I . . . had fallen deeply in love with her," his quiet voice trailed off.

"I know you two had been sleeping together since last October," the sheriff said. "I have the CCTV showing you going into her room late the night of your 21st birthday."

"You're wrong about us, Sheriff. We just spent the night talking and getting to know each other. I told her how much I liked her and that I found her incredibly attractive. She said she liked me too, but she wouldn't make love to me because I was engaged. I honored her wishes. Over the next month, we grew close. Spending time with Carly was what made me realize that I felt more like a brother to Tammy than a bridegroom. Our families are best friends and we had always been expected to marry. But, once I got to know Carly, I realized that I'd never really been in love with Tammy."

"Your father told me that you planned to give Carly the money your grandmother left you in her will. Did Carly blackmail you for the money? Did she use your sexual relationship to get you to break up with your fiancé?"

"Absolutely not. You didn't know her, Sheriff. Carly was an honorable woman. She was struggling to make it with what little she earned at her job plus her child support. I only wanted to help her." The boy's eyes filled with tears.

"If you're not prepared to make an arrest, Sheriff, I'm leaving with my clients," Chastain said. He started gathering up his keys and cell phone.

"Hold on just a moment. Just one more question. Leo, are you prepared to take a lie detector test to prove you have nothing to do with Carly's death?"

"You don't have to answer that." Spencer Chastain looked ready to explode, but Leo nodded, wiped away his tears and said he would be happy to take the test.

"It may not be necessary. One last question. Was Carly going to see someone else after you left?"

"Yes, she was. Her car was on its last legs and she needed a new one. She was looking at used cars and I wanted her to have the money I inherited as soon as possible. Since my dad had to get it out of a certificate of deposit, I asked her to go to the Fowler's house—he's my father's broker—and get the receipt showing that the cash had been transferred to her account."

They were almost there. He could feel it coming. After so many days and nights, he was finally going to learn who killed Carly Yellowwood.

"How far away from Carly's house does this broker guy live?" Pete asked.

"About a five miles," Mr. Sorenson said.

Despite Attorney Chastain's obvious frustration, Pete took a few minutes to think. If Carly left her house immediately after Leo departed, she would have arrived at the broker's house by 8:15. Picking up a receipt couldn't have taken long. She had probably left the Fowler's by 8:30, stopped back at her house to drop off the receipt for the deposit before heading out again. Axel Fowler was the last person to see Carly alive and almost certainly her killer. But, if he had killed her, he certainly didn't do it at the behest of either Leo or his father. *What did he possibly have to gain?*

"Can we go now, Sheriff?" Mr. Sorenson asked.

Pete wanted to ask more questions, but knew he was pushing the envelope. "Yes, but please make yourselves available if I have to speak to you again."

As he followed the three men down the hall, he suddenly remembered Carly's neighbors telling his deputies that two men had visited her house during the fall and winter. One of those men turned out to be her ex-husband, but the second man hadn't been identified.

"Leo," he called out as the men opened the door to exit the building, "What kind of a car do you drive?"

"A navy-blue Chevy Blazer," he said.

Pete felt a curl of satisfaction. Leo Sorenson had been the second man Carly's neighbors saw visiting her house in late fall and early winter. Leo had told him the truth. He and Carly were in a serious relationship. They had fallen in love.

TWENTY-FIVE

"So, do we have our killer?" Victoria asked when Pete walked up to the front desk after the Sorensons and their attorney left.

"I hate to tell you this, Victoria, after everything you've done, but it's not looking like Leo's our guy."

"What?" she said with a stunned look.

"Leo was in a romantic relationship with Carly. He kissed her good-bye when he left that Monday morning, but was on his way back to CMU a full two hours before she died. He texted his dad when he got to M-66. Mr. Sorenson has the text and can prove the location of the vehicle." While no alibi was completely watertight in Pete's mind, it was virtually impossible that Leo was their perpetrator.

"You don't look as depressed as I thought you would," Victoria said, giving him a considering look. Her dark eyes narrowed. She lifted her long red braid and placed it against the back of her neck.

"I'm getting really close. Carly was headed to Axel Fowler's house after Leo left. It's about five miles from her home. He's their financial broker and had transferred $15,000 from Leo Sorenson's CD to Carly's account. She was going over there to pick up the deposit slip. That's the receipt she wanted Joe to find, and it was among the receipts Ben found at her house. We know she got to their house, because Joe said she'd called him as she was leaving and asked him to come by her place after his AA meeting. She said she was going to the grocery store but thought she'd be back by the time he got there. That receipt that was proof she didn't have to collect any back child support from him. Fowler's our killer and I'm going to arrest him today."

"Shouldn't you wait until Sheriff Dodgson arrives?" Victoria asked.

Pete hesitated. Sheriff Dodgson was scheduled to arrive at the Traverse City airport the following evening and he knew should wait for his direction. But, for the first time in his life, he wasn't content to sit back and ask for permission.

"Not this time." He shook his head. "Can you get me a warrant to search the Fowler residence?"

Looking at Pete, Victoria saw the fierce determination in his eyes. If Carly had been drugged by Axel Fowler in his home, the warrant would likely uncover the medications, but if he failed, Victoria was afraid of what it would do to him. It was up to her to slow down this crazy freight train. "Let's think about this a minute. How sure are you that this Fowler guy is the killer?"

"He was the last person to see her before she died."

"Okay, so that's his opportunity," Victoria said.

"Right. And my guess is that when she went into his house, he probably offered her some coffee or tea that he'd laced with the digitalis Dr. Winter found on her toxicology screen."

"If so, you have the means," she said. "Can't you hang in there until Sheriff Dodgson arrives and the two of you can get him together?"

"I know the bastard killed her," Pete said, gritting his teeth. "Just once, I wanted to be the hero who nailed the bad guy."

"You don't have his motive though, do you," she said gently. "And without that, I doubt Judge Hartley will give you a warrant."

Victoria could see that Pete was in misery. She was reminded of a bullfight she and Matt had seen on their honeymoon in Spain. The bull had been backed into a corner, so weakened by a dozen or so spears that all he could do was shake his lowered head and bellow in rage as his knees buckled and his life came to an end.

"How about this, Pete. Let me do a background report on Axel Fowler. Maybe I can tie down the motive. Okay?"

Reluctantly, Pete nodded.

IT WAS VERY LATE THAT EVENING when Victoria finished her background on Axel Fowler. She'd been sitting at their kitchen table in front of her laptop for hours and had completely ignored her husband's multiple requests that she stop working and come to bed.

"You may as well move *your bed down to that darn office*, if this is going to be your work schedule," Matt groused from the bedroom.

She let it go.

"Come to bed, Victoria. Tomorrow's another day."

She didn't respond.

"Or, maybe you should marry your boss and *divorce me and our kids*."

She'd refused to respond to all his complaints until this last jab. This one was just too ridiculous.

"Pete just asked Ashley to move in with him, so unless he's a secret Mormon and believes in polygamy, he's taken," she called, rolling her eyes at her husband's silliness. "And I'm finally done. I'll join you in five minutes."

She sat back in her chair to look over what she'd pulled together. A check of Fowler's birth family revealed that his parents originally had two children—Axel was their first born. Eight years later, they had a daughter named Mary. Tragically, the girl died at the age of six. There was an article in the local paper that described the event. It was July and Axel had taken his little sister to a nearby lake for a swim. Although Mary was a novice swimmer, she had tried to make it across a narrow stretch of the lake to the opposite shore. Axel had been talking with some friends and hadn't noticed her disappearance. Although he searched for her for hours, the local fire and rescue squad had eventually been called. They located her body. She had drowned.

Axel must have been consumed with guilt, Victoria thought.

Despite having regularly attended the local primary and middle schools, she found no evidence that Axel ever went to high school. He showed up again as an eighteen-year-old college student having taken a high school equivalency examination. Such a long gap in his life pointed to a breakdown, major depression and possibly even a stay in a mental hospital.

Checking more recent records, she learned Fowler was fifty-four years old, married with one child and working as a stockbroker. Checking the database for the brokerage he'd listed as his employer, she hit the jackpot. Axel Fowler was no longer employed there. In fact, there was no indication he had worked anywhere since he was terminated from the brokerage six months earlier. With his big home on Lake Charlevoix, a stay-at-home wife and a daughter in college, he would be hard-pressed to meet his financial commitments.

Finding his "in case of emergency" contacts, she saw that Fowler had listed both his wife and his doctor. A quick check showed that the doctor was a psychiatrist. Medical records were inviolable, so she couldn't check her hypothesis that Fowler had serious mental health issues, but the picture was emerging of a desperate man, unstable, unemployed and probably still riddled with guilt for his failure to save his little sister.

Axel's wife's name was Winifred and their daughter's name was Tammy. It was the name Tammy that made everything click into place for Victoria, because Tammy Fowler had been engaged to Leo Sorenson. She stood up, walked into the kitchen and poured herself a glass of white wine. Picking up her phone, she looked quickly through the back issues of the Charlevoix Courier until she saw it—the announcement of the engagement between Leo Sorenson and Tammy Lee Fowler.

Her boss had been right. Axel Fowler was the perpetrator who killed Carly Yellowwood. Laid bare in front of her, blue as the evening shadows of winter trees on snow, Victoria had found the motive. This crime had never been about male sexual jealousy. It was about love, albeit a twisted kind of love, because Axel Fowler drugged Carly Yellowwood when she came to their house to get the receipt for the deposit. He'd done so for his daughter, Tammy, who must have been in despair about the broken engagement.

While there were still unanswered questions, in the police business it was well understood that *love, lucre,* or *loathing* were the motives for murder. As a teenager, Fowler had failed to save his little sister from drowning. The resulting guilt he undoubtedly felt meant he would be willing to do anything rather than fail his daughter. She wanted to call and give Pete the message then, but it was almost one o'clock in the morning and Matt was sulking. Leaving the information on the office phone line would be good enough. Her boss would check it first thing in the morning.

"You were already on the five-yard line," Victoria said at the close of her message. "With this, you can carry the ball right into the end zone. Go get our killer tomorrow, Pete. And don't forget my raise!"

TWENTY-SIX

Tuesday

Pete Manstead woke with a heart-pounding jolt and sat straight up in bed. It was still dark in the room and he could hear the wind howling outside. He'd been dreaming of a hand wearing a black glove reaching down to twist open the cap on a small blue thermos. He'd fallen asleep obsessing about how the drugs could have gotten into Carly's system. Clearly, his mind had been working while he slept, because he woke up knowing how it was done. The drugs had been added to the insulated thermos he'd seen in Carly's sink at her cottage. Poured into her coffee, the bitter taste of digitalis would be masked and the poor woman wouldn't have suspected a thing.

In his mind, he recalled walking through Carly's small cabin the day she died and seeing the thermos in the sink. Had he touched it? He groaned, remembering that he had turned the lid, feeling it screwed on tight. If Carly hadn't rinsed the thermos out, it was possible that Dr. Winter would be able to detect a trace of the drugs, but any fingerprints would have been smudged by his own. *He'd been a damned fool!*

Setting his feet down on the cold wooden floor of his bedroom, he decided it was critical to go back to Carly's place. Throwing on his clothes, he remembered that the date on the warrant giving him permission to search her house had expired and there was no time to get another one. The killer could be trying to get into Carly's house at any moment to remove the thermos. In fact, he realized with a sinking sensation, the killer could have gotten the thermos days ago. It was unlikely though, he told himself, because they had locked Carly's place up tight after the initial search. Because he was trying to get what was, in effect, the murder weapon, he'd manage to get inside her place somehow—even if he had to break in.

Snow was falling heavily when Pete walked outside, grabbed the ice scraper from behind the driver's seat and removed the snow from his windshield and rear window. Then he jumped into his truck, started it up and headed down his long driveway through the row of white pine trees and out to M-66.

To his surprise, when he got to Phelps road, he saw it had been plowed. The county didn't include it in their snow removal schedule which meant someone had hired Inman's to clear the gravel road. It was already filling in with snow again, but the recent plowing made it passable enough that he could drive all the way to Carly's place. As he got closer, he was surprised to see lights on in the house. Was he too late? Had the killer already come to remove the evidence? His heart pounding, he parked the car, walked up to the porch and banged on the door. To his surprise, the long narrow face of Joe Yellowwood appeared in the doorway.

"What do you want?" he asked, testily when he opened the door.

"Can I come in, Joe? I think I've solved Carly's murder, I just want something from the kitchen."

"Come in, then," he said, sounding frustrated.

Pete stepped inside and walked into the kitchen. The sink was empty. *Damn*, he thought. Looking around, he wondered how long Joe had been staying at Carly's house. He was dressed in pajamas and a bathrobe. There were dishes on the table and coffee was perking in the pot. The man's winter coat was hanging on a hook and his boots were on sitting on the book rack. There was no snow on the coat or boots. "This house doesn't belong to you, Joe, why are you living here?" Pete asked.

Joe flushed and said, "I know it's not mine legally. The house belongs to Carly's parents. They bought it for us when we got engaged. I called them and they don't mind me using the place. My mother and I have applied for custody of Chenoa. If we succeed, I think my daughter would be happier living here, with all her little toys and things." He sounded wistful.

Pete frowned. In effect Joe was an illegal trespasser, but he had more important things to do than to evict a squatter. Plus, he suddenly realized, Joe being in residence might actually have helped him. If the killer had come back to get the thermos, he might not have been able to get in. "When did you move in?" he asked.

"The day you told me Carly died," he said.

"When I searched the house, there was a small insulated blue thermos in the kitchen sink. Where did you put it?"

"Carly always kept it in the upper cupboard to the left of the sink. That's where I put it."

Pete stepped forward, swung open the cupboard door and saw the thermos. He was so excited, he almost grabbed it before he stopped himself. Quickly pulling on a pair of plastic gloves and retrieving an evidence envelope from his pocket, he put the thermos into the bag.

"Why do you want this, sheriff?" Joe asked.

"It was the way Carly was drugged," he said. "I hope to hell you didn't wash it. Did you?"

"No. It was the last thing Carly touched. I couldn't wash her fingerprints away," Joe said sounding miserable.

Pete could have kissed him.

"I'm taking this with me. It's possible the drugs can still be detected in the thermos and there might be fingerprints. This is confidential information, Joe, but if I'm right, I can prove who killed Carly, because this little thermos is the murder weapon." He reached out his arms and to the man's surprise, pounded him on the back vigorously.

Once back inside his vehicle, he called Dr. Winter.

"Winter," the man answered sleepily.

"I could use your help this morning, doctor. I think I've found the way Carly was killed. It was by adding drugs to her coffee thermos. I got it from her place this morning."

"Bring it to the hospital now. I just got up and am still at home, but I'll meet you there. I just hope to hell there is a residue of the drugs inside." Pete could hear the pathologist's excitement in his voice.

"There could be fingerprints, too," Pete said. "But, I'm afraid I touched it when I searched her place last week."

"Don't worry about that now," Dr. Winter said. "We'll do whatever it takes to get the bastard who drugged that little woman." The exultation in his voice made Pete smile.

VICTORIA DECIDED TO GO IN LATE to the office. Matt was clearly feeling slighted and she intended to do something about it. Letting him sleep in, she slid quietly out of bed and left the bedroom. She woke the boys, made them bacon, cream cheese and bagels for breakfast, packed their lunches and watched from their living room window as they boarded the yellow school bus. With a cup of coffee for her husband in one hand and a plate of scrambled eggs in her other, Victoria set about making her husband feel appreciated. To her delight, Matt was very pleased. It had been some time since they had spent time together, just the two of them. They talked about the early days of their courtship, becoming boyfriend and girlfriend and then getting married.

SHE DIDN'T PULL INTO THE SHERIFF'S office parking area until mid-morning. Looking for the cars in the lot, she saw both their patrol cars were missing. The office was unoccupied but her boss had left a note at her station.

"Thank you," it read, the word was followed by three exclamation points interspersed with dollar signs. "I figured out how Fowler drugged Carly. I'm on my way to get an arrest warrant from the judge."

Fifteen minutes later, Victoria saw Pete pull in. He was alone in the vehicle. She frowned. If he'd gotten his warrant and made an arrest, Mr. Fowler should have been in the back seat of the patrol car. She wondered if Charlie was bringing him in, but when their deputy pulled in moments later, he was alone in his car as well. Both men slogged across the lot toward the office, looking dejected. Had the judge declined an arrest warrant?

Not likely, she thought. Judge Angela Hartley would have pulled out all the stops to nail a murderer. She was a stickler in most cases, but in a capital crime like this, she would lean in the direction of keeping a killer off the streets.

"What happened?" she asked as the two walked in.

"Fowler's not home. Mrs. Fowler tried to convince us that her husband was out of town visiting clients, but thanks to your background, we know he lost his job six months ago," Pete's mouth tightened.

Victoria felt a surge of sympathy for him. He'd worked the case so hard and now, even with the killer identified, he'd struck out.

"Fowler's wife said she'd taken him to the Traverse City airport, but I don't believe her. I think he's staying somewhere local," Charlie said.

"I think he's in the wind," Pete said gloomily. Being "in the wind" was cop-speak for a suspect who had gone missing.

"What now?" Victoria asked.

"Stake-out. Starting tonight," he said and running his hands through his hair plodded down the hall to his office.

Once her boss was out of earshot, Victoria turned to Charlie. "I'm starting to worry about Pete. I thought me finding the connection between Axel Fowler and the Sorensons was going to raise his spirits. Do you think he's going to be all right? He wouldn't do something stupid like . . . hurt himself, would he?"

"Beats the heck out of me," Charlie said, shrugging his shoulders and headed to the breakroom.

There were times Victoria could have strangled him.

TWENTY-SEVEN

Sitting glumly at his desk, Pete dialed Sheriff Dodgson's phone. "What's your travel situation at the moment, sir?" he asked.

"We have doctor's appointments for my wife's busted ankle this morning. Those should be done by noon and if everything connects, we should arrive in Traverse City on the last flight tonight. What's happening there?"

"I left you a message earlier that Leo Sorenson's not our perp. The DNA test we did on his father shows a genetic relationship between the Sorenson family and the saliva on Carly's upper lip, but the test was unnecessary because Leo told his father he and Carly were in a relationship."

"Hmmm. Is this just your gut feeling that Leo's not our guy, Pete? Or do you have actual evidence?"

"Both. According to Dr. Winter, the drugs in Carly's system would have killed her within an hour or so of her swallowing them. I double-checked the timeline and she would have taken the drugs between 8:30 and 9:00. She was dead by 10:00 a.m. Leo stopped to see Carly and kissed her good-bye that morning, but he'd left her house by eight o'clock. He texted his father when he got to M-66 and

Mr. Sorenson confirmed the car's location on google maps. Plus, Leo was in love with the woman. He wouldn't have drugged her."

"If you're right, Carly met with someone else after her boyfriend left that morning."

"She did. Leo planned to give Carly a legacy he'd received from his grandmother. Her car was barely drivable and she couldn't afford a new one with what she made at the restaurant. Leo couldn't touch the money he inherited from grandma until he turned twenty-one, so his father had invested it in a short-term CD. They called the family broker, whose name is Axel Fowler, and asked him to move the money into Carly's account. Leo suggested that she go by the broker's house to pick up the deposit slip, and she did."

"Great work, Pete. Since the broker was the last person to see her, he's our perp. What are your next steps?"

"The timeline goes like this—after Leo kisses her good-bye, Carly departs for Fowler's place, which is only five miles away. While she's there, Fowler adds the drug-laced coffee to her thermos. I retrieved the thermos from her house this morning and took it to Dr. Winter. He just called me to say that the residue in the thermos tested positive for digitalis."

"You got the murder weapon. Well done! What was Fowler's motive?"

"I struggled with that, but last night Victoria discovered the link. Axel Fowler is emotionally unstable, lost his job a few months ago and is the father of Leo's former fiancée, Tammy. My theory is that Fowler drugged Carly because his daughter was heartbroken when Leo broke off their engagement. Tammy must have convinced her dad that Leo would come back, if only her rival was out of the picture."

"Bravo," Sheriff Dodgson said with a note of satisfaction. Pete could practically see him smiling. Such solid support from the boss felt very good.

"Victoria has asked for a raise and she really deserves it, Boss. She's worked almost as many hours as I have on this case."

"It's okay with me. What have you done so far to nail the bastard?"

"I got the judge to sign off on a warrant to search Fowler's place and arrest him. But, when we got to the house, he wasn't there. His wife said he was out of town. She said she'd taken her husband to the airport over a week ago. It was ostensibly a business trip to meet with some clients in Lansing. That's an obvious lie because Victoria found out he lost his job months ago. We searched the house for the drugs and found an empty prescription bottle for Digitalis in the kitchen trash. Mrs. Fowler picks up the prescriptions for her mother who has congestive heart failure, so the meds were available for her husband to access. In case he was hiding at the house, we walked through every room in the place, including the attic, the basement and the garage. They have no outbuildings."

"You've done fine work on this, Pete. All you have to do now is track Fowler down."

Pete walked out of his office to the coffee room feeling a sense of relief. It had been great to get a pat on the back from the sheriff. For the first time since Carly died, they had been on the same wavelength.

FINDING VICTORIA IN THE BREAKROOM, PETE asked if she would chase down the flight Fowler could have taken when he left Charlevoix. He personally thought the man was hiding out somewhere in town, but flights were worth checking.

"You don't want much, do you?" Victoria said, giving him a look. "I was up until past midnight last night nailing down the background on Fowler and I don't think I heard the word 'please' or 'thank you' come out of your mouth today."

"Please." Pete said. "Please, please, please."

"Oh, all right," Victoria said with an exasperated look. "Mrs. Fowler said her husband left a week ago, right? That's suspicious right there, him leaving the day after the crime."

"He's our guy, all right. So, the three of us, Charlie, Ben and I are each taking an eight-hour shift keeping watch on the Fowler house. The man's been gone over a week and if he's somewhere around here, he must be about ready to sneak back home. Mrs. Fowler said she'd taken him to the airport and if she really did, I'm hoping you can find out where he went."

"Was the Fowler's daughter at home when you were there?"

"No, and I checked with her mother. Apparently she's gone back to college. Why do you ask?"

"Not sure, really, just something niggling the back of my mind. I'll tell you when I think of it."

"Okay," Pete said. "I'm sorry if I haven't seemed very appreciative of your ideas on the case, Victoria. I couldn't have gotten this far without your help."

"It's called women's intuition, I believe," she said with a grin.

Assuming Axel Fowler had flown out of Traverse City, Victoria began by checking departing flights from that airport. It was a long slog through dozens of suspicious and difficult officials before she learned there was no record of Axel Fowler taking any flights that day. She'd have to go further afield. Dreading checking the multiple flights from the Grand Rapids airport, she walked to the breakroom. Although it was in total violation of her self-imposed ban on candy, she put coins into the candy machine and pulled out a Snickers bar. Assiduously crumpling up the candy wrapper, so as not to see the calorie count, she munched on yummy peanuts, nougat, caramel and chocolate.

Thinking about how long she could delay calling the Gerald Ford International Airport in Grand Rapids, Victoria had a brainwave. There was a small private airport in Charlevoix that only flew between the town and Beaver Island. In case that's where Fowler went, she decided to see where he could be staying on the Island as most of the B & B's and hotels were closed in the winter. She had no luck calling the few open inns on the island, but after spending half an hour searching property ownership records, she shrieked "yes" and high-fived the air. The family had a summer place on the island.

"Pete," she yelled and to her satisfaction, the man himself can running down the hall. "The Fowlers have a home on Beaver Island. I'm just about to call the private airport to see if he flew to the island after Carly died. It's probably where he's been hiding out."

"Great idea, go ahead and . . . No, wait. Hang on a minute," he said, looking out the window. "I think that's Axel Fowler pulling into the parking lot right now." He yelled for Charlie who came down the hall from the cells where he'd been chatting with Sgt. Craig.

Watching Axel Fowler walk across the parking lot toward the office, the two men congratulated each other, saying they'd gotten their killer in custody before the sheriff got back. Victoria looked fondly at both of them, even though she knew she deserved at least part of the recognition. *Male chauvinists. You gotta love 'em,* she thought.

Appropriate credit aside, she was thrilled to be part of a team that was going to get justice for Carly Yellowwood. With Fowler in custody, she could switch the calls to the on-call service and would be able to make the appointment she and Matt had made with the psychologist for that afternoon.

TWENTY-EIGHT

Matt and Victoria pulled into adjacent parking places on Lake Shore Drive for their meeting with Dr. Brian Lightfoot Tones. His practice specialized in relationship counseling and settling disputes involving the native population. The appointment had been Matt's idea, after Victoria told him how discouraging the attorney Nancy Barnes had been about the likelihood of their adopting Chenoa.

The office had a splendid view of Lake Charlevoix, now completely blanketed in deep snow drifts. The snow had stopped falling, the sun had come out and the view across the lake was dazzling. They hung up their coats and took seats in a small waiting area. The room had been painted a stark white and decorated with brightly-colored red and yellow tribal artwork. A young male receptionist with straight black hair greeted them and said Dr. Tones would be with them shortly. "Help yourself to coffee or tea on the sideboard," he said.

In just minutes Dr. Tones came into the waiting room. He was a large man who looked to be around sixty, had a well-defined jaw line and dark shiny eyes. His white hair was worn long and he was dressed in an open-collared shirt and blue jeans. He greeted them by their first names and ushered them into the inner office.

"Have a seat," he said gesturing to the round table by the window. It was the only furniture in his office. Noting the look of surprise on Victoria's face, he said, "Sitting at a desk puts an unnecessary distance between a counselor and his clients. I don't use one for that reason. Now, how can I help you?"

"We are hoping to adopt a child named Chenoa Kai Yellowwood," Matt said. "She's First Nations. We are aware of the ICWA law but I am one-quarter Chippewa and have the blood quantum required to qualify as an adoptive parent."

"I know about this child. Her mother died recently, I understand," Dr. Tones said. "A tragic situation."

"I was the person who stopped to help them after the collision. The EMT and I took Chenoa to the hospital that day," Victoria said.

"Since there is a question about guardianship, when she was discharged from the hospital, Chenoa was placed in foster care. She'll be there until the custody hearing," Matt added.

"Our local reservation is not large enough to have ICWA-credentialed social workers, so it was probably the county social workers who stepped in. Where did they place her?"

"With her former baby-sitter, Mrs. Applebee. They are Caucasian, and I asked the social workers if they shouldn't have placed her with a native family. We offered to help, but they said they use only registered foster parents," Victoria said with a rueful look.

"It was a good decision to place her with the Applebees. Since it was only going to be a short placement, I imagine the tribe concurred, thinking the child would adjust more readily to familiar people and surroundings. There are ICWA-licensed social workers in Traverse City, of course, but if they took responsibility for Carly's daughter, it would have involved moving the child further away and would have been harder for her. What family members does Chenoa have here?"

"Her father and grandmother. The Yellowwood family lives on the Chippewa/Ottawa reservation in Charlevoix," Matt said.

"Is there some reason they would be denied custody?"

"Joe Yellowwood was arrested, tried and convicted of an assault a couple of years back. He's served his time and now lives with his mother on the Reservation," Victoria told him.

"I see," Dr. Tones said. "Have you consulted an attorney about this? In an adversarial matter, lawyers are usually best at representing your interests."

"I talked with Nancy Barnes, but she was very discouraging." Regret crossed her face and she looked away, breaking eye contact with the compassionate gaze of the psychologist.

"May I ask why you made an appointment with me?"

"We are trying to decide the right thing to do," Matt said. "We don't want this to be confrontational and hoped you could assist us. As a first step, we met with Chenoa's grandmother."

"What are her plans?"

"Mrs. Yellowwood and Chenoa's father plan to request custody," he said.

"Before I could advise you, I'd like to hear each of your reasons for pursuing this matter. Why do you want to adopt Chenoa, Matt?"

"We have two sons and my wife wants a daughter. Although she loves our boys dearly, I know there is an empty place in Victoria's heart. I stayed with Chenoa in the hospital when Victoria was working and although I was initially opposed, after spending time with her, I found myself warming to the idea. She's an endearing little person."

"Victoria what are your reasons, beyond those Matt mentioned?"

"A little background will probably be helpful to you, Dr. Tones. In case I didn't mention it when we made the appointment, I'm the dispatcher for the sheriff's office. I was on my way to work last Monday morning when I witnessed the accident when the car ran off the road. Walking back to the car and looking into the back seat, I saw Chenoa for the first time. Her eyes were open, but then they snapped shut. It was as if she was afraid of seeing something, or maybe someone. What I'm about to tell you now is confidential information."

"Of course," he nodded.

"Carly Yellowwood was intentionally drugged which led to her death. My boss, Pete Manstead, the Undersheriff, is investigating the crime. The moment I saw Chenoa shut her eyes so tightly, it occurred to me that she might have witnessed what happened. The poor baby went through such a terrible thing, being present when her mother died, that I felt . . .;" she hesitated, "a profound responsibility for her. It was as if God was urging me to be there for this child."

"I understand," the psychologist was quiet for a moment and then said, "My job, as I have come to see it, is to help my clients get clarity about the issues that they struggle with. If I feel I can help, by talking through their problems with them, I will. If I can't, I often refer people to attorneys or physicians. It seems to me that your problem, whether to pursue the custody of Chenoa, is inherently a matter between the two of you. I sense your ambivalence, Matt and your passion, Victoria. Once you two make a final decision, I am happy to talk further with you."

"Thank you," Matt said.

"I have a strong relationship with the tribe. It's not just the family, you know, but the tribe itself that is party to these custody cases. I know the tribal elders and am happy to speak for you with them. I'll make myself available any time you want to meet prior to the custody hearing."

"I believe the court will be meeting on Friday to determine her custody," Victoria said.

"Then the two of you have to make a final decision soon." Mr. Leonard stood up and took a small carved turquoise bear from the top of his bookshelf. "This is a Zuni fetish. The Zuni believe that animal spirits are contained in these small talismans and that they can help people with difficult choices. They have historically used stones in the shape of animals as totems. They have done so for more than 5,000 years. In more modern times, the Zuni carved stone fetishes for religious ceremonies and as artwork. If you wish to petition a fetish for its help, you hold it in your hand, close your eyes and concentrate on the difficult decision you have before you. Sometimes clarity emerges, either as a flash of insight or a gradual clearing that reveals the path you should take."

Victoria smiled as she took the small bear in her hand. "What's the meaning of this tiny red line on the bear's body? It has an arrow point at the end."

"That's called the heart line. Supposedly when the Father of the Sun sent his children down to help mankind by eradicating the large animals who were killing people, he asked that the spirit of the animal be kept alive. The heart line is the representation of the still-living soul of the animal. Please return the fetish to me once you have made your decision. I find it helpful both in my practice and to my clients."

"Of course," she said, feeling the bear's cool smoothness as she slipped it into her pocket.

"Good luck," Dr. Leonard said and shook hands with both of them.

The walked out to their respective cars in silence, but before they parted, Matt gave his wife a hug. "I love you, sweetheart. Can you come home now?"

"I can't get away yet. Axel Fowler came into the office just as I was leaving for our meeting. I want to find out what Pete learned from his interrogation. You know how important this is to me."

"We can talk tonight then," Matt said.

TWENTY-NINE

Asking Sgt. Craig to bring Mr. Fowler into interrogation, Pete flipped on the video capture equipment and took his place across the table from where his sergeant would seat their killer. Charlie took his place standing in the far corner of the room. Neither of them had ever obtained a confession of murder or even been involved in such an investigation before. The atmosphere in the room was intensely charged but totally silent. Both the officers were deadly serious.

In just minutes, Sgt. Craig entered the room with Axel Fowler. It was the first time Pete had seen the man up close and he was surprised. Fowler was not at all what he'd expected. Tall, somewhat stooped and balding, he seemed completely ordinary, like a local citizen you would greet in the grocery store or say hello to at the post office. *Was it possible this seemingly commonplace man had committed premeditated murder?*

"You are Mr. Axel Fowler, correct?" Pete said after Sgt. Craig seated him at the table and left the room.

Fowler nodded, his handcuffed hands in their silver bracelets resting on the table.

"You must identify yourself aloud for the tape," Pete told him.

"My name is Axel Carlisle Fowler," he said.

"I understand you told my sergeant that you came into the office because you have something to confess. Is that correct?"

"Yes. I came to be taken into custody for a crime," he said.

"Mr. Fowler, before you say anything further, I must advise you of your right to remain silent. You have the right to refuse to answer questions or provide information to law enforcement or other officials. You have the right to an attorney, and if you cannot afford one, we will provide you with one. Do you understand these rights?" Pete asked him.

"I do."

"Do you wish to have us call an attorney for you?"

"No, I am here to confess to killing Carly Yellowwood."

Pete was taken aback. This seemed way too easy. He had to get more details or he feared the confession wouldn't hold up in court. "Tell me the circumstances, starting with the date."

"It was Monday morning, a week ago yesterday. Carly came to my house to get a deposit slip for money I had transferred to her account."

"What time was this?"

"She arrived at my house around 8:15. When she rang the doorbell, I opened the door and invited her in. I said I wanted to talk to her about my daughter, Tammy. She said she couldn't stay long because she'd left her child in the car. I asked her to come into the kitchen."

"What was the nature of your conversation?" He was taking this slowly, step by step.

"I told her I knew she'd seduced Leo Sorenson and had coerced him into breaking his engagement with Tammy. She said that wasn't true, they had fallen in love and wanted to be together. You see, Sheriff, when Leo ended the engagement, it broke my daughter's heart. She's my whole life and it killed me to see her in so much pain. All I wanted was for Carly to realize what she'd done and agree to break off her relationship with Leo. I offered her money if she would."

"How much did you offer her?"

"Twenty-five thousand dollars."

Pete frowned. According to Victoria's background work, the man had lost his job six months earlier. It seemed pretty unlikely Fowler had that amount of cash on hand. "I take it Carly didn't accept your offer of money."

"She categorically refused. According to her, Leo had always regarded Tammy as a little sister. He'd come to realize that he wasn't physically attracted to her and had never been in love. The Sorenson family had pressured him into proposing, but once Leo fell in love with Carly, he'd decided he couldn't ethically proceed with the marriage."

"What happened then?" Something felt off about the whole conversation. The man's words sounded pat, like he'd rehearsed what he was going to say many times in his head.

"When Carly refused to take the money, I killed her."

"You are telling me that you killed Carly Yellowwood in your kitchen while your wife and daughter were upstairs sleeping? Weren't you afraid they'd come down? Witness the killing?"

"No, because my wife takes sleeping pills. I knew she wouldn't get out of bed for hours and Tammy never shows her face before noon. Anyway all I did was give Carly a beverage."

"Go on."

"I gave her some coffee I'd prepared it in advance, in case she wouldn't agree to give Leo up. I'd dissolved a half a bottle of Ambien in the mug. I didn't want her to feel any pain and thought it would make her fall asleep and she wouldn't ever wake up."

Pete glanced quickly at Charlie standing in the corner. No Ambien had been present in Carly's toxicology report. The man was lying.

"Did you say you gave the coffee to her in a mug?"

"Yes, and she downed it immediately. Then she said she had to go, reminded me her little girl was in the car, and left."

"So, you're saying that you loved your daughter so much, you were willing to kill a young mother just to make her happy? What about Carly's daughter, the little tyke waiting out in the car, didn't you think of her?" Pete asked. He gritted his teeth, feeling a spear thrust of near-uncontrollable rage growing in his heart. Fowler colored and looked down, but didn't respond. "Where is the mug now?"

"I put it in the dishwasher and turned it on," he said.

Unlikely it had any trace of drugs then, Pete thought. "How did you know you had killed Carly if she walked out to her car? She was obviously alive at that point."

"I didn't find out until several days later. My wife told me Carly died, after watching the ten o'clock news the night you did your appeal to the community for information. She knew nothing about what I did, sheriff. My wife's not involved in this."

"Why not turn yourself in the next day? The community appeal was five days ago."

Mr. Fowler paused and took a deep breath. "It took me a while to realize that I had a duty to confess. I'm asserting my right to silence now. I'm not saying another thing."

"That's your right, Fowler, but you have done nothing but *lie* to us since you got here. Carly Yellowwood didn't die from an overdose of sleeping pills. You didn't kill her." Pete looked at the man in disgust.

"Then can I go now, sheriff?" Fowler asked in a hopeful tone.

Pete wondered briefly if the man was smart enough to have fed him a tissue of lies that held a germ of truth but decided it was unlikely. Fowler was probably covering for someone else, likely his wife or daughter. "You have wasted a lot of valuable police time and I should arrest you for obstruction of justice, but I'm going to let you go after we get your DNA. Don't ever do such an irresponsible thing again. Take him out of here now, please, Charlie."

As he was leaving the room, Pete noticed an odd expression cross Axel Fowler's face. He struggled to think of the exact word to describe it. Then he got it. The man looked like a kid who had gotten away with breaking a window.

THIRTY

Arriving back at the station, Victoria walked down the hall to check the jail cells. They were empty. Frowning, she headed to Pete's office.

"What happened when you questioned Fowler? Why isn't he in custody?"

"The numbskull gave us a false confession so I sent him home," Pete shook his head in barely concealed loathing. "But, I got his DNA before he left."

"Why on earth would he do such a thing?"

"There are three reasons people make false confessions. Either they are looking for media attention, they are frankly delusional, or they are protecting someone else who committed the crime. I think Axel Fowler is covering for someone and he's going to lead us to the real killer. I've asked Ben to tail him. Charlie is flying over to Beaver Island in case he shows there. It's worth checking since you found out he has a house on the island."

"I kept thinking about the dynamics in that family and called Tammy's college roommate. She never returned to the University after Christmas break."

"So Axel's daughter is around here somewhere. She's got to be the person he's protecting. I want to say how much I appreciate everything you've done, Victoria. Can you start working on finding her?"

"Of course," she said. "Remember that dark hair I found in Carly's care?"

Pete nodded.

"Since you got Fowler's DNA, do you want me to ask the lab to do a comparison?"

"Good thought," he said.

ASSUMING THE BEST WAY TO FIND Tammy Fowler was to go to their house, Victoria switched the call line to her cell phone and left the building.

It was a short drive south along the winding road that ran beside the frozen lake to the Fowler's residence. Arriving at the address, she pulled into the driveway of an imposing house set in a large lot directly across the street from Lake Charlevoix. The home was located across from Portside Park where they held an art fair in the summer. She wondered how the Fowlers afforded such a luxurious place when he had lost his job.

Turning off her car, Victoria envisioned the morning Carly had arrived at this house where she was given a fatal dose of drugs. Remembering little Chenoa waiting in her car seat for her mom to return, she felt a wave of intense sorrow for the child and all she had gone through. Had she seen the person who drugged her mother? Was that the reason she closed her eyes so tightly when Victoria opened the car door?

Forcing herself to stop thinking of Chenoa before she started to cry, Victoria got out of the car. Walking up on the porch, she rang the doorbell. It was snowing and the temperature had fallen into the teens. The wind chill made it feel like it was below zero. Through the window in the front door, she could see a woman walking toward her. Then the door opened.

"Hello, Mrs. Fowler? I'm Victoria, the dispatcher from the sheriff's office."

"Yes?"

"The sheriff wants to talk to Tammy. Is she at home?"

"No, she's not." The woman's blue eyes were intense. The woman was thin with dark hair pulled back so tightly, it looked like it hurt. She raised her hand to her mouth and Victoria noticed her fingernails. They were bitten to the quick.

"We just want her help with an inquiry. Is she here?"

"No, she's at college," the woman said and started to close the door.

"I'm sorry, Mrs. Fowler, but I already checked with Tammy's college roommate. She never went back to school after Christmas break."

"You must not have talked to the right person," she said. There was something odd about her delivery, Victoria thought.

"I spoke to a girl by the name of Elaine Stevenson who said she was your daughter's roommate. That's Tammy's car in the driveway, isn't it. Are you certain she isn't home?"

"I think I would know if my daughter was at home or not. Tammy is twenty-one and comes and goes as she likes. She's not accountable to me."

Winifred Fowler was trying hard to sound confident, but Victoria sensed there was something the woman was holding back.

"Tell me where she is, Mrs. Fowler," Victoria demanded. "If you can't produce her, the sheriff is going to bring *you* into the station to be questioned." She held the woman's gaze until Mrs. Fowler dropped her eyes, biting her lip.

"Possibly she's staying with her friend in town. It's been such an awful time for poor Tammy, what with that despicable Leo Sorenson ending their engagement."

Victoria controlled her rising anger with difficulty, gritting her teeth. Whatever Tammy had gone through was infinitesimal compared with Carly, who had lost her life because of this horrible family, and poor baby Chenoa had also suffered terribly. "What's the friend's name and phone number?"

"It's Violet Kochanski. If you come inside, I'll check my phone for her number."

When hell freezes over, she thought. "No, thank you. I'll just wait here while you get it."

There was no way she was going into that house where Carly was drugged. Mrs. Fowler went inside and when she returned, she handed Victoria a piece of paper.

"I want Tammy's phone number too, and as soon as you hear from your daughter, please have her call the sheriff's office." After Mrs. Fowler scribbled Tammy's phone number on the slip of paper, Victoria turned on her heel and left.

Looking back at the house through the windshield of her car as the wipers swished back and forth sending snowflakes flying, she was surprised to see Mrs. Fowler still standing on the porch in that brutal cold. Her eyes caught the light from the sun across the water. They glittered.

If Tammy Fowler was mixed up in this crime, her mother would want to protect her, she thought as she backed out on to the road. Turning north, she reached the field where patrons of the art fair parked on the grass in the summer. She pulled off the road, hoping she wouldn't get stuck in the snowbank, and waited.

Ten minutes later, Winifred Fowler pulled out of her driveway and turned south. Luckily, a truck drove by just as the woman left, blocking her view. Keeping her distance, Victoria pulled out on to M-66.

It was the first time she had ever followed a suspect and she didn't want the woman to know she was being tailed. Taking advantage of the situation, she made no attempt to pass the vehicle that was positioned between their cars. Mrs. Fowler made it through the light at East Jordan, but Victoria got stopped when the light changed. When the truck swung off into the grocery store parking lot, she put on up a bit of speed, afraid she'd lost the woman.

A bit past the town, a van entered M-66 ahead of her from one of the side roads. It was a high-profile vehicle she couldn't see past, but reaching the top of the steep hill that cut through the pine forest at the edge of Antrim Township, she spotted Mrs. Fowler again. She'd stopped at the light by the McDonalds. When the light changed, the woman pulled her mirror down to look behind her before turning right, continuing through the small town and heading south on M 131.

Afraid she'd been spotted, Victoria kept going straight. As soon as she could, she made a U-turn and circled back, following M 131 south. In fifteen minutes, she gave up, realizing she'd lost Mrs. Fowler. When her phone rang, she gave it a quick glance. It was the office number. Pulling off to the side, she'd pushed the button to answer the call just as Tammy's mother drove right past her. The look on her face was one of total shock.

"Hi, Pete," Victoria said morosely.

"Where the heck are you?"

"I am trying to track Tammy down, Boss, which is what you *asked* me to do," she said. "I went to their address to see if she was there. Mrs. Fowler said Tammy wasn't home, although her car was in the driveway. I must have spooked the woman because she left right after my visit. I followed her to Mancelona which could be where her daughter is hiding out. I think she was going to warn Tammy that you wanted to talk with her. Anyway, Mrs. Fowler just drove past, saw me and looked flustered. She's probably heading back to Charlevoix."

There was a short silence and Victoria could hear Pete hesitate before he said, "When I asked you to find Tammy, I meant using your computer and contacts. What I did *not* authorize you to do was to chase a suspect all over the County on slippery roads in a snow storm. What the hell were you thinking, Victoria? You aren't an officer of the law and this is a murder investigation. My God, woman, you could be the killer's next victim," he paused taking a deep breath. "I'll go over to the Fowler's house now and bring Tammy into the post before her mother gets back. She's got to be at home since you saw her car. You are to come back here ASAP," he added in an exasperated voice and clicked off the call.

Ending the call, Victoria sat quietly for a while. She was deep in thought.

The boss is already mad at me, but since I've come this far . . . she thought and restarted her car. Driving slowly down the street past the small homes, she checked the names on each mailbox. No Fowlers. Why had Mrs. Fowler gone all the way to Mancelona? Was Tammy hiding out somewhere in this little town? Is this where Mr. Fowler was staying for the week after Carly died? As soon as she got back to the office, she decided she'd check Winifred Fowler's maiden name. Maybe her parents lived somewhere south of Mancelona.

VICTORIA DROVE INTO THE PARKING LOT at the sheriff's office as Pete drove past her in a patrol car. He waved but didn't stop. Once inside, she encountered Sgt. Craig. "Where was the boss headed?" she asked.

"To pick up the sheriff and his wife. They are landing in Traverse City in an hour."

"I thought he was going to bring Tammy Fowler into the station," she said.

"Already did. She's here. We're keeping her overnight. Pete and the sheriff are going to interrogate her together tomorrow morning."

"How did she come across to you?" Victoria asked. She was curious about this girl who seemed to be the impetus for the entire tragic debacle.

"Seemed perfectly at ease. Walked inside the post as if she was bullet-proof. Everything Pete said to her when he read her rights just slid off her like rain on a duck's back."

"Should I get her DNA?"

"The boss already did. The sample's on your desk. He asked that you take it to the lab."

"No problem. Mind if I talk to her?"

"Sorry, Victoria, but the Boss said not to let you within twenty feet of her cell."

"I'm headed home then. I'll drop off Tammy's DNA sample at the lab on my way. See you tomorrow. Could be we finally have our killer in custody."

THIRTY-ONE

Wednesday

It was 10:00 a.m. and Victoria, Deputy Ben Wilcox and Sgt. Craig were hanging out in the main lobby of the station. They were trying to look like they were working, but in truth they were just waiting for Sheriff Mike Dodgson, Undersheriff Pete Manstead, and attorney Spencer Chastain to emerge from the interview room after conducting Tammy Fowler's interrogation. The officers were discussing a recent hockey match and laughing.

Before she left for work, Victoria had called Friske's Farm Market looking for donuts to bring to the office. Their bakery pies and donuts were delicious, made from scratch with ingredients from their orchards, but the store was closed. Although not in the same league, she had stopped by Family Fare and picked up a dozen donuts to welcome the sheriff back. She was rearranging the parkas and jackets on their hooks inside the front door when she heard the conference room door open. Quickly shushing the men, she returned to her desk.

"Good morning, Sheriff and welcome back," she said with a warm smile when Sheriff Mike Dodgson came down the hall into the lobby. Pete was with him. Attorney Chastain and Tammy hadn't emerged.

"Morning, Victoria," he said. "Staff meeting in fifteen minutes everyone."

"Okay if I join you?" she asked and the sheriff nodded.

When Mr. Chastain and Tammy Fowler entered the lobby, Victoria cast Pete a quick questioning look, asking non-verbally whether they had gotten a confession. He shook his head.

Hands were shaken, coats donned, and reminders given about the possible need to talk to Tammy again before the attorney and his client left the building. Victoria scurried from her station to the breakroom where she picked up the pot of coffee, the box of donuts and took them into the conference room. On the white board on the conference room wall someone had placed Tammy's picture dead in the center. Her parents' photos were to her right and left. All their previous suspects' pictures had been removed. The direction in which the investigation was now focused was clear. She pulled out her phone and took a quick snapshot of Tammy's face. She'd had an idea and needed a photo of the woman to confirm her suspicions.

Normally staff meetings were a time for banter and teasing, but all of them took their usual seats in complete silence. Sheriff Dodgson sat at the head of the table, Pete was at his right hand and Sgt. Craig was on his left. Ben and Victoria took positions on either side of the rectangular table. Charlie wasn't with them. He'd returned to Beaver Island.

"Good morning, all. This has been my second-in-command's investigation from the outset, so I'd like to have him brief you on where we are at the moment. I want to say that I've been impressed with the work done by all of you on this case and particularly you, Pete. It's very easy in murder cases to have tunnel vision and stay focused on the initial prime suspect. You didn't fall into that trap and it's paid off. It's been a hard slog and nobody took their eye off the ball. I originally planned to take over the investigation when I got back, but am leaving it in the capable hands of my undersheriff. My wife's medical condition requires further tests and possibly surgery, so I'll be in and out of the office over the next few days. Go ahead, Pete," Sheriff Dodgson said.

Their undersheriff cleared his throat and said, "It's been nine days since Carly Yellowwood ran off the road, struck a tree and died. She'd been given a fatal dose of Digitalis that caused a loss of consciousness and her eventual demise. Since then, we have questioned, interrogated and dismissed five prime suspects: Joe Yellowwood, Pat O'Connor, (Carly's boss at the White Swan), David Webster, (the city attorney for East Jordan), Walter and Leo Sorenson. All of them have been cleared, either based on impeccable alibis or DNA evidence. We are now focused on Axel Fowler and his family. We got to him because he was the last person to see Carly Yellowwood before she died. We were about to fly to Beaver Island, where we thought he was hiding out, when Fowler himself came in to the post and confessed to killing Carly."

"For any of you who don't know, it was a false confession. He lied," Sheriff Dodgson said. "Go on, Pete."

"Mr. Fowler told me that he'd dosed Carly's coffee with Ambien, a sleeping pill, but we know from her toxicology report that she died from an overdose of Digitalis. We also know that the drugs were added to her blue thermos, whereas Fowler said he'd given her the drugs in a coffee mug. Fowler's daughter, Tammy, was engaged to Leo Sorenson. Leo broke off the engagement when he fell in love with Carly Yellowwood, leaving Tammy furious and wanting revenge. We assume she was the instigator for the crime since Axel Fowler told me he'd killed Carly to ease Tammy's despair. He denied any involvement in the crime on the part of either Tammy or her mother, although we are suspicious of both of them. Would you like to bring the staff up to date on what we learned this morning, Sheriff?"

"Yes. Pete and I just spent a solid hour with Miss Tammy Fowler. That girl is one cool customer. Between her and her attorney, most of our questions were met with her saying 'no comment.' Obviously, Chastain has advised her to say nothing. In my opinion, the girl is a sociopath and incapable of empathy. To her, people are simply tools to be used if they will do her bidding, or dismissed if they won't. The one question she answered was where she was on the morning Carly died. She said she was in Mancelona at the home of her grandparents, Mr. and Mrs. Gerry Henderson. Pete ducked out of the interrogation for a few moments and called her grandmother on the phone. She concurred that Tammy was there on Monday morning when Carly was drugged but we have to tie down the exact time. Whether it's true or not, as Tammy's grandmother, she's likely to stick to her story."

"I followed Mrs. Fowler to Mancelona yesterday, Sheriff," Victoria said. "Now that we know her parents live there, I assume she was going to warn them that Pete wanted to speak to Tammy. By the way, she lied to me when she said her daughter wasn't at home."

"It's a crime to lie to the police, but we have bigger fish to fry here," Sheriff Dodgson said.

"I'm going to press down hard on both Mr. and Mrs. Henderson, Tammy's grandparents, when I speak with them. If they admit Tammy wasn't with them the morning Carly died, we plan to place her under arrest today," Pete said.

"Both Pete and I assume that Tammy's jealousy and thirst for revenge was the impetus for this crime, but whether she was the one who added the drugs to Carly's thermos is as yet unproven. We have to have evidence of that to arrest her."

"Unfortunately, the only fingerprints on Carly's thermos, which was in effect, the murder weapon, were hers." Looking embarrassed, Pete added, "Except for one smudged fingerprint on the cap that was mine." He was still feeling pretty irresponsible about touching the thermos.

"Any further ideas? Victoria? Ben? Todd?"

"I wondered whether the Fowlers had an outdoor camera system for security," Victoria said. "When Carly went to the Fowler's house the morning she died, she left her car running and presumably unlocked. Nobody around here locks their cars in snowstorms. It takes too long to unlock a vehicle in freezing conditions. It occurred to me that either Mrs. Fowler or Tammy could have gone outside to her car and added the drugs to Carly's coffee thermos. I'm assuming Carly left it in her vehicle when she went in the house to talk to Mr. Fowler."

"Excellent thought, Victoria," the sheriff said.

Imagining Tammy opening the door to Carly's car in that snowstorm, removing the cap from the blue thermos and dropping in the pills one by one, Victoria thought she would have noticed Chenoa in the back seat. *Had she said something to her? Told her to not to look? Was that the reason the little one closed her eyes tightly? Was there any way of finding out what Chenoa knew without traumatizing her?*

"Anyone else?" Sheriff Dodgson asked the team.

"Are we concerned that Tammy Fowler could be a flight risk? If so, I'd be willing to keep an eye on their house over the next couple of days," Ben offered.

"Thank you, good idea," Pete said.

"What about you, Todd?" the sheriff asked.

"Before I locked that little gal into her cell last night, we confiscated her phone. Pete and I figured there might be some evidence on it, if the crime was planned in advance, but she'd wiped the device. I expected her to kick up a fuss at losing her phone and all she did was look down her nose at me."

"Tammy Fowler is like a prisoner of war. Name, rank and serial number is all we'll get out of her. She is never going to confess. Our only hope is to find actual evidence that she poisoned Carly's thermos, or that her father or mother will point the finger at her, if we threaten to arrest them," Sheriff Dodgson said. "Sorry to leave you guys, but my wife has an appointment with the surgeon today. I'll be back when I can."

"Okay, here are the assignments, people," Pete said. "Victoria, please check whether there is outdoor security at the Fowlers' place. I'll do the same when I talk to the grandparents. If Tammy left her parent's house for the grandparent's place on Monday morning, it will show the time she left on their security video. Ben, I agree with you that a stake-out is in order. Please start watching the family today."

Victoria handed out coffee and donuts to the men as they left the room.

THIRTY-TWO

Pete drove to Mancelona directly after the staff meeting. He'd gotten the address for Winifred Fowler's parents place from Victoria. It was located on Starvation Lake off Carmichael drive. Despite its dismal name, Starvation Lake was a beautiful body of water, good for fishing, water skiing and swimming in the summer. From the hill on which the house had been built, Pete could see the whole cove. The frozen lake was topped in snow and outlined in forest green pine trees enveloped in ice. The icicles shone brilliantly in the sunshine. On the beach were sections of an expensive floating dock which had been removed from the water for the winter.

Mrs. Fowler's parents' house was a cedar-clad place, large enough for multiple bedrooms and baths. He checked the eaves, spotting three cameras and felt a warm sense of satisfaction. If Tammy came to see her grandparents after drugging Carly's thermos, they would have the evidence of the time she arrived on that camera. He might even have the proof today, he thought hopefully, although he knew unless Mr. and Mrs. Henderson were willing to show him the video feed, getting it would require a subpoena.

He wondered what Winifred's father did for a living to afford this grand place. Then it dawned on him. The money in the Fowler family wasn't Axel's. It must have come from Winifred. When Axel Fowler offered to pay Carly Yellowwood a quarter of a million dollars to give Leo Sorenson up, it hadn't been an idle boast. He walked up to the front door, knocked and waited until the door cracked open. Pete was expecting an older woman, but it was Winifred Fowler who stood in the doorway.

"Good morning, Mrs. Fowler," he said, recovering from his surprise. "Are your parents at home? I want to speak with them."

"My father is at a doctor's appointment. My mother is here but she's not well. What do you want to know?" Her tone was hostile.

Police officers were always advised to say that they just had some questions, but Pete had had enough of being lied to. He edged past her into the house. "Please get your mother for me."

When she left, he looked around at the open great room with its floating staircase ascending to the second floor. The place was as impressive inside as out. He spotted the control panel for the monitoring system to the right of the front door and was just about to open the panel when both women returned.

"This is my mother, Henrietta," Mrs. Fowler said.

"Good morning, I'm Undersheriff Pete Manstead. We spoke on the phone this morning. I'm sorry you're not feeling well." The woman was white-haired and obviously not in good health. Her breathing was labored, and she was walking very slowly using a cane.

"I've got congestive heart failure. I already told you that Tammy was here last Monday morning," she said. "When my husband and I came down to breakfast, she was making pancakes."

"Do you remember what time that was?"

"Around 9:30."

"I am here to view your security camera footage for the morning of January 9th to confirm what you are saying. Most of these systems have a calendar for the month, and you can just push the day you want and it will give you the playback. Do you mind if I check the date in question?"

"I am not comfortable with that, Sheriff," Winifred said crisply. "My father is the only one who knows how to work the system. He will be back later today. I suggest you call and make your request when he's available. I would like you to leave our home now."

Seemingly bested, Pete turned toward the front door. Then he stopped, turned around and pointing to the back yard said, "That looks like a bald eagle perched in your oak tree." Both women walked toward the window and in that instant, Pete flipped open the panel to the security system and snapped a photo with his cell phone. The picture would show the brand and model number.

"There was no eagle there," Winifred said, looking back at him suspiciously.

"Sorry, I guess I was wrong. It's just an oddly formed branch with a tuft of snow on it," he said. "Thank you for your time this morning, ladies."

Walking back out to his car with his breath forming a white mist in the frosty air and blinking at the bright sun, Pete smiled to himself. He was pretty sure you could see what was on those security systems remotely and that Victoria could figure out how to do it.

It was mid-morning when Victoria left the station to check whether the Fowlers had an outdoor security system. She hoped she could see the cameras without speaking to any of them, but unfortunately, when she pulled in, three cars were parked in the driveway. The whole family was at home. Getting out of her car, she looked up at the roofline. There were spotlights on each of the corners of the house, but nothing that looked like cameras although it was hard to tell. Walking up onto the porch, she rang the doorbell. Mr. Fowler came to the door.

"Yes?" he asked.

"The sheriff sent me to ask if you have a home security system."

"We do. It sounds an alarm whenever someone opens one of the exterior doors. It keeps ringing until we enter the code. If we don't punch in the number in five minutes, it calls the security company who sends someone out."

"Which company do you use?"

"Acme Security. Is that all?" he asked.

"Do you also have cameras on the outside of the house?" she asked.

"No," Fowler said and closed the door in Victoria's face.

Discouraged, she returned to her car. Starting to back out of the driveway, she looked up at the second floor. One of the women, either Tammy or her mother, was standing by a curtained window. Whoever it was pulled a cord and the drapes snapped shut.

Impossible to tell which one of them was watching, she thought, realizing Tammy and her mother had the same height and build. If Mr. Fowler had lied and Tammy or her mother came out to Carly's car to drug her thermos, it would still be tricky to identify which of them it was, especially dressed in winter apparel.

ALTHOUGH MATT WOULD HAVE TOLD HER not to, Victoria decided to drop by Mrs. Applebee's house. It had been a week since she'd seen Chenoa and she was missing her. She hoped to set eyes on the tyke and find out how she was doing. Accelerating slightly on M-66, her car fish-tailed. She slowed down to forty mph. When she reached the intersection at County Road 48, she turned left into the small snow-bound village of East Jordan. Driving across the bridge where the Jordan River ran through the marsh, she saw an open patch of cerulean blue water. Two stately swans were bending their long, elegant necks deep into the water, prodding the lakebed for something to eat. Passing the White Swan restaurant, where Carly had worked, Victoria felt a piercing wave of sorrow for the young woman whose life had been stolen from her. *Carly should have had another half century to live and see little Chenoa grow up.*

Rose Applebee lived a block past the town. Hers was a two-story house clad in baby-blue aluminum siding. The front yard was enclosed in a black wrought-iron fence. Only the tops of the black shiny posts showed above the snow. A mostly-buried sign in the front yard read, "Rose's Child Care." Victoria pulled into the driveway. Looking through the front window of the house she could see a woman in the living room. She was bending down to say something to a little boy. Opening the car door, she walked up the shoveled sidewalk and rang the doorbell.

"I'm coming," she heard a woman's voice say and the heavy wooden door cracked open. "Hello, you must be Rose. I'm Victoria Treadwell. In case you aren't aware, my husband and I are hoping to adopt Chenoa." The pleasantly smiling woman looked to be in her early forties and wore a T-shirt with an apple tree print under a pair of bib overalls.

"I don't know if I should let you in," Rose said, looking uncertain

"That's okay, I just wanted to set eyes on her. Could you call her into the living room?"

"I know you were the person who rescued her in the storm," Rose said and called, "Chenoa, come here, darling."

Victoria could hardly breathe seeing the toddler in bright blue dungarees and a yellow shirt run into the room to stand by Rose's feet. In a voice skating on the edge of tears she said, "Hi, darling. Do you remember me? I'm Victoria. I was with you in the hospital."

Chenoa gave her a wide smile, looking up at her with dark shining eyes. Then she dashed back down the hall, calling out something to another child that Victoria didn't catch.

"Do you know when the custody hearing will be?" Rose asked.

"Friday morning. How is she doing?"

"Remarkably well, really. She keeps asking about her teddy bear. It wasn't with her things when the social workers brought her to us."

"I got her a little pink teddy bear when she was in the hospital. I'll make sure you get it. What does she tell you about what happened?"

"She asks for her mother from time to time, mostly at bedtime, and when I tell her that Mommy is up in heaven smiling down on her, she gets quiet. I think she's amazingly resilient, given what she's been through."

"In case you aren't aware, I work at the sheriff's office and we're investigating Carly's death. I have a picture of a woman on my phone that I could send you if you are okay giving me your number. It's important to the case."

"No problem," Rose said and gave her the number.

"Thank you. Could ask Chenoa if she saw this woman open the door to Carly's car the morning of the crash? If you think she seems upset or frightened, please don't push it." Chenoa couldn't testify, of course, but it might help them decide which one of the Fowler women they should concentrate on.

"Well, I guess that would be okay," Rose said. Just then a gust of wind blew into the home disturbing some magazines on the coffee table.

"Sorry, Mrs. Treadwell, it's too cold to stand here any longer," she said and gently closed the door.

THIRTY-THREE

Pete and Victoria were sitting at the conference room table reviewing the security footage they had obtained from the Mancelona property. When Pete spoke with Tammy's grandfather, he agreed to give them the codes to access the CCTV. The two of them were intently watching the screen on her laptop when his phone rang. He switched the call to speaker mode.

"Hi Ben. What's happening?"

"I'm tailing Mr. Fowler. He's driving out of town and there's a woman with him in the car. She's wearing a hooded parka, so I can't tell if it's his wife or his daughter. Hang on a minute . . . They just pulled into the road that leads to the Island Airways airport. They are on the run, Boss."

"Great work, Ben. I'll fly over there later today and haul them back in. Better go back and watch the house. I want you to keep an eye on whoever stayed behind."

"Will do," he said and hung up.

"Look at this," Victoria said. "Just a second while I re-wind." When she started the footage again, both of them saw Tammy's car pull into her grandparent's driveway. The time-code on the footage showed it to be 9:25 a.m. She parked, got out of the car and walked into the house.

"It's a half an hour's drive from the Fowler's address to her grandparents' home in Mancelona, so there was just enough time for her to have poisoned Carly's coffee and still get to Mancelona to make pancakes for grandma and grandpa," Pete said.

"In which case, her grandmother didn't lie to you."

"No, but what we really need is the security footage from Tammy's parents' place. Didn't you tell me all they had was an alarm that went off when the doors opened to the house, but no exterior cameras?"

"That's what he said, but he's a slippery customer. He lied before. Maybe he lied again."

"Better double check on that, can you? I'm calling Charlie."

Victoria nodded, hearing the phone ring until their deputy at the Beaver Island police post picked up the call. Pete put the call on speaker.

"Hi, Charlie. Ben just called and Mr. Fowler with either his wife or his daughter are on their way to fly to Beaver Island. I'll come over later today. Looks like we got them. It should be your collar, since it's in your jurisdiction," Pete said.

"Well, I am the law on Beaver Island," Charlie said with a self-satisfied chuckle. "Congratulations, we did it."

"I'm going to go check in with the Beaver Island airport now."

AS SOON AS PETE LEFT FOR his office, Victoria pulled open her desk drawer. Inside lay the evidence envelope with the long dark hair she had lifted from the seat of Carly's car. Pete had originally dismissed her find, saying Carly hadn't been drugged in her car, although he'd wanted it kept in evidence. In light of recent information, it was looking like he was wrong. In fact, the car could have been the scene of the murder. Since they'd obtained Tammy's DNA when she was initially brought into the station, Victoria could ask the lab to see if the hair was a match. She quickly sent Pete a text asking if she should request the comparison. In just moments, he texted her back with an uppercase YES! She smiled to herself thinking that if it was a match, Pete would have to make her officially part of the investigative team. A single hair could be the evidence to prove Tammy was their culprit.

PETE AND CHARLIE WERE BOTH FREQUENT flyers with Island Airways, the private carrier that flew between Charlevoix and Beaver Island. Charlie used their service so often, he even had one of the ten-ticket books that gave him an eleventh flight free. The airport was a local business and had been owned by the Welke family since 1965.

"Undersheriff Pete Manstead calling. I want to get to Beaver Island later today, weather permitting. Can you book me a flight?" he asked the Welke's granddaughter who answered the phone.

"Let me check with the pilot. Hang on."

While he was on hold, he checked the weather map on his phone. Flying looked possible to him. The temperature had plummeted to zero, but the wind was steady and the next storm coming from the Upper Midwest was twelve hours away. The flight from Charlevoix to Beaver Island only took twenty minutes.

"If you can get here by 4:00 p.m., we'll fly you over," she said. "Is this going to be a one-way or a round trip?"

"Round trip, and I'll be bringing a firearm. Will that be a problem?"

"Not for law enforcement," she said. "Are you returning today?"

"Sorry, I don't know yet. I'll call you as soon as I know."

"Okay, you will have to be here a few minutes ahead of time so we can run through the weapons check and the paperwork."

Pete left the office to pack a suitcase in case he ended up spending the night, which seemed likely. There was a big hotel in Jamestown, the village near the port where the Beaver Islander ferry docked in the summer. He wondered if the hotel was open in the winter. If not, he'd have to rely on Charlie's hospitality. He'd stayed overnight at the Beaver Island police sub-station once. If memory served, there was a jail cell in the building. If worse came to worse, that cell had a single, very short and lumpy bed.

Checking his phone, he noticed the time. Ashley would still be teaching, but he had to tell her that Carly Yellowwood's killer was about to be arrested. He dialed her number and left a message saying, "The murderer has been identified and is in our sights. I'm going to Beaver Island today to pick him up. There will be a celebration for Carly's life on the reservation on Saturday afternoon. I'd like us both to attend. I did it, Ashley. I got the bad guy. Love you."

IT WAS JUST FOUR O'CLOCK WHEN Pete drove into the parking lot for Island Airlines. The skies were lowering and very dark. The wind had risen and was howling. A branch cracked off a tree and skittered across the parking lot.

"Is the weather all right to fly?" he asked the girl at the desk.

"So the pilots tell me. Did you bring your firearm?"

"I did." Pete took out his permit to carry and filled out the paperwork on the weapon.

"We've had the runway cleared on Beaver Island," Ms. Welke said. "You shouldn't have too much bumpy air on your way over. What with the storm coming in, I recommend you return as soon as possible. You don't want to be stuck on the island until the ice breaks up in the spring," she grinned adding cheerily, "It is *the dead of winter* you know, Sheriff."

Pete felt an unpleasant cold tingle run down his spine.

When the pilot and co-pilot were ready, he followed the two men as they walked outside in an icy wind. He climbed the short metal staircase and ducked his head to enter the plane. Looking at the rows of seats, he saw that he was the only passenger.

Once airborne, Pete texted Charlie asking him to meet his flight.

"My girlfriend and I will pick you up," Charlie texted back.

They were already out over Lake Michigan when he clicked off the call. It was mostly frozen over, but some sections of the crust had irregular borders, thinner sections of the ice floating on the water. It resembled a child's map of white islands outlined in dark gray charcoal.

The big lake looked so innocent beneath its blanket of snow, but Pete knew full well how treacherous it could be. For a moment, he couldn't stop his mind from going back to the day the snowmobile fell through the ice. He'd pulled the child up to the surface and pushed his little body away from the opening onto solid ice before diving down again. It had been a desperate struggle to lug the heavy adult up from the lakebed. When Pete's head broke the surface for the second time, he saw a slender adolescent who had placed the child's body on a toboggan. The boy pulling the sled was taking steps gingerly, pausing between each one. He remembered hearing the ice crack and seeing the teen-ager's terrified expression. He'd screamed for help again before the water-logged body of the dead man became too heavy to hold and pulled them both back down under the water.

The therapist he worked with afterwards told him he had PTSD. He'd been in such bad shape he couldn't work for nearly a year. One of the symptoms that still remained, more than a decade later, were nightmares that woke him gasping for breath. Now that he and Ashley were going to be living together, he would have to tell her what happened. He dreaded it. Reliving the experience with her was the reason he'd delayed so long before asking her to move in.

Just then the pilot spoke, breaking his train of thought. "We're coming up to some bumpy air, Sheriff. Buckle your seatbelt."

Once through the rough clouds, Pete could see the tear-drop outline of Beaver Island laid out below them. They were coming in fast and low. Tall stands of pine and fir looked like black toothpicks standing in a white pelt of snow. The plane touched down and pulled to a stop near the small rectangular building that served as the airline office.

The pilot emerged from the cockpit into the passenger area and said, "We're going to turn around and head right back ahead of the storm. Hang on a second while we lower the steps."

Pete exited the plane into a wildly blowing gale. Charlie was standing there waiting and led the way toward the building with a sign over the door reading, Beaver Island Airport.

"Pete, this is Cyndi Jeffries," he said, introducing the petite dark-haired woman who was waiting for them inside.

"It's nice to meet you, sir," she said holding out her small hand to shake his. He removed his gloves to shake her hand.

"Call me, Pete," he said. "Thanks for coming to pick us up."

"Cyndi's the paramedic on the Island," Charlie said. "She runs the clinic and only rarely has to call the mainland to request a doctor. Whenever she calls, a doctor flies over, or if the patient requires immediate surgery, Cyndi accompanies the patient to Charlevoix by air." Turning to his girlfriend, he asked if she was hungry. She said she was and mentioned a local eatery.

"We're going to Stoney's," Charlie said. "It's just off the King's highway near Donegal Bay. If Fowler patronizes any local restaurants, this is the only one within walking distance of his house."

Pete nodded, but felt uneasy. He hadn't had time to check whether Fowler had a permit for a firearm. The last place to try to take a desperate man into custody was a busy restaurant. If there was a shoot-out, civilians could be at risk. Sitting in the back seat of Cyndi's car, he texted Victoria, asking her to check whether a 'permit to carry' had been issued to Axel Fowler.

THIRTY-FOUR

When they arrived at the restaurant, Pete asked the bartender if he knew the Fowler family.

"Sure do. Mr. and Mrs. Fowler come in often. Hope he isn't in some kind of trouble." They lied, assuring him that Mr. Fowler was helping them with their inquiries about a crime in Charlevoix.

Waiting to be seated, Pete said quietly, "Ben just texted me. He's still watching the Fowler house and has seen the wife there which means it's Tammy who's here with her father."

Charlie nodded.

When the hostess asked where they wanted to be seated, Pete requested a table with his back against the wall. He was feeling apprehensive and wanted to watch the door.

"Patrons usually like facing the lake," she said. "But it's totally dark already. No view from inside this late."

Both men ordered hamburgers and fries. Cyndi had the perch special.

After dinner she drove them to the police station where Charlie kept his patrol car and his weapon. Pete was relieved when she dropped them off. The arrest could turn ugly and he didn't want anyone else endangered. It was bad enough he and Charlie were taking the risk. They were after a dangerous, unpredictable perpetrator, a man who had been party to the premeditated murder of a young mother.

To his consternation, when Victoria called him back, she told him Fowler had recently acquired a concealed weapons permit. Both he and Charlie found that troubling. It was pitch dark and bone-chillingly cold with two feet of snow on the ground. If either Axel or Tammy got away and ran, they would never find them. The perpetrators could die of cold or exposure, and he would have failed to bring Carly Yellowwood the justice he'd promised her.

"Do you know the Fowler house?" Pete asked his deputy.

"I do. It's on Donegal Bay. It's a big place with an unusual shape, a rhombus I think it's called. The original owner of the lot poured the basement walls. When that family couldn't afford to build, the place was abandoned. The Fowlers bought the property several years later and built on top of the existing structure. The main floor has huge floor-to-ceiling windows that look out over Lake Michigan. The lower level of the house is the garage for their cars. It's quite the place."

"I assume there's a road that runs behind the house," Pete said.

"Lake Drive," Charlie said.

"How do you get inside?"

"There's two sets of stairs, one outside and one inside. The interior stairs lead up from the garage to the kitchen. Are you thinking we should go out tonight? It will be completely dark by the time we get there."

"I think so. Have you ever been inside the place?"

"Not inside," Charlie said, "but I got called out last summer to quiet down a beach party. According to Cyndi who made a house call there once, the upper level has an enormous great room with a kitchen at the rear. The whole place is built out of poured concrete. It's like a WWII bunker."

"Since you've been there, how about you go up the outside staircase and knock."

Charlie took a moment to react. "I guess that would be okay," he hesitated. "Why should I tell him that I'm there?"

"You could say it's because an alarm on one of the uninhabited houses on the street went off and ask Fowler if he's seen any lights on in the house."

"Should I tell him he's under arrest?"

Pete could hear Charlie's anxiety in his voice. He felt the pressure of making a wrong decision.

"No, let's hold off. Do you think you could get one of the garage doors open?"

"Possibly. I'll give it a try."

"Okay," Pete said feeling on steadier ground. "If you can get me into the garage, I'll go up to the kitchen using that interior staircase and wait until I hear you knock. When Fowler answers the door, he'll have his back to me. Keep him talking. Use the burglary story and ask him if he's noticed any activity that seemed suspicious. I'll sneak up behind him and have the cuffs ready."

The two men drove the rest of the way in silence until they reached the Fowler residence. It was set on a forested sand dune high above Donegal Bay. The driveway angled sharply down from Lake Drive terminating at the garage level. There was only a single pin-point of light visible in the big dark house that loomed over Lake Michigan.

"Hold on. We don't have a warrant, do we," Charlie said.

"No, there was no time. But these are what they call exigent circumstances. We have tracked down a killer or killers who ran to avoid arrest. We are within the law."

"Okay. Here goes nothing," Charlie said as he parked the patrol car on the side of the road. "I'm going to grab flashlights. Here's one for you."

FLASHLIGHTS IN HAND, BOTH MEN TRUDGED through deep snow down the steep curving driveway to the garage. The cement forecourt hadn't been cleared and there were no visible car tracks. If it hadn't been for the tiny light upstairs, no one would have known the house was occupied. Their suspects were keeping their presence on the island a total secret.

Reaching the garage, Charlie gave a sudden grunt of surprise. With his heart in his throat, Pete moved closer to his deputy.

"I forgot there was this entrance door down here," Charlie whispered. He removed his gloves and tried the handle. "It's locked, but I'm going to use my credit card and see if I can open it. Train your flashlight on the lock."

It took some time and Pete could hear him sliding his card up and down in the iced-over groove, but then to his surprise he heard a tiny click and Charlie's white-toothed grin shone in the flashlight beam.

"Okay, you walk up that outside staircase now and knock on the door. I'll take the interior stairs up to the kitchen." Pete took a breath, trying to still his rapid heartbeat. His knees felt wobbly. "Listen, Buddy, in case this doesn't end well, I want you to know how much I . . ." his words trailed off.

"Yeah, me too," Charlie said and they shook hands.

"Let's go," Pete whispered and disappeared through the door into the garage. The bobbing light from his flashlight showed dimly in the darkness.

Charlie walked up the outside staircase slowly. He wanted Pete to have enough time to get upstairs and into the kitchen before he knocked. His heart was hammering in his chest.

PETE GOT TO THE TOP OF the stairs leading to the kitchen without incident where he encountered another door. Luckily, it was unlocked and he opened it silently. He heard voices and thought the television was on, but then he realized it was two men talking. He edged inside, leaving the door behind him open in case he had to escape. Crouched over, he crossed to the far side of the kitchen.

By peeking over the lower cabinets, he could see the living room and beyond that a balcony which ran around the entire perimeter of the upper level. Silently standing up beside a vertical cabinet, he noticed the living room was recessed a foot below the kitchen level. He'd have to be careful not to trip when he stepped down into the room. The fireplace was burning brightly and two men were sitting on the couch. Their backs were to him and both of them had whiskey tumblers in their hands. They were speaking in near whispers and Pete strained to hear what they were saying.

"I can only stay one more day." Pete thought he'd heard that voice before. He frowned, trying to remember who it was.

"I know and I appreciated you flying over here with me."

"Tell me what happened," the man said.

"She just wasn't listening to me," he said and Pete could hear the desperate frustration in Fowler's voice. "All I wanted Carly to do was break off her relationship with Leo Sorenson. I offered her a king's ransom, but I didn't kill her, Spence. When she backed out of my driveway, she was alive."

That's who the second guy is, Pete thought. It was Spence Chastain, the attorney.

"Why run all the way over here if you are innocent?"

"I'm being completely honest with you. After Carly left the house to go out to her car, I heard Tammy come back into the house through the side door. When she walked into the kitchen, she was holding her grandmother's prescription bottle in her hand. I asked her what she was doing with it and she said she was going over to Mancelona to bring her grandmother the medicine."

"But you suspected that what actually happened was that she'd used the drug to poison Carly."

"Tammy had been so distraught when Leo broke their engagement, I feared she'd do something desperate." His voice was filled with despair.

"Have you talked to Tammy about this since?"

"I've tried, but got nothing out of her. As soon as Carly backed out of our driveway, Tammy told me she was leaving and I watched her pull out and turn in the direction of Mancelona."

"I'll have to talk to Tammy if you want me to defend her, that's in case she's brought in to be questioned," Chastain said.

"She's sleeping, but I'll wake her up if you want to speak to her now."

"Let's wait a bit. Why do you have a gun on the coffee table, Axel?"

"For protection."

"Wouldn't think you'd have to have any protection up here. There's no crime on Beaver Island to speak of. Is it loaded?" Chastain asked.

From his position behind the couch, Pete's stomach clenched when he saw Fowler nod.

"You should lock it up in a gun safe when I leave. Guns are nothing to fool around with."

Seeing the gun resting on the glass coffee table, Pete felt the hairs on the back of his neck rise. The faint light coming from the fireplace gave just enough illumination for him to see it was a .22 pistol. When Fowler heard Charlie knock, he'd bring the gun with him to the door. His deputy was walking into a death trap. Their only means of communication were cell phones. He pulled his from his jacket pocket and scrolling rapidly down to Charlie's number, he texted, "He's got a gun!" He heard the doorbell ring and one of the men rose to go to the door.

Pete's heart was racing and he was poised to act, but taking quick look at the coffee table, he saw Fowler's gun was still there.

"Good evening, sir," Charlie's voice was hearty. "Just making the rounds this evening. The alarm went off in the neighbor's house two doors down. I drove over to see if it was a real emergency or just a glitch. The alarm is set to ring the police station if it's not turned off in five minutes. By the time I got here, their place was dark and locked up tight. Are you Axel Fowler?"

"No, a friend," Chastain said.

As they continued talking, Pete stepped carefully down into the recessed living room and knelt behind the couch. He peeked around the end of the sofa and looked at the coffee table again. The gun wasn't there. *Dammit, where was it?*

Pulling his 9mm from his jacket pocket, Pete stood up. Charlie was still engaging Spence Chastain in conversation. He looked all around the darkened room, finally spotting Axel Fowler's silhouette. He was standing by the expansive glass doors looking out toward Lake Michigan. Silent as a cat, Pete headed toward him.

"Hands in the air, Fowler," he said in a low voice.

Then, from behind him, he felt a cold round gun barrel prod against his back and heard a woman's voice say, "Put your gun down, Sheriff."

He turned around very slowly with his hands in the air. Tammy Fowler was holding the .22 pistol in a firm grip. Her hands were rock steady.

"Let's just talk about this, Tammy. Nobody had to get hurt here. Look, I'm putting my gun down now," he said and bent to lay his 9mm on the wooden floor.

At that moment, the girl raised her arms and pulled the trigger. The gunshot was enormously loud. He felt a searing pain in his shoulder and fell to the floor screaming. For a moment, he almost passed out. Touching his shoulder, he felt warm wet blood. Keeping his hand on the injury, he dragged himself across the floor toward the couch. He managed to pull himself into a sitting position, grabbed a couch pillow and put it against the wound. When he looked up, Tammy Fowler was crouching down by him, the barrel of the gun only inches from his forehead. He could smell gunpowder on her hands. Looking into her eyes, he saw madness.

"Put the gun down, Tammy," he heard Charlie say.

Tammy stood up from her crouching position and swung around, pointing the pistol directly at Charlie's chest.

"I didn't kill Carly Yellowwood," Mr. Fowler said. He had walked over and was standing beside his daughter.

"No, but your daughter did," Charlie said. "Carly died from the drugs Tammy put in her thermos and you are an accomplice since you helped cover up her crime with your false confession and running over here to avoid arrest."

"It's all gone wrong," Fowler said in a bleak tone. There was a terrible look on his face, the look of a cornered desperate animal. "Give me the gun, Tammy. You have to leave here now. I'm going to kill both these men before I turn the gun on myself," he said. Without a second's thought, the young woman tossed her father the gun and ran toward the sliding glass door.

Pete knew he had only seconds. Still on the floor, he kicked his booted foot at Fowler, but felt only air. Dragging himself into a better position, he kicked again desperately. This time he felt his boot connect with the man's ankles. Fowler yelped in pain, falling forward. Charlie struck at the man's gun arm and the weapon skittered across the floor. In one controlled motion, he grabbed Fowler's arm, twisted it and in a split second dropped the man to his knees. Even in the heat of the moment, Pete was impressed that he'd used a maneuver called a wristlock takedown.

Still holding the pillow against his shoulder with one hand, Pete scrambled for Fowler's weapon. "I've got his gun, Charlie," he said, as his deputy pulled a struggling Fowler to a standing position and put the cuffs on him. Then he looked for Tammy. She was opening the sliding glass door to the balcony. Spencer Chastain was ahead of her, already going down the snow-covered steps.

"I'm arresting you for aiding and abetting the murder of Carly Yellowwood," Charlie said. Pete felt the room going dark and forced himself to stay conscious. As if the voice came from far away, he heard Charlie's voice reading Fowler his Miranda rights.

Struggling to pull himself up on the couch, Pete saw Tammy and the attorney in the floodlights. They had reached the landing halfway down the stairs. Tammy was desperately hanging onto Chastain, her face a mask of fury. Mr. $1000 suit pushed her off.

Charlie crouched down beside him and asked, "Where are you hit, Pete? Is it your shoulder?"

"Tammy and Chastain are outside, they're getting away. Go

after them." The pain was so intense, he groaned.

"They'll be all right. I'm calling my girlfriend now, and . . . yours."

Don't do that, Pete thought, before he remembered that Charlie's girlfriend was the paramedic on the island. He felt a powerful rush of relief. Medical help was on the way.

THIRTY-FIVE

Thursday

It was brightly sunny and bitterly cold with gusting winds when Pete, Charlie, a hand-cuffed Tammy Fowler, her father, and a deeply-chagrined Spencer Chastain walked across the snowy tarmac toward the light aircraft that was coming to take them back to Charlevoix. Normally, in the case of a shooting, a helicopter would have been sent to the island, but the heavy snow and intermittent turbulence had grounded the aircraft.

The events of the previous night came back to Pete in discrete images, like a panel of snapshots at the bottom of a cell phone. He remembered seeing Cyndi in the kitchen of the Fowler house and hearing her say she'd driven there in the Beaver Island ambulance with an EMT. She and her colleague had spotted a coatless Spencer Chastain and Tammy stumbling down Lake Drive heading toward town. She'd texted Charlie who told her to lock them in the ambulance. They'd done so.

Pete still couldn't recall how Cyndi and the medic managed to get him down the stairs into the garage and outside, but he remembered the cold air hitting his face just before the ambulance doors were slammed. He'd heard the siren come on and felt the blessed relief of the shot of morphine Cyndi expertly inserted in his upper arm.

He had no memory of where he spent the night or where the Fowlers and Chastain were housed. It wasn't important. They'd nailed their killers and were on their way home. Wincing slightly at the pain in his shoulder, Pete adjusted his arm sling and followed his deputy as they walked across the runway at the Beaver Island airport. The plane was just coming in and they watched as it landed and taxied to a stop. The engine died and moments later the pilot opened the exterior door. Approaching the aircraft, Pete recalled something Charlie said the night before. "I'm calling my girlfriend . . . and yours," he'd said. At the time, he thought he misheard.

But he hadn't, because Miss Ashley Hamilton came dashing down the silver steps from the plane and ran toward him, her curly mane of blonde hair blowing wildly in the wind. All the color leached from her face when she saw his arm in a sling.

"I just can't let you out of my sight, can I," she said, half laughing and half in tears. Then by standing on her tallest tiptoes in the blowing snow, she kissed him over and over again. Charlie escorted the prisoners and the attorney onto the aircraft. Pete and Ashley followed them, walked to the very back of the aircraft and took their seats. All the way across Lake Michigan, Ashley never let go of his hand.

"I'm okay, really I'm fine," he kept saying.

"You're not just fine, you're a hero," she said.

"No, I'm not. All the credit all goes to Charlie. I almost screwed up the whole thing. It was Charlie who saved us from getting killed. He was the one who arrested Axel and Tammy. I was no help at all."

"That's not what I heard. According to Charlie, if you hadn't knocked Fowler's feet out from under him, you would all be dead. You're the hero of the operation," she said. "And that's what I'm going to tell your mother."

He considered his maternal parent and hoped she and his dad were happily at home. "She's not here, is she?" he asked, in a voice filled with trepidation.

"Oh my God, Pete, of course she's here. She took a bus down from the Upper Peninsula last night. I called her as soon as I heard from Charlie. She'll be waiting in the car to go with us to the hospital."

He could just imagine the two women fussing over him and sat back in his seat. There was no avoiding it.

Twenty minutes later, Charlie escorted the prisoners and the attorney across the blowing snow on the landing strip and put them into the waiting patrol cars. When Pete and Ashley exited the aircraft, his mother was waiting. There was a thunderous expression on her face. He remembered that look. It meant he'd screwed up again.

"Hi, Mom," he managed in a quaver.

"I'm barely speaking to you, Peter James Manstead. It goes without saying that you will be quitting your job, or at a minimum going back to full-time paperwork. You are never doing this to me again. I nearly had a stroke!"

"I'm fine, Mom."

"Not another word," she said, glaring at him, before turning her furious boot-button eyes on Ashley. Rearranging her features into a smile she said, "I'm certainly glad I have *one* family member who's not a complete nitwit."

At the Charlevoix hospital Emergency Room, Pete learned the bullet had gone straight through his body. No trace of metal had showed up on X-ray and he wouldn't require surgery. The doctors removed the dressing Cyndi had applied, saying complimentary things about her field work, redressed his wound and gave him a new sling. He'd asked for a replacement, not wanting his mother to see blood stains. He'd been thoroughly evaluated and observed for several hours before he was released.

"I have to stop by the office," he told Ashley as they were leaving the hospital with his mother seething in the back seat. "The bullet has to be located at the Fowler's Beaver Island house for the ballistics match."

"Oh no you don't, Peter Manstead. You can call them when we get to the house, but that's it. I talked to Victoria already. Sheriff Dodgson's going to interrogate both Fowlers, place them under arrest and schedule the arraignment. They're still trying to figure out something they can charge Chastain with, but your job is done. What you are doing now is recovering. Your mother and I are seeing to that."

"Exactly," his mother said from the rear of the vehicle.

PETE'S LITTLE CABIN IN THE WOODS on the Jordan River looked very welcoming when they drove in. The driveway had been plowed, the lights were on and he could see a little finger of gray smoke rising from the chimney. His mother had been hard at work. No doubt she'd brought groceries and probably cleaned the kitchen as well.

Once inside the house, he told both women he was tired and although they stripped him naked, to his acute embarrassment, he managed at least to keep both of them from accompanying him into the bathroom.

Falling asleep to the sounds of their voices talking at the kitchen table, he heard them chatting about the need for an addition to the house. The cabin had to have a master bedroom and a second bathroom, his mother said. He knew better than to protest and drifted off into an uneasy sleep punctuated by nightmares of chasing men escaping into the snow-bound wilderness.

When he woke up, it was completely dark. He caught the scent of a pot roast, potatoes and carrots. Seeing his cell phone on the nightstand, he decided to call his father, Pete Sr. It rang for quite a while, and he envisioned the old man working his way toward their old black phone sitting on the end table in the living room.

"Hi, Son. How's it going?"

"Fine, Dad. The doctors discharged me with no follow-up. It all worked out. The killer is in custody and there won't be any problems with the conviction. Tammy Fowler's going down for the rest of her natural life for killing Carly Yellowwood."

"Why did she kill the poor woman?"

"It's a bit of a long story."

"I've got the time," his dad said and Pete could hear him settling in his leather La-Z-Boy chair in their comfortably dated living room.

"I don't know if you knew, Dad, but Carly had been married, had a little daughter and subsequently got divorced. I knew from the report done by the pathologist that she had a lover. After dismissing several other suspects, I settled on a young man named Leo Sorenson as our prime suspect. At the time of his 21st birthday, Leo was engaged to Tammy Fowler, but shortly thereafter he and Carly started having an affair. At first I thought Carly was blackmailing him to get him to end the engagement, but I was dead wrong."

"Go on."

"The Sorensons and the Fowlers were best friends as couples and Leo and Tammy were raised together. In the parents' minds it was a foregone conclusion that they would end up together. He proposed to her last summer. However, when Leo turned twenty-one, he met Carly Yellowwood. His birthday party was held at Turtle Creek Casino and Carly had been hired to serve drinks for the event. Leo was instantly attracted to her and late that night went to her hotel room. They spent hours talking and as time went on and they continued to see each other, he realized that he had never been in love with Tammy. It wasn't long before he broke their engagement. Tammy Fowler conceived a violent hatred for Carly who she considered had seduced Leo."

"With you so far," his dad said.

"Leo inherited $15,000 from his grandmother and planned to give it to Carly because she desperately needed a new car. Leo's father had invested the money in a CD and had to get his broker to move the money into Carly's account. Axel Fowler, Tammy's father, was their broker. On the morning she died, Carly went over to the Fowler's house to get the deposit slip for the money. That's where she was given the fatal dose of the drugs. We have yet to get a confession from Tammy, but the sheriff's interrogating her tomorrow."

"What happened on Beaver Island?"

"Once Axel and Tammy learned we were closing in on them, they took a flight to the island where they own a summer home. My deputy, Charlie Pierce, is the law on the island, and when I flew over, we went to the Fowler's house together. I got the drop on Axel, but Tammy came up behind me with his gun. She was the one who shot me. Her father took the gun away from her and threatened to kill me and Charlie before turning the gun on himself. I kicked his legs out from under him and Charlie took him down."

"Where was Tammy while all this was happening?"

"She and their lawyer ran out of the house and were hiking down the road toward town when Charlie's girlfriend, she's a paramedic and was on her way to help, found them and locked them in the ambulance. From the conversation I overheard between Axel Fowler and his attorney, we are virtually certain it was Tammy who drugged Carly, but we still lack definitive evidence."

"That's quite a story, son. I'm sure it'll make the papers. Are you okay now?"

"I'm fine, but can you do me a favor? Ashley's here and between her and my mother I'm not going to be allowed to leave the house. They are already driving me crazy. Any chance you could come down here and get mom?"

He heard his father's dry chuckle. "I'll drive down to get her in the morning, although I must admit I'm enjoying a little quiet time to myself. But you definitely have the greater need. By the way, congratulations on having Ashely move in. Mom and I are both happy for you."

"Thanks, Dad." Pete hung up the phone smiling. Now that his father was coming to get his mother, he thought he could talk Ashley into letting him go to the post to observe Tammy's interrogation and to Carly Yellowwood's funeral. He felt a rise of self-confidence in his manly ability to handle the females in his life. Unfortunately, his feeling of male superiority was totally shattered when he got out of bed buck-naked and had to call the women for help getting dressed.

THIRTY-SIX

Friday

The temperature was hovering around twenty degrees and there was a cloudless blue sky as Deputy Charlie Pierce drove down the long driveway to Pete Manstead's hunting cabin on the Jordan River. The white pine trees that bordered the drive were coated with snow. Icicles hung from the needles on the lower branches, catching the light from the sun. He pulled into the graveled parking area in front of the house and got out of the car. Knocking on the front door, he was met by Pete's girlfriend Ashley. She looked none too pleased to see him.

"The doctor told Pete that he wasn't to do any work for two weeks," she said firmly.

"All he's going to do today is sit and watch an interrogation. The sheriff wants him there in case he has questions."

"Which you could answer yourself, Charlie Pierce, since you were on Beaver Island when he was shot," she said, narrowing her eyes. "Pete better not have called and asked you to drive out here to get him. Did he?"

Pete emerged from the bedroom saying, "Hi, Charlie. Thanks for coming." He looked almost pathetically glad to see his deputy.

"I can't believe you are doing this," Ashley said, shaking her head.

The men left before she could lodge another protest.

Driving toward town, Pete asked Charlie for an update.

"The sheriff has placed both Tammy and Axel Fowler under arrest. You would think it would shake her, but so far, Tammy is saying nothing. Axel keeps insisting she's innocent and trying to take the blame himself. It's transparently obvious he didn't kill Carly Yellowwood and that he's covering for his daughter."

"Did Victoria get any CCTV from their house?"

"She sure did. Turns out Axel Fowler lied about having no cameras on the eaves of his house. Acme security told us they had installed them, but we had to get a subpoena to acquire the footage. The video shows Carly getting out of her car and going into the Fowler house. Then we can see a woman coming out the side door of Fowler's place, going over to Carly's car, opening the driver's side door and leaning into the vehicle. She's obviously adding the pills to Carly's thermos, but according to the sheriff there's a problem."

"For God's sake, what is it?"

"Mrs. Fowler and Tammy are exactly the same height and weight. The woman on the closed-circuit footage was wearing a purple parka with black fur around the hood and dark gloves. We know it's Tammy's coat, but she says it wasn't her. She and her mother borrow each other's clothes, apparently."

"Cripes sake," Pete growled.

"It's possible all we can get her for is shooting you. That is incontestable, although she maintains she shot in self-defense. Since I will testify that I witnessed you lay your weapon down on the floor before she fired, we have her for shooting a serving officer of the law."

"Is Chastain defending her?"

"No, he bailed. He isn't willing to represent either Axel or Tammy. In fact, I've heard they are having a hard time getting an attorney."

"That's one good thing anyway. But she can't get away with this, Charlie. As far as I'm concerned, I don't care one iota if she gets off for shooting me. All I want is to see her convicted for the cold-blooded, premeditated murder of Carly Yellowwood."

"I agree, but proving it is going to be tough. We did take custody of Tammy's laptop yesterday and I took it to Victoria last night."

"Let's hope she finds something," Pete said.

They pulled into the station parking lot and walked inside.

SHERIFF DODGSON CAME OUT OF HIS office when they arrived to greet them. "Great to see you, Pete." He was about to shake his hand before he spotted the white sling and resorted to a pat on the shoulder. "I checked with the Prosecuting Attorney about whether you could be in on the interview, but since you were a victim, he said would be a problem in court. You can observe."

"Thanks for sending Charlie to get me."

"I would have left you at home to recover, but he said you'd called wanting to be here."

With a guilty look Pete said, "I just wanted to hear what she has to say."

When the sheriff added that Charlie hadn't been cleared to interview Tammy either, they walked down the hall to the interrogation room. Both of them took seats in the viewing box adjacent to the interview room. Looking through the one-way glass, they saw Sergeant Craig bring Tammy into the room.

"Where's Victoria?" Pete whispered.

"In court. It's the day of the custody hearing for Carly's daughter. She's coming in after the decision is rendered. She just texted me that she has something for us from Tammy's computer."

SGT. CRAIG WAS STANDING IN THE corner of the room as Sheriff Dodgson read Tammy her Miranda rights and made sure she understood her right to remain silent.

"You have a right to an attorney. Do you want me to request one for you?"

"No," she said, shaking her head. "I am innocent."

"That is yet to be determined. Now, I want you to take me through the day that Carly Yellowwood came to your house to get the deposit slip for the money your father put in her account. We know she arrived shortly after eight o'clock on Monday morning last week. We also know from the closed-circuit data taken from your outdoor security cameras that while she was inside talking with your father, you left your house from the side entrance, walked over to Carly's car, opened the driver's-side door and leaned inside the car. Can you tell me if this is correct, so far?"

"I was in the house all morning and never went outside until I left to visit my grandparents," Tammy said coolly.

"We'll be talking about that later. Right now, I want you to see the video in which you come out the side door and walk over to Carly's car," the sheriff started the video from his laptop. "That's you, Tammy," he said.

"No, that isn't me. It must be either my mother, who often wears my clothes, or another woman. I was in Mancelona that morning."

"What time did you leave home for their house?"

"Shortly after eight," she said. Her lips were set in a determined line. Despite the fact that the heat in the room had been cranked up to eighty degrees, a common practice intended to make suspects uncomfortable, Tammy Fowler hadn't broken a sweat.

"We have evidence that you didn't arrive at your grandparents' place until close to 9:30. According to your grandmother, you were inside the house making pancakes when they came down to breakfast."

"I often visit them on week-ends. They are getting older and need my help." She sounded so piously sanctimonious that Pete cast Charlie an incredulous look.

"Actually, I've checked with them and they were surprised to see you. They said you haven't been to visit since your folks *made* you come at Christmas. What you were doing was trying to establish an alibi, but it won't hold, Tammy. We know you poured your grandmother's Digitalis pills into Carly's thermos and that you waited until she drove off before you left for Mancelona."

Tammy looked at the sheriff and in a pedantic tone said, "You have no proof that I drugged her, Sheriff. You have no fingerprints on the thermos or on the handle of the car door. There are lots of parkas that color and style. It's possible it was my mother. She hated Carly, you know for what she did to me. Perhaps you should talk with her."

"We already have, Tammy. Your mother spent Sunday night with your grandparents. We checked and their security system shows her arriving Sunday morning. Her car never left their driveway until around noon on Monday. You stole your grandmother's congestive heart failure medicine to use on Carly and because she ran out of the drug, you damn near caused your poor grandmother to have to go into the hospital."

Tammy shrugged. "She's old. Old people die."

From their position, Charlie and Pete could see the sheriff clench his hands in his lap. They watched him take a deep breath. What he'd tried so far wasn't working. He was about to change direction.

"Let's see if you and I can agree on some basic things. I can understand why you hated Carly Yellowwood. She used her sex appeal to seduce Leo Sorenson and made him break your engagement. Leo shouldn't have done that to you. The two of you had known each other forever and you are much prettier than Carly."

Tammy gave the sheriff a brief sloe-eyed glance, pushed her dark hair back and inclined her head. It was as if she considered the compliment to be nothing less than her due.

Pete and Charlie sat up straighter. The sheriff was getting traction. His body was completely still and he seemed to have entered a space where nothing existed except Tammy and her story.

"That slut took him away from me. She had no right," Tammy said in a cold tone.

"You really must have hated her," the sheriff said quietly.

She nodded.

"Leo Sorenson wasn't worthy of you. He was weak. He should never have cheated on you, but he succumbed to Carly's sex appeal. I don't blame you for drugging her. She deserved it, didn't she?"

"Leo belonged to me. She had no right to lure him into her bed. The little tramp was nothing but a cheap whore."

"I am with you, Tammy. In fact, Carly's the one who should be prosecuted. In the old days, a publicly reported engagement was a formal contract and breaking it was against the law. If only you hadn't given her those drugs, she would be sitting here instead of you."

Tammy opened her mouth. She had arrived at the saw-toothed edge. Then she stopped herself. "You aren't going to trick me into confessing, sheriff. I didn't murder Carly Yellowwood and I don't know who did. I'm not saying another thing."

"Take her back to the cells, Sergeant," the sheriff said.

Walking into the observation room, he said, "Both Tammy and her father are under arrest, and will be brought before the judge tomorrow morning for arraignment. We can definitely nail her for shooting you, Pete. That was witnessed by Charlie. But, unfortunately Tammy Fowler is right when she says we can't prove she drugged Carly. We have nothing but circumstantial evidence. I know she did it, you guys know it, but we have no actual evidence, no trace and no forensics. Unless something comes in soon, the little psychopath could get away with it." He ground his teeth.

"We can't let that happen, Sheriff," Pete said in a desperate voice. "Tammy Fowler committed premeditated murder. I owe it to Carly, we all owe it to Carly, to put her killer behind bars."

"I know how you feel, guys. I feel the same, but all we can do is to go back to the beginning and try to find something, anything, that will convict Tammy Fowler of Carly's murder. I promise you, Pete, we will get there. That girl is living on borrowed time."

THIRTY-SEVEN

STANDING BY HER KITCHEN WINDOW LOOKING out at their snow covered back yard, Victoria picked up the small turquoise bear fetish from his place on the windowsill and slipped him into her pocket. It was the day of the custody hearing, and she was still struggling to decide whether they should petition the court to adopt Chenoa. She hoped the final answer would come to her before the judge asked them to make their presentation.

"Boys, come in here and get your lunches," she called and when her sons dashed into the kitchen, she checked that their faces and hands were clean before telling them to put on their boots and coats. She and Matt were driving the boys to school that morning since it was on their way to the court.

"Mind your teachers," she called as they climbed out of the car. "We love you."

"Tell your mother you love her," Matt said. They did, but in whispers, before running into the school with a pack of their friends. Apparently, telling your mother you love her was too embarrassing to say aloud. Given the uncertainty of the outcome of the court's decision, they had decided not to tell the boys they were considering adding a little sister to their family. They had told them about the dog though, and they were wildly excited.

Pulling out of the school's driveway onto the main street and heading toward the center of town where the Charlevoix Court was located, Matt said, "We're almost out of time, Victoria. Are we going to request custody, or not?"

"Oh, Matt, I've driven myself crazy trying to decide the right thing to do. I even brought Dr. Tones' fetish with me today, hoping the decision will come to me in time."

"I want you to know, honey, if we are awarded custody of Chenoa, I promise to be the best father I can be to her. I had hoped you would have made your decision before now, but I can live with whatever the judge decides."

Minutes later, they drove into the parking lot by the 33rd Circuit courthouse. Unlike many traditional courthouses that are usually white and crowned with a dome, this one was an unprepossessing two-story tan brick structure located in the center of Charlevoix. Six pillars supported the flat-roofed overhang for the entrance. The couple got out of the car, their breath making clouds in the frosty air. They walked inside the building. Following the signage, they found the courtroom. Dr. Tones standing in the corridor waiting for them.

"Good Morning, Matt and Victoria. It's good to see you both. I thought it might help you to know the process for these hearings. The judge will start by asking Greg Nokomis, he's the attorney for the tribe, to agree to have the matter of Chenoa's custody settled in circuit court, rather than tribal court. After that, Joe Yellowwood will be asked to speak. As you know he plans to request custody of his daughter. Then I will be asked to present my support of your case. You will be the last to present, before the judge makes her final decision."

"Good to know," Matt said. "My wife will be speaking for our family today."

"Victoria, you told me when we spoke on the phone yesterday that you are still struggling to know the right thing to do. Hopefully, after hearing the other presentations, the answer will come to you. Let's go in."

The three of them walked into the courtroom. Like many courts of law, it was paneled in wood with multiple rows of seats for attorneys, clients and observers. Behind the judge's raised bench, the white oak paneling had been done in vertical strips.

Victoria noticed the Yellowwoods were seated in the front row of the court. Joe was nicely dressed in a charcoal suit and a red patterned tie. He appeared stoic and determined. His mother looked daunted and a bit frightened. She had brought her oxygen machine with her. Mr. and Mrs. Applebee were seated behind them. They wouldn't be asked to speak, but had to know who was awarded custody. Little Chenoa, whose whole life would be determined by the outcome of today's deliberations, wasn't even there. The social workers, Mrs. Robbins and Sharon Tucker were present, as was a man Victoria didn't recognize.

"Who's the guy in the black suit?" Victoria whispered.

"Probably the attorney for the tribe," Matt said.

The Bailiff walked into the court and said, "All rise, Session 21398 of Juvenile Court. Case number 409318, Judge Martha Mason presiding." The Judge, a tall woman dressed in a black robe with a white collar, entered the court from her chambers and took her seat. She wore her shiny brown hair in an elegant twist. Victoria had done hers in French-braids on the crown and wore the remainder tied tightly in a ponytail. Despite her efforts, multiple curly strands had already escaped their rubber bands. *What I wouldn't give to have the sleek look of the Judge's tresses*, she thought.

"You may be seated," the Bailiff said.

The Judge began, saying, "The purpose of today's case is to make a decision regarding the custody of two-year-old Chenoa Yellowwood. I understand both parties requesting custody are present. Please stand as I call your names and remain standing until I call the next party to the claim. Mr. Joe Yellowwood, father of the child, and Mrs. Doris Yellowwood, grandmother."

They stood up. "Thank you, please be seated. Now, Mr. and Mrs. Matthew Treadwell." Victoria's heart was pounding as she stood up. She slipped her hand into her jacket pocket to touch the small bear fetish. "You may sit down. Representing Charlevoix County, Mrs. Gretchen Robbins and Sharon Tucker." Both women stood up. "Lastly, representing the Traverse City Chippewa/Ottawa band we have Mr. Gregory Nokomis, attorney at law and Dr. Lightfoot Tones, who is present as liaison between the tribes and the Treadwells. Mr. Nokomis, you may begin."

"The Indian Child Welfare Act (ICWA) is a federal law from 1978 that explicitly gives tribes the right to intervene in any court proceeding relating to custody of a Native American child. Absent good cause, state courts must grant petitions from the tribe or a Native American parent to transfer these proceedings to tribal court. In the case of Chenoa Kai Yellowwood, since the mother was Caucasian, the tribe and Mr. Yellowwood have consented to have the case heard in your Court, Judge," Mr. Nokomis said.

"Noted and appreciated, Mr. Nokomis," she said. "We will begin today with the petition from Mr. Yellowwood, the child's father. You may stand and present your request."

Joe's voice trembled as he read from a typed sheet of paper, "I, Joe Redwing Yellowwood, request custody of my only child, Chenoa Kai Yellowwood. Her mother, Carly Jane has passed away." His voice was heavy with emotion and he swallowed. "I am Chenoa's father and have seen her regularly every week since I was released from prison. I know her mother would want me to have custody. In support of my request, I would remind the court that Carly gave our daughter a Native American name, listed my mother as her primary contact in case of a medical emergency, and had her participate in all the age-appropriate ceremonies on the reservation. I have a good job at Ace Hardware and am being considered for an assistant manager position. I got into a fight in a bar a few years ago and lost my temper when a man came at me with a knife. When I got the knife away from him, I injured him, something I deeply regret. I pleaded guilty to the assault and served my sentence. At the time I was an alcoholic, but I have been recovering and sober for three years. If the court grants my request, I plan to continue living with my mother so that Chenoa can be cared for by her grandmother when I am at work." Joe looked up at the judge and in a plaintive voice said, "I wish it to be known that I have never relinquished my parental rights and beg the court to be allowed to have custody of Chenoa."

"Thank you, Mr. Yellowwood. Dr. Tones, do you wish to make a presentation on behalf of your clients?" the judge asked.

"Yes, thank you, Your Honor. I have met with Mr. and Mrs. Treadwell and know them to be a stable, loving family. They have been married for ten years and have two sons. Mrs. Treadwell is the dispatcher for the Sheriff's office. Mr. Treadwell is a guide for tourists who hunt and fish locally. He is one quarter Chippewa, and a card-identified Native American. He also speaks the language of the tribe, having learned it from his grandfather. If the judgement of the court rejects the claims of the child's father, due to his incarceration for a violent crime, I can attest that the Treadwell's will provide Chenoa with a fine caring family," Dr. Tones said and sat down.

Listening to Dr. Tones' remarks, Victoria touched the fetish in her pocket. It seemed to have grown warm against her fingers, like the forehead of a febrile child. An image flashed into her mind of a time when her baby son had a fever and she was rocking him to sleep. She remembered feeling an overwhelming love for him and realized her emotions exactly mirrored Joe Yellowwood's love for his daughter. What she had to do came to her in a blinding flash of certainty.

"Mrs. Treadwell, I understand you are presenting the case for your family adopting Chenoa. You may stand and begin."

"Thank you, Your Honor. I was on my way to work a week ago Monday when I saw a small black car in my rear-view mirror. The conditions were icy and the car was fish-tailing across the road. It ran into the ditch and came to an abrupt stop against a tree. When I went back to help and reached into the car to check Carly Yellowwood for a pulse, I saw Chenoa for the first time. She was in her car seat in the rear. If I hadn't taken the side roads that morning, it could have been hours or even days before Chenoa was found. I believe I saved her life," she paused to take a breath.

"My husband and I stayed with Chenoa both days she was in the hospital. Matt took the day shifts when I was working, and I stayed with her at night until she was placed in foster care. It was during that time we came to the decision to adopt her, if the court agreed. However," Victoria stopped and looking directly at Judge Mason said, "I apologize to the court for wasting Your Honor's valuable time this morning by going forward with our request. Having heard the profound love Joe Yellowwood has expressed for his daughter, I find myself unable to be a party to any action that would take a Native child from her family."

"Very well," the judge said in a dry tone. "Custody is hereby granted to Mr. Joe Yellowwood, with the following strictures. He will remain sober, attend regular AA meetings and with his mother's help, will teach Chenoa about her tribal legacy. I was personally raised by my grandmother and know how critical they are in the lives of children. Case dismissed." She banged her gavel down.

Leaving the courtroom, Victoria and Matt thanked Dr. Tones for his help, and handed him the fetish. To her surprise, it had turned cool again. Having helped her find the right path, the totem had become nothing more than an elegantly carved piece of stone. "I appreciate you lending me the turquoise bear. I found him to be very helpful."

"Perhaps you should buy one for yourself. You can purchase them on eBay," he said and smiled at them both.

Walking back out to the parking lot, Matt asked Victoria if she was all right.

"I'm a little sad, but feel I made the right decision. I'd like to go home for a bit before I go back to work." They were looking for their car in the parking lot when she noticed Mrs. Applebee walking toward her.

"Good morning, Victoria. As you requested, I showed Chenoa the picture of the woman you sent me. She recognized her and told me that when that woman opened their car door, she told her to close her eyes. 'Don't peek' was what she said."

"Thank you very much, Rose. Of course, Chenoa is far too young to testify to what she saw, but this supports what I've thought all along. Are you bringing Chenoa to her mother's memorial service on Saturday?"

"Yes, we will be there and the Yellowwoods will officially take custody then."

"We plan to attend at well," Victoria said, blinking back an unexpected rise of tears. "Thank you for caring so well for her. We have to go." Turning to her husband she said, "Ready, to head home?"

"Not quite yet, sweetie. I got to thinking about you wanting a little girl and decided it was up to me to get us one," his eyes twinkled.

"What on earth are you talking about, Matt?"

"You are right about the high price for a trained pointer, so I purchased us a female Vizsla puppy instead. She was only a fraction of the cost. I'm going to train her myself and we'll have a little girl in the family after all."

"Oh my goodness, that's wonderful. I knew there was a reason I married you," she said in a laughing voice. "What does the puppy look like?"

"Vizslas are the ancient dog of Hungarian royalty. They are a sleek golden red color and have no doggy smell. The breed is known to be especially loving around the house and intense when hunting. I decided we should name her Willow, which is Chenoa's middle name," he said and Victoria felt a wave of fondness for her dearly loved husband.

"Is Willow old enough to come home yet?"

"She's eight weeks old, so we could have her now, although there might be less crying at night if we waited a couple more weeks."

"I don't want to wait another minute. Let's call the breeders and let them know we're coming. And we should get the boys from school to come with us. It's a perfect day to pick up our little girl, the newest member of the family."

ALTHOUGH VICTORIA WAS DUE BACK AT the station, she found herself unable to pull away from the adorable tableau of her husband and sons playing with baby Willow. The love in the kitchen was so concentrated that it seemed to make the air in the room shimmer. She decided it would be enough to email her findings to Pete.

She'd gone through Tammy's computer late the previous night. It hadn't taken long. In her search history she found multiple searches tying down the dosage of digitalis it would take to cause a fatality. Tammy Fowler had been doing her homework.

Logging into her own computer, Victoria went to her email. She was tickled to find the report from the lab for the long dark hair she'd found on the seat of Carly's car. It was a match to Tammy Fowler's DNA. Pulling up the group email list that included the sheriff, Pete, Charlie, Ben and Sgt. Craig, she attached the lab report and her summary of Tammy's searches on digitalis. On the subject line she typed the words SHE'S NAILED.

In the body of the email she wrote: "I believe this information will be enough to convict Tammy Fowler of the murder of Carly Yellowwood. In return, I request a raise and an informal promotion. If we have any more violent crime in Charlevoix County in the future, which I know is highly unlikely, I request to be considered an integral part of the investigating team. Please let me know your decision."

She sent the email off and spent a little time going through the rest of her inbox. When she'd finished responding to her mail, she checked her incoming emails. Charlie, Ben and Sgt. Craig were all on board with her request, and Sheriff Dodgson had written, "Nice work, Victoria. It will be an honor to have you on the team." She was a bit disappointed to see that Pete hadn't responded.

Let it go, she told herself. After all, she didn't have to have his agreement. Sheriff Dodgson would be in charge of any further cases and he'd already warmly supported her request.

Walking back into the kitchen, she saw Gavin sitting on the kitchen floor petting little Willow.

"Mom, come hold her. She's so soft."

Victoria, with a big happy grin on her face, did exactly that.

THIRTY-EIGHT

Saturday

It was the day of Carly Yellowwood's memorial service, a celebration for her life to be held on the reservation and Victoria Treadwell was awaiting the return of her husband, Matt. He'd gone ice-fishing early that morning, taking both boys. It was still snowing, but lightly, and the sun was coming out through feathery clouds. Assuming part of the service would be taking place outside, she'd dressed in a black turtleneck sweater, warm slacks and boots, accented by the turquoise jewelry her husband had given her the day of their wedding. The smoked whitefish and berries she was bringing to the service were on trays covered with foil. Looking in the mirror, Victoria took a deep breath and spoke the words she'd been using as a calming mantra of late.

"You are calm and confident," she said taking a deep breath. Lowering her shoulders, she felt her breathing slow. Today she was going to speak with Joe and Doris Yellowwood and ask (beg, really) to be a part of Chenoa's life. She knew it was a big "ask," but since she had withdrawn her petition to adopt the child in support of the Yellowwoods' custody claim, she hoped the woman would agree. Plus, she had a gift for Chenoa's grandmother. She'd made a little photo album with copies of all the pictures she and

Matt had taken of the child in the few days they had spent with her in the hospital.

They had been keeping baby Willow in the kitchen, which was now gated to prevent her leaving the tiled area. At the moment, the puppy was happily destroying an old leather shoe and Victoria knelt down to pet her smooth head. Matt had brought the children's plastic wading pool into the house from the garage and after a thorough cleaning, lined it with towels. They were using it as the puppy's play and napping area. Willow's crate was stationed beside the wading pool, but it was only used at night, or if both of them had to leave the house. Victoria's husband was in charge of potty training and had shoveled the snow from a space in the yard behind the back steps for Willow's bathroom. He'd set a timer on his watch and was taking her outside every two hours during the day. Victoria had watched her two rambunctious sons sharply to be sure there was no pulling of ears or stepping on tails.

The discussion of what to do with the puppy at night had been loud and contentious. Matt was clear that he and Victoria were not sleeping with the dog. The boys, who had bonded instantly to the smooth, red-coated puppy, begged to be able to sleep with her. Matt finally agreed to bring her crate into their bedroom at night and place it between the boys' twin beds. He grinned at Victoria after acceding to their pleas. They both knew it would only be moments after they kissed the boys good night until Willow was broken out of her cell and allowed to cuddle with their sons.

Somewhat to her surprise, Victoria had fallen hard for little Willow herself. As a child, her parents had cats and this was her first puppy. Bemused, she found her maternal feelings for Willow were as strong as they had been for her own babies. If Matt hadn't been able to stay at home with Willow, she would have had a hard time going to work and leaving her.

A movement caught her eye and she raised her eyes to look out the window. There was a bright yellow flash at the bird feeder and Victoria was surprised to see a goldfinch. She didn't think they migrated as far north as Charlevoix. A shiver ran quickly across her shoulder as she recognized that the goldfinch was the spirit of Carly Yellowwood. She had come to say good-bye and thank her for rescuing Chenoa. For the rest of her life, every winter when the snows came, or whenever she saw a goldfinch, Victoria knew she would remember the brave young woman.

Matt drove up the driveway. "Ready to go?" he asked cheerily when she opened the door.

"I have to pee," her son Gavin said and dashed into the house.

"Help me with these food trays, will you?" Victoria handing Matt the foil-wrapped trays of fish and fruit. Then looking around the room and seeing everything in its place, she smiled. Calling her son Gavin, she said, "I'm all set."

PETE'S GIRLFRIEND, ASHLEY, HAD TAKEN A leave of absence from her job and was now decisively ensconced at his place. She'd had taken over supervising his recovery after receiving detailed instructions from his mother who'd protested mightily at being removed from the cabin when his father appeared to take her home. The couple were sitting at the kitchen table, discussing Pete's intention to attend Carly Yellowwood's funeral. Ashley was insisting it was too soon.

"You can drive me, but I have to be there," Pete said. He rubbed his hands tensely on his pant legs under the table. His only hope was convincing Ashley to drive him. The doctors had prohibited him from driving for two weeks.

"The sheriff's office will be well represented without you. Sheriff Dodgson, Charlie, Ben, Todd and Victoria are all going. The event is taking place outside, is expected to take several hours, and you'd have to be on your feet the whole time. You're not going." Her face wore a mulish expression.

"I'm in no pain, slept well last night, and you changed my dressings this morning. Not a drop of blood on the gauze," he said.

"The reason you are in no pain is because I caught you taking two Vicodin this morning," Ashley said, shaking her head. "It's only been four days since you got shot! And I distinctly remember the doctor in the ER saying you had to rest for a week."

He was getting nowhere and felt desperate—because the circle around the case hadn't been closed. There was one open spot. He had to say a final farewell to Carly and tell her they had her killer in custody. "I have to tell her good-bye, Ashley and tell her we have her killer in custody. If I don't, I'm afraid this will never be over for me."

She looked at him for a long time before taking a deep breath and saying. "Fine, but only for an hour. I'm driving and I swear I'll shoot you myself if you don't leave when I say it's time."

Pete ducked his head to hide his smile.

THEY DROVE ONTO THE HILLY RESERVATION amid a long cordon of other cars. Two patrol cars were in the line. Riley Donovan was driving his big red snow plow, no doubt remembering the day he'd pulled Carly's car from the ditch. Altogether there must have been thirty vehicles heading to the reservation. Many citizens of the town, it seemed, had turned out to say a final farewell to Carly Yellowwood. Sadly, Carly's mother, Mrs. Lynley, has taken a turn for the worse and was in the hospital. Her father had called the sheriff's office to say they wouldn't be able to attend. They had sent a huge floral wreath.

"Roll down the car windows will you?" Pete said.

Ashley did so and they could hear the distinctive resonance of funeral drums floating on the snowy air. The drums were created by stretching deer hide tightly across a round frame. Driving closer they heard the high transcendent music of a flute and saw a bonfire burning brightly on the knoll above the social services building. Most of the people standing outdoors were in winter parkas, but one man was clad entirely in a tribal costume that looked like it had been made from white leather.

"That's got to be the chairman of the tribe," Pete said, looking at the man who was standing next to Will Leonard, the slender tribal police officer he'd met at the casino. They parked, got out of the car and walked over to join the police contingent. All of them, with the exception of Victoria, were in uniform.

"I'm glad you were up to coming, Pete," Sheriff Dodgson said. He held out his hand to shake, but remembering his injury, clapped him on his left shoulder instead. "I'm going to say something about how Tammy Fowler was captured and announce that you are being awarded a medal for being wounded in action."

"There's no need for that. Really, sir, please don't. I'm embarrassed about the whole thing. Not about figuring out who killed her, as you know that was a team effort, and I pulled my weight. The night we arrested Axel and Tammy Fowler, though, was all down to Charlie. It was his quick action that kept me from a second bullet that could have killed me. He even used the wrist takedown on Fowler. Very impressive in that tense situation. Charlie deserves the award, not me. On another note, have you decided what to charge Axel Fowler with?"

"I've spoken with the Prosecutor and he believes we can make a case for his collusion in the murder, based on his false confession and his attempt to evade justice by flying over to Beaver Island. He'll definitely be convicted and serve time."

"What about Spencer Chastain, the attorney. Is there anything we can at least cite him with?"

"Unfortunately, no. He was only there in his role as legal counsel. Once Tammy shot you, he decided he wouldn't represent the Fowlers."

Pete looked around for Ashley who had gone back to the car. She was opening the trunk. To his acute embarrassment, when she came toward them she was carrying a folded lawn chair.

LEAVING THE OFFICERS STANDING BY THE bonfire, (and the lawn chair leaning against a tree) Pete and Ashley went inside the social services building where the food was being set out on tables in the gymnasium. Rose Applebee, carrying Chenoa, and trailed by her husband and children, arrived and asked Pete if he'd seen Joe Yellowwood.

"He's over there with his mother," he said, gesturing to the area by the food.

"Look over there, Chenoa. It's your Daddy," Rose said and Chenoa's face broke into a huge smile. She struggled to get down and Rose released the tyke. She was wearing her pink snowsuit, and her rambunctious curls had escaped Rose's careful combing.

"Daddy," she shrieked and ran to him. Joe turned toward her and Pete could see his joyous response. He bent down, picked up his daughter up and kissed her. Then Mrs. Yellowwood held out her hands for the child who was handed over. Pete could see the shine of tears in the grandmother's eyes.

Victoria Treadwell approached the three of them tentatively and Pete could hear Chenoa's delighted voice calling out, "Where is my teddy bear? Did you bring him?"

He heard Victoria laugh and saw her give the little girl a pink teddy bear. When she extended a hand to Mrs. Yellowwood, the grandmother took it with a gentle smile. They talked for some time. Pete couldn't hear a word, but by watching the body language of the two women, he could tell it was going well.

When Victoria presented Doris Yellowwood with the small photo album, the gift seemed to be appreciated because Mrs. Yellowwood leaned down and said something to Chenoa who held up her arms saying, "You can pick me up now." Deeply moved, Pete saw Victoria Treadwell lift the little girl in her arms.

IT WAS ALMOST AN HOUR BEFORE the formal presentations for the celebration got underway. People had been chatting and enjoying the banquet foods when they heard the low booming of the water drums calling the group to the fire. Leaving the comfort of the building, the mourners trudged up the rise as the wind whipped through the reservation. The group stood four deep in a large circle around the bonfire.

"I want to welcome you all on behalf of the Yellowwood family," the chairman said. His gravitas came across in his deep voice. "This is Joe Yellowwood and his mother Doris. With them is Joe's daughter, Chenoa. He wants to say a few words."

Joe was obviously having trouble controlling his emotions, but after clearing his throat said, "I met Carly Lynley on the first day of high school and for me it was love at first sight. We started dating as freshmen and I was thrilled when she agreed to marry me four years later. We were married right after graduation. She and I were soul mates and when Chenoa came our family was complete. Carly was a perfect woman, loving, principled, beautiful and brave. I know she fought to the bitter end to save her life for our daughter. It was terribly wrong that she didn't get to see Chenoa grow up. I will always . . . mourn her loss." Joe turned away, unable to speak through his tears. The tribal chairman patted him on the back and turned back to the group.

"Will Leonard from the Traverse Band tribal police would like to say something now. Go ahead."

"I wish to congratulate the Charlevoix Sheriff's Office for their work in apprehending the evil coyotes, Axel Fowler and his daughter Tammy, who took the life of Carly Yellowwood. I understand that the Fowlers were captured on Beaver Island through the brave efforts of Undersheriff Manstead, (Pete flushed) and his deputy Charlie Pierce. I hope in the future that we can work together to solve crimes, irrespective of the white man's concept of *jurisdiction*," he said. He cast a grave look at Pete who nodded.

"Sheriff Dodgson, would you come forward?" the chairman asked.

"Thank you. I'd like to reassure everyone here that the safety of our communities, both white and Native American, were protected in this case. Tammy Fowler and her father have been arrested, arraigned and are being held in custody. Mr. Fowler has confessed and will serve a sentence. While it is crystal clear that Tammy Fowler was the culprit who caused Carly Yellowwood's death, she has yet to express any remorse for her crime or to confess. However, the evidence against her is overwhelming. While the final outcome won't be decided until the trial, we are convinced she is guilty and will likely spend the rest of her life in prison. Justice will be done. My men . . ."

"And women," Pete interjected.

"And women, thank you Victoria. You did fine work on the case. In recognition of her efforts, I'm promoting her to Evidence Tech. I am proud of them all."

"Thank you, Sheriff. Victoria Treadwell has also asked to say a few words," the chairman said.

Victoria made her way up through the crowd that parted to let her pass. "As most of you know, I first saw Carly Yellowwood when I opened the door to her car the morning of the car accident. As the investigation proceeded, I identified closely with Carly and my husband and I considered adopting Chenoa. I spent much time searching my heart to know the right thing to do, but in the end I knew she belonged here with her father and her grandmother. I've recently learned that grandmothers are especially revered on the reservation for their roles in the education of young children. Chenoa Kai Yellowwood belongs with them. Never again should a tribal child be stolen from her people."

There was long applause from the crowd and very few dry eyes as Mrs. Yellowwood and Joe walked over to stand beside Victoria. Chenoa took her rightful place between them, holding both women by their hands.

"It's time to go now, Pete," Ashley whispered.

"Just one more thing," he said and walked to the fire. "May I say something," he asked and the chairman nodded.

"As all of us know, we are very fortunate to live in this beautiful place with little to no crime. I've never had to deal with a case of murder before and hope to never have to deal with another. Sheriff Dodgson and Will Leonard have congratulated me on the arrests of Axel and Tammy Fowler. It was kind of them, but all the credit for the arrest goes to Deputy Charlie Pierce who made the collar. I also want to thank Victoria Treadwell, without whom we wouldn't have obtained the final piece of evidence that will convict Tammy Fowler of the murder. It was a privilege for the whole unit to get justice for Carly Yellowwood." He stopped, feeling overwhelmed, before adding in a tear-choked voice, "Good-bye, Carly. May God be with you in the world that lies beyond ours, and with your family here on Earth."

After accepting the congratulations of the group, Pete and Ashley walked slowly back to their car just as Mr. and Mrs. Sorenson pulled into the parking lot. Leo was sitting alone in the back seat. Mr. Sorenson got out of the car, spotted Pete and came over to shake his hand.

"It's good to see you here," Pete said.

"We wanted to say good-bye to Carly and I've decided to give Joe the money that Axel Fowler tried to get Carly to accept to break up with my son. The Yellowwoods can use it to raise Chenoa," Walt said in a gruff voice.

Pete could tell Mr. Sorenson didn't seem to want to have a big deal made about his generosity and just laid his hand on the man's shoulder. "How are you doing, Leo?" The handsome young man who had been Carly's lover looked positively broken.

"It's my fault Carly died," he said wearily, looking down at the snowy ground.

"You didn't kill her, Leo," Pete said.

"In a way I did, Sheriff. By falling in love with Carly and breaking my engagement to Tammy, I initiated the tragedy that led to her death. I am having a hard time forgiving myself."

"It will take time, but I want you to keep in mind who dealt the final blow. It wasn't you, Leo. That's down to Tammy Fowler. You're a Catholic, right?" Pete asked and Leo nodded.

"Perhaps it's time for a visit with Father Jake. I understand Catholics priests are in the business of forgiveness," he said and added, "With his help, I know the time will come when you can forgive yourself, Leo. I'm quite certain Carly already has." He put his arm around the young man whose shoulders were shaking. Saying good-bye, he and Ashley headed back to where their car was parked.

As Ashley drove them back to the cabin, Pete took her hand. He was feeling happier than he could ever remember being. While Tammy hadn't confessed, they had solid evidence which he was certain would convict her. The District Attorney said that he saw absolutely no issues that could possibly obscure the proof the sheriff's office had collected. The DA was especially complimentary about the searches Victoria found on Tammy's computer regarding fatal dosages of Digitalis and the DNA match to her hair she had collected from Carly's car seat. That hair proved it was Tammy who leaned across the driver's seat to drop the Digitalis pills into Carly's little blue thermos. The DA's office was seeking life in prison.

As they drove toward East Jordan in comfortable silence, Pete felt a fierce pride. He'd actually helped solve a case of murder. In the hierarchy of crimes, murder was the big one. No matter what happened in his future in law enforcement, he would always have this success to look back on.

He was equally delighted with his personal life. He and Ashley were closer than ever. She was going to move in with him in June and he could hardly wait.

"Ashley, you know you are my forever person," he said.

"I know," she replied, "And you are mine."

On that beautiful morning as a curtain of snow fell softly around their car cocooning them in beauty, Pete was confident that only long tranquil days lay before them.

Read Chapter 1 from the next
Lyn Farrell mystery

THE SILENT SOLSTICE

One

The scent of lilacs drifted in through the open bedroom window and sunshine slanted through the slats of the venetian blinds placing golden ribs of light across the quilted bedspread. Cuddled in an antique bed that was clearly too small for them, Sheriff Pete Manstead and his girlfriend Ashley Hamilton were still asleep that morning. When Ashley opened her bright blue eyes, she smiled. *Pete looks so young when he's sleeping, just like a little boy.* She watched him breathe for a while, seeing his fair eyelashes resting on his cheeks.

Pete was in his late thirties with the broad countenance and faded blue eyes of his Norwegian ancestors. Ashley was tall and willowy with blonde hair. Thick and luxurious, her tresses were sun-streaked and curly. Her hair was one of the things that first attracted Pete when he saw her across a crowded bar five years ago. They had recently moved in together after Ashley landed a job working for the East Jordan public schools. She'd been teaching first grade in Gaylord, but once Pete asked her to live with him, she sold her place and joined him in his log cabin on the Jordan River. Their cabin was located in northern Michigan, near the delta where the river entered Lake Charlevoix.

Ashley touched Pete's shoulder to wake him.

"What?" he asked, coming awake instantly. It was one of the habits he'd acquired during his police academy training.

"We haven't entertained anyone since we moved in together, and these long summer evenings are so lovely. Let's have Charlie and Cyndi over for a Solstice picnic on Saturday night."

"What is the Solstice? I know it's something celestial," Pete said. He sat up, leaned back against the carved rosewood headboard and rubbed his eyes, trying to remember.

"The Summer Solstice occurs when the earth is fully tilted toward the sun in the northern latitudes," she told him. "It's the longest day of the year. A perfect time for a twilight get-together."

"You sound just like a teacher," he smiled and reaching out his long arm tousled her hair.

"I sound like a teacher because I *am* one. So, can you call and invite Charlie when you go into work this morning?"

"Sure thing."

"You best get going, Sheriff," she said. "You're the head of the station now, so you can't
be dragging your butt into the post late."

"You'd think a man could come in late to work when he's the boss," he said, sounding hard-done-by. His promotion to Sheriff of Charlevoix County was recent and he was just getting used to it. He'd been undersheriff for a decade until the former Sheriff Mike Dodgson retired. His decision came after they'd successfully solved the Yellowwood case the previous winter. Most people believed it was the arrest of the culprit that caused the sheriff to step down, but Pete knew better.

The sheriff's wife had insisted her husband resign after Pete was shot through the shoulder by the perpetrator of the Yellowwood murder. Despite the fact that northern Michigan had one of the lowest crime rates in the country, Mrs. Dodgson had experienced enough worrying about whether her husband would come home in one piece. She put her foot down and the sheriff had turned over the reins.

Somewhat of an oddball in the cynical hierarchy of the police force, Pete believed all people were essentially good at heart. He invariably excused juvenile indiscretions, putting them down to youthful rebellion. With respect to drugs, he was of the opinion that people used drugs today the way the older generation had used alcohol—self-medicating to blunt the pain of mental or physical illness. When hunting for a perpetrator of a violent crime, however, he was single-minded and obsessive. Like a bloodhound, he never gave up. But once the person was in custody, he often felt compassion for them, and if they were young offenders, he usually petitioned the Judge for shorter sentences.

Wishing he didn't have to show up to work that morning, he pulled the strap of Ashley's pink nightgown down and kissed her on the shoulder. "I wish I had the summer off like *some* people and could lie around in bed all morning," he said.

"Anytime you want to teach stubborn little first-graders how to read, you can have my job," Ashley said heartlessly. He sighed, and despite the distractions of his beautiful girlfriend, got out of bed.

THE FOUR OF THEM, PETE, ASHLEY, Charlie and Cyndi, dined *al fresco* on their screened-in porch Saturday evening, enjoying the rippling sounds of the river that ran past the rear of the property. The scent of the white pine trees that surrounded the cabin and the candles on the table created an island of peace as the twilight lingered.

Charlie Pierce was Pete's deputy, responsible for law and order on Beaver Island. He was a retired Navy Seal with a short beard, twinkling olive-green eyes and a weakness for a practical joke. Although Pete was Charlie's superior officer, since the previous winter when they apprehended the Yellowwood killer, they had become close friends. Charlie's longtime girlfriend Cyndi Jeffries, was the paramedic on the island. The couple had taken the Emerald Isle ferry over to the mainland from Beaver Island to celebrate the Solstice with Pete and Ashley.

The women had refused the guys' half-hearted offer to help with dishes and the two men talked quietly as they walked toward the river in the long pale twilight. Sunset rays illuminated the pine trees, setting alight the deep green needles on the branches. Blue shadows lay on the pale sandy ground. Light streamed from the windows in the cabin behind them and the men could hear the women's voices, the clink of plates and glasses. One of them laughed aloud.

Walking closer to the crescent of riverbank on Pete's property, they heard the lapping of the water as it gurgled over stones on its journey. The warm summer night and the moving water made Pete feel serene and tranquil. Everything in his life had worked out exactly as he had hoped, and indeed predicted, after a life sentence was handed down to the perpetrator who killed Carly Yellowwood. It had been the first murder in the county in close to two decades. Pete had been in charge of the challenging case, his first and he fervently hoped, the only major crime he would ever have to investigate.

"Do you and Cyndi want to stay with us tonight?" he asked. The remodeling of his old hunting cabin had been instigated by his mother who came down from Michigan's Upper Peninsula to supervise the renovation. She insisted that Ashley, who she kept referring to as her daughter-in-law, couldn't possibly be happy in Pete's old place. They now had a fancy new kitchen, master bedroom and bath, leaving the original bedroom available for guests.

"No, I promised my folks we would stay with them. In fact, we should get going pretty soon. Excellent grilled white fish, potato salad and corn on the cob, by the way. You're one lucky bugger. Ashley's a good cook. Cyndi thinks women spending time in the kitchen only reinforces the male patriarchy," he shook his head with a grimace. "She says either I can cook, or we can eat out. I was surprised when she offered to help do the dishes."

"Anything out of the ordinary happening on the island?" Pete asked, changing the subject. Beaver Island was the largest island in Lake Michigan. It was inhabited by some five hundred people, mostly summer residents, and located thirty miles across the big blue lake from the town of Charlevoix.

"Couple of snatch and grabs of tourist purses by local hoodlums, but nothing of importance. Not compared to last winter anyway." Charlie's voice went quiet.

Pete met his somber eyes and nodded. It had been the two of them who had apprehended the murderer on the island in the dead of winter. The injury from the bullet that went through his shoulder throbbed slightly, reminding him of his near escape.

"That was a once in a lifetime event," he said firmly. He still felt embarrassed about the award he'd received for being wounded in action. In his view, Charlie was the one who got control of the situation, took the man's gun away and prevented his threat to kill both lawmen. Pete's sole contribution, as he lay bleeding on the floor, had been to kick the killer's feet out from under him. Charlie maintained that without Pete's tripping the culprit, he couldn't have subdued the man. All Pete's efforts to have the award given to Charlie had been in vain. Sheriff Dodgson had insisted it was his by right, saying, "You were the officer injured in the line of duty."

"Let's hope we never have to deal with a murder case again," Charlie said quietly. "We better head back to the house."

"In a minute," Pete said, spotting the wooden measuring stick he'd left resting against a big oak tree. Picking it up, he inserted it into the water by a large boulder and marked the level. "Water is up from last year. Should be good fishing this summer."

"I'll be happy to join you any time you want to pull some trout out of the water," Charlie said with a grin.

They walked back toward the clean well-lighted home.

HALF AN HOUR LATER, THE FOUR of them were standing outside by their parked cars. Ashley had insisted on their guests taking the left-over whitefish which she had put in refrigerator dishes and loaded in a paper sack. She hugged Cyndi and the men shook hands.

"Come again soon. It was great seeing you," Ashley said. Her thick blonde hair was lifted by the evening breeze. Pete put his arm around her and drew her close. He had moments when he couldn't believe his luck. It was a miracle having her fall in love with him.

"We will, but you two need to make a visit to the island this summer before fall arrives," Cyndi said. "Pete, I assume when you were walking down to the river that Charlie told you about the incident on the ferry."

"No, he didn't. What happened?"

"Do you know Riley Donovan?"

"Sure do. He works for Ed's Snowplowing service. Met him last winter. Nice guy. What about him?"

"He passed out near the men's bathroom on the ferry," Charlie said. "When he didn't come around, Cyndi checked him out and called 911. Emergency services were there when we docked. Riley's former girlfriend, Janey Hillberg, drives the ambulance now. She took him to the ER."

"Why do you think he fainted?" Ashley asked.

Pete gave her a look. "Women faint. Men pass out," he said and Charlie nodded in agreement.

Cyndi rolled her eyes. "Male chauvinism aside, Riley was lying face down in the corridor outside the men's room when he was found by two guys who work on the ship. They assumed he'd been drinking. Luckily, one of them thought to call for medical attention because when I got there, I found the numbskulls trying to pour coffee down his throat. In my examination, I discovered he had a wound to the back of his head."

"How would he have gotten an injury like that?" Pete asked frowning. As the lone paramedic on Beaver Island, Cyndi handled virtually all medical issues there. He trusted her medical acumen, but her observation was troubling.

"Well, either he slipped and fell or someone hit him over the head with something," she said. "He was pretty groggy. Unless he was fully conscious in the ER, I suspect he would have been admitted to the hospital for a CT scan to rule out a brain bleed."

Pete nodded. The couple got into their vehicle, waved and drove off. Watching the red taillights of the car disappear down his long driveway, he said, "Honey, I'm sorry but…"

"You're going to the hospital aren't you," she said in a resigned voice. He nodded.

It was coming up to nine o'clock and dimly light when Pete headed north on M-66 toward the town of Charlevoix. His cell phone rang and he grabbed it, seeing the face of Ben Wilcox, his deputy who policed Boyne City Ben was a good-looking guy in his twenties, tall with a receding hairline and a ribald sense of humor. He and Charlie were constantly engaged in friendly competition and practical jokes. Due to the minimal amount of crime in Charlevoix County, the sheriff's office staff had just five employees: the sheriff, their jail sergeant, the two deputies and Victoria, their dispatcher and evidence tech.

"Hi, Ben. What's happening?"

"I was driving toward Charlevoix from Boyne City about half an hour ago when I spotted a bicyclist limping down the road. He waved me down. Guy's name is Jordan Reese. He said he was the victim of a hit-and-run, insists he was deliberately targeted."

"That's disturbing. Is he up to giving you a statement?"

"No. Poor guy was in pretty bad shape. He had a broken arm with a compound fracture. I saw the bone sticking out through the skin on his forearm. I took him directly to the hospital in Charlevoix. It was faster than waiting for the ambulance. I'm there now."

"I'm headed to the hospital myself. Hang on. I'll meet you."

Continuing down the road, Pete considered the two casualties, one man with a head injury and one run off the road. *Nothing but a coincidence*, he thought, but wondered uneasily if there could be a link between the men.

"Stop borrowing trouble," he told himself aloud. It was one of his mother's favorite maxims. The older he got, the more he found himself sounding like her. He smiled thinking of his parents. They were still in love and held hands even while shopping at the grocery store. The empty road shone in his headlights as he continued toward the town of Charlevoix. Much later he would recall that it had all begun the night of the Summer Solstice, the longest day of the year.

Lyn Farquhar—penname Lyn Farrell—holds a Ph.D. from Michigan State University and is an experienced author, having published the seven book series (the Mae December mysteries) with Epicenter Press and four books in the Rosedale Investigations series. She has also published one women's fiction book, "The Cottonwoods." To date, seven of her books have been picked up by a secondary publisher, Harlequin. Lyn worked for Michigan State University's College of Human Medicine for 30+ years before retiring to pursue her dream of becoming a published fiction author. She is the mother of two daughters, has six step children and twelve grandchildren. She loves gardening, playing with her Cavalier King Charles spaniels and is always on the look-out for paintings by her famous artist grandfather (Eugene Iverd) who painted covers for the *Saturday Evening Post* in the 1930s.

www.ingramcontent.com/pod-product-compliance
Lightning Source LLC
LaVergne TN
LVHW031538060526
838200LV00056B/4547